THE
DEPENDENTS

THE
DEPENDENTS

A Novel

KATHARINE DION

Little, Brown and Company

New York Boston London

Copyright © 2018 by Katharine Dion

Hachette Book Group supports the right to free expression and the value of copyright. The purpose of copyright is to encourage writers and artists to produce the creative works that enrich our culture.

The scanning, uploading, and distribution of this book without permission is a theft of the author's intellectual property. If you would like permission to use material from the book (other than for review purposes), please contact permissions@hbgusa.com. Thank you for your support of the author's rights.

Little, Brown and Company
Hachette Book Group
1290 Avenue of the Americas, New York, NY 10104
littlebrown.com

First Edition: June 2018

Little, Brown and Company is a division of Hachette Book Group, Inc. The Little, Brown name and logo are trademarks of Hachette Book Group, Inc.

The phrase "We end in joy" on page 277 is from Theodore Roethke's poem "The Moment."

The publisher is not responsible for websites (or their content) that are not owned by the publisher.

The Hachette Speakers Bureau provides a wide range of authors for speaking events. To find out more, go to www.hachettespeakersbureau.com or call (866) 376-6591.

ISBN 978-0-316-473873
LCCN 2017963616

10 9 8 7 6 5 4 3 2 1

LSC-C

Printed in the United States of America

1.

HIS WIFE HAD died in June and there was to be a memorial service for her in two weeks, at the end of the summer. Gene's daughter had come out from California with his granddaughter to help make the arrangements, and he found himself dismayed by his general helplessness, which was not exactly the same as resenting what his daughter did for him, but the feelings existed along the same continuum. He hadn't been able to find his swim trunks that morning, so he was wearing a pair of pants Dary had chopped off at the knee. She had cut them unevenly and the left side hung lower than the right, in a skew of brown corduroy fringe dampened by sweat against his slack thigh.

He was also wearing real shoes, probably the only person on the entire beach. A bulky pair of sneakers made of foam and glue, the sort that older people were punished with and expected to submit to meekly, as if they were no longer discerning. On Dr. Fornier's recommendation Dary had driven all the way out to the freezing mall, the one with the potted palms, because it was easier to do something for his weak ankles than his grief. He had fought only a little about whether he would wear them, because when he and Dary had started to bicker, his ten-year-old granddaughter had shouted from the back seat of the car, "If you're going to fight, leave me home!"

Now Annie was playing down the beach with a group of boys and girls who were still unselfconscious about being a group of boys and girls who played with one another. Dary had gone to get her because they were going to meet the Donnellys at the miniature golf course. He had little interest in miniature golf, but as long as his daughter was in town it seemed that he was a type of appendage to her, expected to go where she went unless she made other arrangements for him. He had promised to meet up with his daughter and grand-daughter later, and they had left him behind with their towels thinned by too much washing and a single glass jug filled with what was now very warm water.

The beach was crowded, a cluttered heap of pink skin, chipped toenail polish, ice chests, crumpled tin foil, silver cans wearing coats of sand halfway up their sides, shovels and buckets in primary colors, and striped umbrellas that stammered in the uncool breeze. A group of teenage girls had established a colony nearby. They were arrayed on their stomachs in a line surrounded by the incredible amount of stuff that had come out of their bags, the water bottles, energy bars, sun lotions, women's magazines, hairbrushes, inflatable pillows, diet sodas, reed mats, and radios. At times they would roll over each other like seals to point out something in one of the magazines, and from them arose a collective shriek that he vaguely recognized as a form of laughter.

Not far from them a good-looking youngish man with bronzed forearms was helping a little girl build a sandcastle with multiple towers and walkways. Whenever the man did something that pleased the little girl, she cried out, "Mommy, look what Roy did!" Then a woman sitting just beyond them with a puppy in her lap would gaze up at Roy with an expression of complete contentment, and she would lift the pudding-fleshed puppy so it too could gaze on Roy with dumb bliss. She was older than Roy but aggressively attractive; her swimsuit squished the tops of her breasts into little meat pies above the elastic. It was difficult to tell how long she and Roy had been together, and whether he had been inaugurated already into a fatherly role or was merely auditioning.

Gene's interest in other people lay primarily in the mystery of their happiness. Happy children, happy parents tending happy children and small animals—had they always been such evangelists of joy? He now reserved a special kind of misery for the sight of a happy couple. This particular human configuration seemed to have been invented to draw out the despair in everyone else.

A scrum of ball-playing men moved up and down the beach, spreading out and coalescing an expansive territory. You could smell them before they passed by and again afterward, a mass of warm air cabbagey with sweat. Even men who didn't play sports in their regular lives, the ones with the narrow bony chests white as the bite inside a pickle—even they would play with a ball at the beach. Every now and then, when they stampeded across a blanket, some lifeguard would stand up and bullhorn about it.

When Gene was in college the lifeguards on this beach had been lazy party boys, scornful of enforcing rules made by somebody else, especially the state of New Hampshire. On their breaks they smoked cigarettes and sipped beer from bottles in paper bags. But something had changed. Now the beach seemed part of a larger state public service effort to deliver a serious message about health and safety. Last summer, a mobile health clinic had been stationed in the parking lot and to get to the beach you had to pass cheerful volunteers in matching T-shirts, handing out flyers promising various free screenings. It had been one of the last memorable fights between him and Maida, a fight that began when one of the volunteers asked if she could give them a flyer and Maida said yes and he said no. Maida took the flyer and read aloud about the screenings as they stumped over the dunes and he was aware of the way his *No* had sharpened her *Yes,* had made it oppositional. "They're free," Maida said. "Why not?" But nothing was free and he said so.

Maybe if they had left off there, sparring halfheartedly about money, he would have forgotten the argument by now. Instead they jumped tracks and the argument became about what it was or wasn't useful to know. If you could know something, Maida said, she didn't understand why you wouldn't choose to know it. "Not knowing won't save you," she said, at a moment when neither of them knew she would die the next summer. Instead, he had taken a certain needling pleasure in assailing her logic. He pointed out that no test would be able to tell him precisely when he would die, or provide the details for how the *how* would unfold. The tests would only increase his fear, which in his estimation was generally worse than pain of a physical kind. "For a smart person," Maida said, "sometimes you aren't."

Now he picked his way down to the water through a maze of blankets, discarded cups, and scavenger birds. Airy tangles of dark seaweed crisped by the sun nested in the indentations in the sand, trapping small bits of litter, froth, and shells—mostly surf clams but also some mussels. When he was ten years old, the year his father died, Gene had gone to the beach for a week with his father's family—the French-speaking aunts, uncles, and cousins who came from the same small town in Canada— and his cousins had told him the secret that if you held a seashell to your ear, the ocean would speak to you. All that week he collected horse mussels, dog winkles, and moon snails, and after he had rinsed them off he tested each one, thinking that if he found the right tiny, smooth, hollowed-out body and held it to his ear, he might hear instead of the cry of the ocean, the voice of his father. It astonished him that even now, more than sixty years later, he couldn't see a seashell without experiencing the flicker of an urge to pick it up, in case the shell was the one that would return his father to him.

A woman in a sun hat and slacks sauntered toward him along the edge of the surf. Some aspect of her gait triggered a flash of recognition, and the seas inside his cells rose in response. For a fleeting moment the woman was Maida. But when she came nearer, the illusion was shattered. Her face, her expression, was wrong, and she was round in the places where Maida was trim. Yet even after the illusion had been dispelled there remained in him a reckless hope that his wife was alive somewhere, that the person who had died in the hospital wasn't her, and that the real Maida was making her way back to him somehow.

There were things he hadn't told her. Like how a week after their fight about the free screenings he had gone back to the mobile health clinic. He wanted to say he had gone back out of devotion to her, out of the kind of love that is a radical openness to someone else's ideas, but the truth was closer to something like superstition. After you had talked so much about the idea that there might be something wrong with you, it took on a fatalistic dimension. On some level he believed that if he emphatically refused the screenings, the universe would punish him. He went back for the free blood-pressure and diabetes screenings, and then—because the frowning stethoscoping doctor recommended it—he paid for an EKG that revealed an irregular heart rhythm. Except the doctor wouldn't tell him what was wrong with him and would recommend only that he see his regular doctor. But by the time the appointment with Dr. Fornier came around, Gene was having trouble with his ankles, and he was relieved to allow this to become the all-consuming problem.

There were also things he hadn't asked Maida. Like if it had been, on the whole, a happy life. He didn't mean the outward life, but the life within the life. The tucked-away life, secret even to oneself most of the time. Had it been happy enough?

A wave, leaping out of nowhere, crashed against his feet. The water coursed over the tops of his shoes, penetrating the webbing. He waded in and the chill grabbed at his corduroys. His body convulsed in the strange liquid way it always did when the water approached his navel.

There were people who told him his grief would diminish, but he didn't believe them. That his father's death was still an experience reverberating inside him after all these years suggested that the distance a person traveled from death was just along a circle, and all it took was one new loss to show you that you were still traveling the same line. Only now he was older and more broken down and less able to absorb the devastation. Because there was only so much room inside the body to accommodate all the deaths you had to accommodate to go on living.

A wave flung toward him and broke against his chest, splashing water in his face. He tasted the blunt gift of its salt, the roughness cutting into his nose and mouth. Then the ocean reeled back, spinning, a membrane pulled in every direction, sucked low and flat by a deep inner drain.

No couple had played a more important role in his and Maida's lives than Ed and Gayle Donnelly. The two families had vacationed together for years at White Pine Camp, the Donnellys' property on Fisher Lake, and they had been initiated together in the summer rituals of family happiness—swimming, boating, fishing, birding, croquet, card games, night swimming. On these trips they had shared responsibility for sick children, mosquito-bitten children, and plain old whiny children. The handed-down clothing and baby items had traveled both ways between the families. Dary, born just over a year after Ed and Gayle's oldest, spent much of her first year outfitted in Brian Donnelly's old clothes. Later, the two younger Donnelly boys, Michael and Colin, inherited the best of Dary's toys. And just as there was a key to the Ashes' house in the top drawer of the Donnellys' secretary (beside the roll of Charles Demuth stamps and the mother-of-pearl letter opener), there were keys to the Donnelly homes in the Ashes' front closet in the pocket of an oversize men's coat, the circumstances of whose acquisition no one could recall. Sometimes to outsiders the Ashes and Donnellys gave the impression that each family was an extension of the other, and in moments of crisis they tended to rely on each other without waiting for an invitation.

The first weeks after Maida's death, Ed and Gayle had often appeared whenever Gene needed a competent stand-in. Gayle quietly went about concluding Maida's institutional relationships in the world. She returned library books, transferred memberships to Gene's name, canceled automatic payments to the gym he had never gone to, and generally handled the things he would have never remembered to do, though somehow it would have drained him to have left them undone.

Ed kept the infrastructure around the house in working order. He took Gene's car to be serviced when it was supposed to be and got an estimate for the repairs to the roof. He replaced the refrigerator the same day it discharged a foul-smelling puddle under the freezer drawer during a heat wave. By the afternoon the floor was clean and dry and the new model was restocked with everything from the old one, plus some nice beer and cold cuts that hadn't been there before.

All this generosity from his friends should have inspired more tenderness in him, and it puzzled him that instead of gratitude he often felt something closer to irritation. It was mostly Ed who aroused it in him, though Gene knew his friend was just trying to be helpful. But the more his irritation grew, the guiltier he felt, with the result that often he found himself balking at some proposed kindness that was in his best interest, or he would be late to some engagement his friends had arranged on his behalf. As he was now late to meet them at the miniature golf course, having waited past the reasonable moment to heave himself out of the ocean.

The course was across the street and down the block, not far from the band shell where free summer concerts were held. He had expected the boardwalk to have emptied in the midday heat, but it was as crowded as the beach and dense with oiled bodies jogging and strolling and lolling at the rail. He had never gotten entirely accustomed to it, the sight of women walking down the street in nothing but bathing suits, the initial shock not from seeing so much flesh but from thinking that here was a person who had forgotten to wear clothes. A tanned bride-to-be in a ruffly white bikini, tiara, and sash announcing her bachelorette status posed for a photo, flanked by a group of equally tanned bikini-clad women, none of whom looked like they needed another minute in the sun. A large muscular man wearing an airbrushed T-shirt depicting a woman with obscenely large breasts was accompanied by a woman half his size wearing an identical shirt.

Gene stepped into the street and was nearly run down by a Rollerblader in the bicycle lane, who shouted at him, "Don't die, dude!"

In front of the penny arcades, everyone seemed to be eating something: three scoops in a waffle cone, or fried dough, or steaming slices of pizza served on doubled paper plates. The seafood restaurant that served the same food under a new name still had a twenty-foot blue marlin surging from the roof. A teenage boy wearing a sandwich board shaped like a piano handed him a flyer for a bar with private karaoke rooms.

There was more than one miniature golf course on the strip, but only one had a pirate theme. A skeleton missing a hand greeted him at the entrance, and the attendant offered him a complimentary paper visor with a skull and crossbones, which he declined. There was no good shortcut through the course, so he simply walked the holes in order, passing entire parties in the skull-and-crossbones visors. There was a hole that had to be played through a shipwrecked boat; another that required hitting the ball through an enormous skull; another that skirted the tentacles of a monster squid. He crossed a wooden bridge and found his family putting next to a waterfall, groundwater tumbling down beige plastic rocks.

"Well, well," Ed said. "The beachcomber arriveth. We started without you, hope you don't mind."

His granddaughter handed him a bright orange ball. He

kissed Gayle hello on the cheek and asked what he had missed.

"Ed's threatening to sell White Pine Camp," Dary said.

"Well, you can't," Gene said. "You can't sell it until I'm dead."

"Not until we're *all* dead," said Gayle.

"I counted," Ed said, "and last summer we were only there a total of ten days. And you"—he pointed to Gene—"we could hardly get you out there for a day."

"It's the kids' fault," Gene said.

"Thanks," said Dary.

"It's true. It's their fault for growing up. It was different when they were young."

"Now I resent that," Ed said. "I resent the idea we were living for them."

"Not *just* for them," Gayle said.

"Just *mostly*," Ed said with a wry, disdainful smile.

"You'll regret it if you sell," Gene promised.

"How is that possible," Ed said, "when I've never regretted anything in my life up to now?"

"It's not just the cabin you'd be giving up," Gene said. "It's the whole experience. The air and everything in it."

"I have plenty of air. The trees make it for me every day."

"It's that deep lake smell, isn't it?" Gayle said wistfully. "It makes everything all right." She went to the tee and played her turn, a solid if unremarkable hit. There was some speculation from Ed about whether she could have done better if she hadn't been chatting (the Ashes abstained from this conversation), and before long Gene found himself hitting the orange ball up a ramp and over a waterway. He thought he had hit it with good power, but it plunked into the water.

"Your head," Ed said.

"What?"

"At the last moment you moved your head."

Ed stepped up to take his turn. He was a tall man, over six feet, and the putter looked too small for him. In the last decade he'd lost some muscle but he still projected an aura of good health, the leftovers of a lifetime of exercising every day. For years he had tried and failed to persuade Gene to get up with him at five a.m. to run along the river, a circuit that ended at a coffee shop where a group of sedentary retirees greeted him reverentially. Now he hit the ball with a swift, precise stroke. It cleared the waterway and came to rest about a foot from the hole. "See if you can do any better," he taunted Dary.

She played her turn. Her ball cleared the waterway easily and rolled to a stop between Ed's ball and the hole.

"Not bad," Ed conceded.

"Spoken humbly by the man who taught me to play," Dary said. "Telling me it was important in life to excel at one or two pointless games."

"If you hadn't listened," Ed said, "you wouldn't have seen a unicorn."

"What unicorn?" said Gene.

"Are you talking about the time Mom saw the pony?" Annie said.

"Yes, honey."

"*She* knows?" Gene said.

In the end, Ed told the story. It took place when Dary was not quite a teenager and Michael and Colin were still little boys. One day Ed had driven with the kids out into the country, looking for a miniature golf course they had heard about. It turned out to be a run-down farm that the owners had attempted to convert into a tourist attraction, a strange little place with a hay-bale maze and a rudimentary nine-hole course that was open only during the summers. There was also a small, derelict petting zoo on the grounds—the kind of place, Ed said, that had been developed with more attention to the billboards than the paddocks for the animals. One of the penned-up animals was a very forlorn-looking pony. Its coat was slick with gelatinous gray patches, as if something under its skin was rotting, and there was a horn affixed to the center of its forehead, which had become partially unstuck. The pony began stamping and thrusting, twisting violently in an effort to throw it off. This terrified young Michael and Colin. Ed was making an effort to redirect their attention when without any warning Dary reached over the fence and tore off the pony's horn, ripping off some of its skin along with it. The animal bared its teeth and brayed malevolently at them. Where the horn had been stuck to its head, little orbs of yellow pus started to spring up on a wound. Ed ordered everyone back into the car.

"How awful," Gayle said.

"But that's just it—it wasn't," Dary said. "Not in the end." She told them how in the car on the way home, Ed had talked about how good intentions sometimes have unpredictable consequences. He reassured her this wasn't her fault.

"Well," Ed said, looking pleased. "I guess I do all right sometimes."

Someone changed the topic, and the game resumed. Ed and Gayle were taking Annie and their son Colin's daughters camping over the weekend, and there was some talk among the adults about what preparations remained for the trip and whether the mosquitoes were likely to be bad that year. Gene didn't hear the rest of it. His mind veered away, drawn back to an aspect of Ed's story he couldn't explain. He was still thinking about the wretched pony, how it had existed for the others for a very long time. Had Maida known about it? If the others knew, it seemed likely she did too. But then why had she never mentioned it to him?

On the way home the Ashes stopped in Wheeler, a seaside village with unpretentious shops and restaurants, the same attractions that had drawn Gene and Maida to it for their honeymoon half a lifetime ago. Annie wanted Dary to buy her a souvenir, a novelty T-shirt or maybe a ceramic figurine of leaping dolphins. While they were inspecting trinkets in a shop, Gene told them he was going down the road to see something and would be back in a bit.

"Don't forget," Dary called after him.

"I know where the car is," he said.

"I mean to come back," she said.

He walked down the row of shops with their sun-bleached signs and casual disarray just inside the door, the retail spaces dense with racks of brightly colored swimsuits and beachy sarongs, and sometimes a wall covered with what was now called "active" footwear. The little shops all looked like a variation of one another, which maybe in some counterintuitive way helped explain their survival. If the town was to be redesigned, it would never have five versions of the same shop, and maybe not even one survivor from among the current contenders. But there was something inherently charming, almost calming, about pausing in front of the Beach Stop or Seagull Alley or Wave Haven and knowing before you walked through the door that somewhere inside there would be a towel blazoned with an orange-to-pink sunset and a marked-down bodyboard in soft blue foam. He hoped these shops would go on surviving forever, in part because his memory of the town depended on them.

He walked on, passing a bar where happy hour began at 11 a.m. and ended at 6 p.m. every day of the summer. Two teenage girls standing on the street corner were selling melons from the back of a dusty pickup they didn't look old enough to drive. A convenience store advertised the sale of "ice cold Ice." After three blocks the commercial strip dwindled and ceded to bushes and shrubs marking property lines. The sidewalk disappeared, leaving him beside the road in a gully sprinkled with gravel and strips of old tire jerky.

It wasn't much farther.

He turned down a gravel drive, and there was a boy in a dun-colored uniform coming the other direction carrying a bicycle over his shoulder. The way he carried it seemed to rob the frame of any weight, and this same quality of weightlessness was borne into his body as he mounted the bicycle in the street. He didn't appear to jump and throw his leg over it so much as resume his natural form. The boy's figure grew small against the row of bushes. It was beautiful how from a distance his legs seemed to become part of the bicycle, as if he was spinning his own disappearance, a boy creating a rent in the horizon with that steady, circling motion of the wheels that were also his legs. A nick of silver, a smudge of air—then the boy was free, on the other side of the visible world. Gene couldn't say why it moved him. And yet there it was, the swollen feeling in his chest.

This too was grief and it was this infusion of it, even more than the suffering, that made the experience of sorrow a kind of madness. Why this freak susceptibility to ordinary dull occurrences suddenly revealing themselves as the world's valentine to itself, the splendor tossed off so casually it made you feel that incidental, unwarranted gorgeousness was actually the hidden power of the universe? Why the avian commotion in his chest? The sheer rawness of his senses didn't explain it. He couldn't understand why, in the midst of feeling it might be desirable to die, the splintering of the air in the late afternoon by a boy on a bicycle could exist as a complete joy. Each time he had narrowed it down, saying grief was *this* or *that,* it sent him a flock of birds in his chest.

He crossed an island of shaggy grass that diverted cars onto a crescent of gravel running along the front of the Sandpiper Inn, a two-story white clapboard that wasn't overly maintained. The shutters were lopsided, the porch sagged, and the seat cushions on the porch rocking chairs had faded to a colorlessness that conveyed rustic charm. There was a restaurant on the first floor and during their honeymoon the smell of frying grease in the mornings had overpowered the sea air and clung to the linens. The cottages, with quaint names like Eagle's Lookout, Plover's Perch, and Crane's Cranny, fanned out behind the inn along a winding boardwalk. Gene recalled that the path led to a small gray beach craggy with jagged rocks.

He still remembered the clerk who had checked them in after the wedding. The reception had taken place in the backyard of the house belonging to Maida's uncle. With the exception of a few friends, most of the guests were family and the party had the stifling atmosphere of a family occasion. When Ed cued "Earth Angel," the song Gene had picked out for this moment, he was too uncomfortable to dance with his bride in front of his family and hers, and they had only held hands and looked at each other, smiling stupidly, until the Penguins cooed their last note. Having escaped the party at the earliest possible moment, they arrived at the inn giggly and breathless, and the boy at the front desk—he was a young man, really, jocular and handsome—had checked them in with a knowing half-smile. Gene in his nervousness got confused about whether he was supposed to pay for the room before or after, and the boy said, "After what?" with a smirk. As Gene fumbled first with his checkbook and then with the pen, Maida started a conversation with the boy about the tattoo on his arm. It was a kind of mermaid, a buxom woman naked from the waist up with a green fish's tail, and as they talked, a teasing rapport sprang up between them. When Gene looked up, the clerk was lifting his shirt to show Maida how the tattoo continued around his torso. The end of the tail was buried in his pants, and for a moment Gene wondered if he was going to take these off too. Suddenly his head felt stuffy and his throat burned. But just as he thought he might have to sit down, Maida slipped her hand into his and gave it a squeeze. Then he understood she was entertaining the boy's story as a sideways flirtation with him. It was a kind of performance to excite him for what was about to happen between them in the cottage.

Now in the humid office of the inn, with the late-afternoon sun streaming through the blinds, Gene explained to the woman behind the desk his connection to Cottage No. 5, the Pelican's Nest. He asked if he might pop his head in and take a look around. She told him there was some work being done on the plumbing, but if he didn't mind that, the cottage was unlocked and he should go ahead.

Some mud-streaked towels lay on the floor but the cottage was empty. It was as simple as he remembered it. The windows had no glass, only screens, and if you wanted to shutter them you had to do it from the outside by releasing the hook-and-eye closure that kept the hinged boards from flopping down in the wind. The single room was adjoined by a closet-sized bathroom lacking a tub, and both the walls and the floor were painted a watery coat of white that the knotty pine showed through. The mattress on the full-size bed wasn't very firm and when he sat down he sank until it seemed his tailbone would connect with the box spring.

How strange those first hours of marriage were! There had been the rush to put miles between them and the wedding guests in Colton. But alone in the cottage the demented urgency he had felt in the car evaporated. Somehow having what he wanted within reach—not only within reach but *expected*—dampened his desire.

For several long minutes they sat on the bed wordlessly holding hands. Maida was wearing a white satin top overlaid with lace and her mother had braided matching white ribbons into her hair. Her expression took refuge behind all this ceremonial white. He realized he would have to be the one to take responsibility for their loving.

Already he had been intimate with her mouth, her breasts, her stomach, her inner thighs, and two days before the wedding he had reached his hand inside her. In response, she had wriggled around in an accommodating way. She had also tried to bring him to pleasure using her hands and been almost successful. But in the end he had to help her, because their rhythm was off.

In the cottage she closed her eyes when he touched her and this was a relief, the potential for awkwardness somehow halved if it was only felt but not seen. To surmount his own sense of absurdity, the absurdity that so much courtship and ceremony came down to *this,* he found it easier to concentrate on her pleasure rather than his own. She was quiet and acquiescent, and her silence roused him to more frantic activity. He imagined motors in his hands, small motors under his tongue, and he told himself he couldn't stop until she cried out in pleasure. But she remained virtually soundless, her quiet absorbing not only any sound she might have made but also his grunts and whimpers. He had no idea that he would feel so alone.

But later, drifting in and out of the balmiest sleep, he wondered in a kind of rapture what exactly had taken place. There were various names for what had transpired between them and none of them was satisfying. None of them explained why his tenderness for her had enlarged when it was already full, or why his innermost life felt more deeply bound up with the woman sleeping next to him.

2.

ED HAD INTRODUCED them.

Gene had met Ed in the spring of his junior year at the University of New Hampshire, after they were matched by a student organization that offered academic tutoring. Gene's course of study in business communications allowed him to take some English classes toward the requirements of the major, and he was determined not to waste the opportunity. Somewhere—and not from his parents, neither of whom he could remember ever reading a book—he'd gotten the idea that to be a person who read books was to be someone who was alluring to other people. The allure had something to do with solitude, but also with intimacy—the flash of connection that was possible between two people who had read the same book. (It hadn't escaped him that the prettiest girls at the college were studying literature.) The power of books was mysterious, and the mystery had an almost erotic dimension, because it required a kind of relentless pursuit that might or might not result in the book giving itself up.

The year before he'd done all right in a class on the

nineteenth-century novel and slightly better in a Shakespeare course in which they got to watch films of the plays. Neither, however, had prepared him for his junior-year survey class in poetry, in which the withered, shrunken appearance of the aging professor provided a startling contrast to the unsparing, blunt comments he scrawled across Gene's papers. Each time one of these heavily annotated papers was returned to him, Gene was disappointed that the sense of momentousness he had hoped to capture hadn't been adequately conveyed. He was embarrassed to have wasted everyone's time—the professor's, but also his own—and his contrition was not any less because of the general irrelevance of poetry. He found a tutor and began to spend Thursday afternoons in Ed's apartment tracking ankles in Dickinson, apples in Rilke, and birds in Stevens in order to find out which ideas these ankles, apples, and birds stood for.

The apartment was a run-down series of rooms that Ed and his flatmate, Braxton, ironically called "Old Glory" for the American flag the previous tenant had left pinned crookedly to the wall above the fireplace. Gene didn't know many students who lived in their own apartments—either they lived in the dorms, as he did, or they lived at home. Ed's apartment had a peculiar odor, a sophisticated amalgam of the cigarettes smoked nearly constantly by Braxton, doughnuts fried each morning in the bakery down below, wet coffee grounds left all day in the sink, a sweet chemical smell that Ed said came from the mouse-traps in the kitchen, and the moist, earthy emanations from the potted plants Ed had stuck all over the apartment to combat the other smells. The apartment was often missing the pieces of furniture you might think were crucial to student life—sometimes the desk, often the chairs—and if a missing piece was inquired about, the inevitable answer was that it had been borrowed by the neighbors down the hall or broken during one of Ed and Braxton's frequent parties. There were not enough chairs, but a section of the living room floor was covered in pillows made of richly textured fabrics. Whenever by some automatic habit Gene picked one up and set it on a chair, Ed said mildly: "Leave it on the floor, Ashe. That's where it goes."

It turned out that Ed was not a literature student—he was majoring in molecular biology—but since he had done well in literature courses (and in art history, political science, philosophy, and economics, as well as in the courses required for his major), the academic organization had listed him as available to tutor in any subject. Ed's off-campus housing and general fluency with college academics had led Gene to believe that Ed was older than him and probably from a city. But neither turned out to be true. Ed was just a junior like him, and he had grown up in the small town just across the river from Colton.

Ed had joined the tutoring organization rather impulsively, because the two young, attractive women who ran it had asked him to. He had skipped the training session, resolving to participate according to his own style. His manner of teaching was indirect—so indirect that Gene sometimes worried that he wasn't learning anything. Inevitably their conversations drifted away from the text they were supposed to be studying toward any number of unrelated topics: whether it was relevant to know they would eventually die, whether happiness was something the self manufactured or whether it was largely the function of your relationships to others, whether romantic love was a worthy pursuit and if so whether that made it interesting or dull. By the time they returned to the text Gene would have forgotten about ankles and apples and birds altogether, and he would have to prod Ed to consider whether a particular line was or wasn't trochaic meter.

Ed had offered to hold their meetings at the library, but then Gene would have been deprived of the opportunity to feed his covert fascination with Ed and his off-campus life. There were enough books in the apartment to keep a person busy for years. Books about religion and medicine and philosophy, about gardening and theater and political economy. During their lessons Gene's eye habitually came to rest on certain volumes: a thin, cream-colored copy of *Siddhartha,* or the black spine with white capital letters of *Thoughts Out of Season.* An entire shelf was devoted to books about photography, and set up permanently in a corner of the living room was a large-format camera with a flash umbrella. Gene heard it first as a rumor and later from Ed directly that if Ed wished to make a portrait of someone he encountered, he invited the person in off the street. Gene began to nourish a private hope that Ed would ask to make a portrait of him.

There were no photographs, however, on view in the apartment, only paintings whose selection had no underlying principle that Gene could discern. Some were still-lifes with crockery pitchers and gleaming tumbled fruits, as boring as anything you would see in a textbook, while others were abstract assemblages of gruesomely paired colors, chartreuse and crimson, bronze and bird shit. Sometimes Gene caught himself involuntarily complimenting Ed's taste, voicing some opinion that he didn't recognize as his own.

"You like it?" Ed said. "I like it too."

It turned out that everything on the walls had come from junk shops. Most of it would go back to them when Ed got sick of it.

Once in a while Gene would remember that he and Ed had both come from small New Hampshire towns, and this fact, freshly landing for the sixth or sixteenth time, astonished him. It seemed impossible that someone like Ed could have had a childhood like his, in which children who complained of hunger were sometimes given a washrag to suck on, and pants were patched with flour sacks, and for amusement in the evenings kids would go to the park to count how many gypsy moths had been caught in the light traps by the men who were studying why all the trees had lost their leaves. To be a child born in 1931 in Colton was to be born into a town losing its life. One year the Amoskeag mill in Manchester shut down on Christmas Eve and never opened again, and three years later the last mill making cloth in Colton was closed for good. Gene's mother said it wouldn't be long before the men who worked at the tannery like Gene's father would be cutting gooseberry bushes with the other ragged men on the side of the road. Gene was just a child then, he didn't understand how it all connected, but he remembered the feeling in the rooms where adults met and addressed each other in low voices, the mood of fear and confusion that made them suddenly wheel around and speak angrily to a child who wanted to know why he couldn't have a cup of cocoa before going to bed. Colton was men without jobs and women minding children, it was churches and waterways and the closed-down mills, and it and places like it were noticeably bare of the kind of cultural objects Ed felt at ease around. So he thought of Ed as a sort of changeling, a person whose origins didn't entirely match his presentation, and for Gene it was a pleasant dissonance, one that inflated his admiration of Ed. He was always a little disappointed when Ed mentioned his boyhood excursions in the White Mountains or playing Skee-Ball at the beach arcade, anything that suggested they had not grown up in distinct universes.

Once after they had not really discussed "The Wild Swans at Coole" but had engaged instead in a conversation touching on the aspiration that something, *something,* could be accomplished in a life, Gene asked Ed why, when it was evident he was so stimulated by poetry, he was studying biology.

"You can't spend all day mooning over poetry," Ed said, "and expect to be accepted to a good medical school."

It couldn't have surprised Gene more than if Ed had said he was planning to live in a cave for a career. Actually, Gene could picture Ed living in a cave more easily than he could picture him as a physician, with the inflexible hours, fixed protocols, never-ending training, and regular supervision. Ed's father was a doctor, a nephrologist, and it occurred to Gene that Ed's decision might have something to do with that, but Ed denied it.

"Isn't there some part of you," Gene said, "that wants to be a writer? Or if not a writer, an artist?"

The look on Ed's face told him the question had hit its mark, but the expression was so fleeting that if Gene hadn't been certain of having seen it, he would have wondered a moment later if he'd imagined it.

"The world doesn't need more writers," Ed said. "Has any writer solved a single problem we know of? I'm going to be a doctor because I want to *do* something with my life. It's all probably going to end sooner than we think anyway, and before I go I'd like to know that my existence made some little difference to this freak show on earth. When you're a doctor, you can do that. You can make people live and die. What's a painting or a poem compared to that? I'm going to learn the human body well enough to tell it how to do its job."

"But isn't there something noble about art?" Gene said.

"Don't ask anyone else that question, Ashe. You can ask me, but if you ask the wrong person, they're going to shove your balls into your throat quicker than you can picture the *Mona Lisa.* Here's my advice to you: if someone starts talking to you about how noble art is—or worse, how noble *their* art is—run the other way."

"I don't think of artists as being especially dangerous."

"That's why you have to get away," Ed said. "Nobility is a concept tossed around by people who are terrified to smell their own shit. You aren't one of those people, are you?"

"I—"

"Don't answer the question. Just smell everything."

One day, from the window of Ed's apartment, they watched a woman passing on the street below. She wore loose batik pants that were tight at the ankles, and in her arms she carried a Manx cat that was clawing at a pile of silver necklaces on her chest.

"What do you think?" Ed said. "On her way to break up with her boyfriend and give him back her Valentine's Day present?"

"Maybe she's going to the vet," Gene said.

"Should we invite her up? Her and—Whiskers?"

"What—right now?"

"Did you have another time in mind?" Ed said, putting on his shoes.

"We don't have chairs."

"I'll sit on the floor. Or you will."

"Why don't you invite her up," Gene said, "and I'll just slip out the back?"

"Are you afraid of women or something?"

"If you don't go down right now, you'll miss her."

"That's all right," Ed said, and he took off the shoes he had just put on. "We'll let this one go." He settled himself on a pillow on the floor. "What I want to know, my friend, is why when I start to talk about that girl on the street, you start looking like you want to jump out the window. Isn't there a woman, any woman, you could call up right now?"

"And say what to her?"

"You're having a party, and you'd like her to come."

"But we're not having a party."

"We could be, in ten minutes. I'll just go down to the liquor store and have Freddie send up a few bottles. Whiskey okay? Normally I'd do one whiskey and one vodka, but the only vodka they have down there is imported from a country whose politics are lousy, so my little act of disobedience is to refuse to buy it."

"What's wrong with it? Are they socialists?"

"Yes, but they've lost their imaginations. I was buying their vodka as long as their ideas were good—but now their ideas sound the same as everyone else's. What's the girl's name?"

"Who?"

"The name of the girl you're inviting over! When I go down there and get the Manx, I'd like to be able to tell her who her sister will be."

Gene thought for a moment. There was a girl in his poetry class who once had given him her notes when he was sick. Encouraged by this, he'd invited her to go to the movies and a date was chosen, but then she had canceled the day before, saying she wasn't feeling well. It was quite possible that she was legitimately ill, but he had been deflated by the experience nevertheless, and the next time he saw her in class he was convinced she was trying to avoid him. He considered who else he might call. "I could call my cousin," he said. His cousin Rose worked in an insurance office in Manchester; she might come on short notice if he explained the situation.

"Ashe, you're not going to invite your cousin, for Chrissake! What's wrong with you? Haven't you been paying attention to anything we've been reading? And here I thought you were a smart guy."

For an instant, forgetting he was being teased, Gene felt the glow of Ed's compliment. A person he regarded as well above average in intelligence and discernment thought that *he*, Eugene Ashe, was smart. The rapture of the praise increased his eagerness to please his friend. "I think you'd *like* my cousin."

"I don't need you to do my fishing for me, Ashe. But it seems like I have to do yours. What's your type? Tall and skinny? Short and fat? Brown hair, blond hair—every last hair plucked away?"

Gene wasn't sure if he was supposed to take the question seriously, or if he was being teased again. "I'm not stuck on a girl's hair," he said. "As long as you like her, I'm sure I will too."

"You're breaking my heart, Ashe, and the only ones who are allowed to do that are beautiful women I've never seen naked. You understand? In the meantime, let's have you work on being a little less skittish, okay? I don't want to invite the girl over for you and then have you running down the stairs."

In the weeks that followed, Gene perceived that he had failed some tacit but nevertheless definitive test of the friendship. But if after that their conversations ranged a bit less widely, there were other explanations besides an unspoken rift. The semester was coming to an end, finals were upon them, and summer jobs had to be found. They parted on friendly terms and promised to look each other up in the fall.

In the fall Gene was relieved when, first thing after he had settled on his classes, he went by Ed's apartment and the two of them stayed up talking into the night. A lot had happened during the summer—Ed had applied to medical school and gotten two interviews, with more potentially coming, and Gene had gone on a few dates with one of his cousin's friends. Ed, for the first time in a while, had a steady girlfriend, whom he'd met at a costume party at which she was dressed as a bottle of No-Cal and he as a straw. Gayle Carey was nineteen years old, she had a job processing work orders at the naval shipyard, and Ed promised that Gene would meet her soon. Ed also had another girl he wanted Gene to meet, someone he knew from high school who he felt "shouldn't go to waste." Gene figured there had to be something wrong with this girl if Ed didn't want her for himself. She was probably ugly or slow-witted or mean-spirited or ratty.

None of these turned out to be true. Maida Halloran was attractive and intelligent. She had a lovely neck shown off by short blond hair, and there was a restraint in her manner that came off as a form of acquired dignity, as if she had been injured once and had decided not to allow it to happen again. She didn't talk often about herself, but she had spent the previous two years at Bates before she'd had some sort of disagreement with the administration. Gene took her general reticence on the topic as an indication that she didn't particularly mourn her collegiate life. She had come to Durham because her father had been able to find her a job with one of his contacts, and she was working in the office of an architect and had acquiesced to Ed's proposal to take her around and introduce her to people.

It was a cataclysmic interruption in Gene's life that he should suddenly come to know not one but two delightful women at the same time. He liked Ed's girlfriend almost as much as he liked Maida. Gayle was the kind of person who stood up to greet you when you entered the room even if you'd only been gone long enough to get limes for the drinks. When you insisted she sit down, she didn't listen, helping you with your coat and whatever you were carrying and then fixing you a drink when you were the one who was supposed to be making drinks for everyone else. Maida was pretty, but she was also slender, and some thin girls carried a perpetual tension in their bodies that made him feel like the slightest touch would send alarms up and down their nerves. Gayle had that pleasing roundness that was the opposite. Gene wasn't accustomed to touching women casually, but Gayle hugged or patted or tugged at people with the affection of a puppy. No one could be afraid of a person like her, a sentiment that was close to feeling that she could be an ally for the rest of your life.

Gayle was terribly naive about certain things—she thought food stamps were a kind of postage, and a pessary a type of fish—and this aspect of her personality galled Ed. Of particular dismay to him was Gayle's tendency to regard the naval ship-yard where she worked as an independent entity rather than as a branch of the armed forces. Ed was convinced of the widespread, amoral collusion of politicians and military personnel, and in an attempt to bring Gayle's views more in line with his, he collected news reports about the unconfirmed hydrogen-bomb test on Enewetak Atoll in the Pacific. "Now how do you think the bomb got to the middle of the ocean?" he said to Gayle, who just laughed as if to say Ed couldn't seriously expect her to opine on something she knew nothing about. "Think," Ed said.

"Just stop and think for a minute." Gayle pretended to study the article. Then in a tone of mild surprise she said, "It sounds like there was a fire on the island. Maybe it was set by the people who live there." Ed responded by turning from her and asking Maida what she thought of the treaty with Japan. Gene understood Ed's frustration, but he personally found Gayle's lack of intellectual posturing refreshing.

Sometimes Gene had the sense that Gayle didn't have a *No* in her body, that her body would give and give and never turn someone back no matter what they asked, no matter how enormous or desperate their need might be. One evening, when the four of them had spent the day together and she was the last of his passengers to drop off, he asked her if he could come inside to see her apartment, which she shared with two other girls on the first floor of a large house. He asked her mostly because he was curious about her life, but also because he just wanted to know what she would say. Her kitchen was cozy and cheerful, with striped yellow wallpaper bursting with yellow roses, and a yellow sugar bowl on the table in the shape of a bird. She made a pitcher of fresh lemonade, though it was already quite late and she had to get up early for work the next day. It was only when he noticed her rubbing her neck that she admitted she had a headache. He led her by the hand into the dark sunporch and had her sit on the bench, facing out toward the night. He started at her temples, rubbing gently, allowing his palms to brush against her cheeks, the lobes of her ears, her neck. There was something thrilling about her vulnerability to him. He brought his face close to the back of her neck— it smelled of the lemons she had squeezed. His hand swept down to her waist, the suppleness there surely just a prelude to the suppleness of her breasts. But abruptly she was back on her feet. She said she couldn't stand to have a fuss made of her.

Not long after this he asked Ed a question that had been on his mind a while: Why did he like Gayle? Gene understood why *he* liked Gayle, but it was something of a mystery to him why, out of all the women Ed had dated, he'd chosen Gayle Carey to be his girlfriend.

"I guess it might seem improbable at first," Ed admitted. "She can be a little square, right?" He smiled a brittle smile. "Don't be fooled," he said. "The square ones—they're the ones with the darkest stuff in here." He tapped two fingers against his chest. "All their wholesome piety is hooey. They're the ones with the most to repent for, the most to hide. I like to crack them." The brittle smile expanded. "And I think they like to be cracked."

Gene figured it would not take Ed long to crack Gayle and move on, putting an end to the fun the four friends had together. But Ed and Gayle were still dating six months later when Ed invited Maida and Gene to spend a few weeks of the summer with them at White Pine Camp, the Donnelly family property. Gene still hadn't acted on his amorous interest in Maida and he took Ed's invitation as a gentle ultimatum— either he would make something happen with Maida that summer, or he would have to give her up.

The four friends went to White Pine Camp for two and a half weeks in July, and continued their tradition of blundering around. There were hikes up Mount Orry to hunt for birds' nests and snake eggs; monologues delivered on the old stone foundation of the local factory that had once produced bobbins and clothespins; tramps through the woods and marshy bottoms to collect wild strawberries; trips down to the millpond choked with pickerelweed to cut its rangy purple flowers for the table; canoeing and horseshoes; and of course escaping from the sun's heat every day with a dip in the lake.

Just before the trip Ed had been offered and accepted a spot in medical school at the University of Michigan, and there were times when he and Gayle entered into a contentious conversation about the future of their relationship. At those moments Gayle looked at Ed with such forlornness and longing that it seemed everyone in the room was slightly embarrassed for her. Selfishly Gene couldn't help feeling dismay whenever the topic arose because it always threatened to ruin what otherwise could have been another perfect day. Evidently, Maida felt the same annoyance. One afternoon when Gayle began to adopt a familiar injured tone, Maida said, "Oh, enough already, Gayle. Let the rest of us have some fun." Unfortunately Ed chose this precise moment to smile, prompting Gayle to run off crying—though not before she had said, "If everyone is against me, then why am I here?"

The next time the conversation veered in this direction, Maida and Gene removed themselves from the scene. In theory this was a promising development—it gave Gene an opportunity to spend time alone with Maida—but in reality it was a source of enormous anxiety for him, because as soon as she wasn't expected anywhere she went for a long swim. He was left watching her slip away from the shore while he stood hesitant in his swim trunks on the beach, feeling like a confirmed land animal.

At twenty-two he swam exactly one stroke. It wasn't the crawl or the breaststroke; it was some hybrid in which his arms and legs moved as completely different systems whose only unity was the goal of keeping his head above water. His hands dug for purchase, his legs abruptly sucked together, and his feet landed a firm wallop on the water every few seconds. Maida teased him for it.

She had learned to swim before she could read. Her strokes were beautiful, effortless shearings of the lake's surface, and she treaded water in that efficient way that barely betrayed any movement beneath the surface. In the summers a floating dock was anchored some twenty yards from the shore and she could pull herself up onto it without using the ladder. When she had sunned herself there a little while, some urge would propel her back into the lake, and she would begin swimming toward the opposite shore, sometimes catching up to a canoe if the paddler was intermittent in his efforts. She always turned back before she lost sight of their little beach.

That day, after they had left Ed and Gayle, he asked her if she wanted company on her swim. "Do what you like," she said and then plunged beneath the lake's coppery sheen. But she was not as indifferent as she made herself out to be, and when he paddled haphazardly after her she tried to help him develop his stroke.

It was pure humiliation and torture, striving to succeed at something he knew he would never experience at the level of success other people did. There was simply no getting back those childhood years when the limbs and the brain were on closer terms. When Maida told him he was tiring himself unnecessarily and would never stop being slow unless he put his face in the water, he hated her for having no idea how difficult this would be for him. He inhaled a mouthful of water and it came back out his nose, painfully. He began to cough. She grabbed him and towed him toward the floating dock, deepening his shame.

But once they were sitting on the floating dock together with their splayed knees brushing occasionally against each other's, he recalled how she had tried to help him. The same words that in the water had seemed to him lacking in sympathy and patience now struck him as generous offerings. Her actions, too, had been generous—she had acted to save him from harm. At any moment she could have swum off by herself, leaving him behind. Instead she had stayed beside him and accepted his limitations as her own.

It was early evening. The lake floated beneath a sky not yet drained of light. Children were dragging rafts out of the water and tying them up to piers. People were heading home. There was a great settling all around them. The water deepened to a mossy darkness as fragrant as soil, and the trees bowed over this darkness, releasing the last of the light from their crowns. The earth's surrender of its color quieted something that Gene hadn't realized had previously been loud, making a space in which his own body was more alive to him. He felt the electricity of their two bodies in proximity, an immense feeling born of the tiniest motion, the way his skin leaned toward hers in the gap between their touch and sometimes found nothing but air. There was a physical sensation, a type of pain, associated with not touching. At first it was no more than a minor discomfort, akin to a tickle. But as they sat there the sensation deepened, until it manifested itself as a physical pain in his chest. He saw that his body had become an object of hers and would always be an object of hers as long as she was near. It was then he understood he loved her. He had skipped all of the steps: dates, phone calls, a first kiss. He knew her character, and he was as certain of her good qualities as he was of his own deficits. He was already in love.

In many ways, that period between when he knew he loved Maida and when he told her was the most thrilling, excruciating time in his life. For two weeks, whenever he saw her his whole body entered a harrowing state of wakefulness. Everything she did he interpreted in relation to him, an exalted state of suffering that took the form of a complete disregard for himself except as an extension of her, which also had the strange effect of at once increasing and diminishing his sense of himself. He was everywhere and everything when she acknowledged him with a gesture, and he was nowhere and nothing when she failed to glance in his direction.

He knew he would have to tell her before long—the enormity of the secret was too great. The moment when the secret passed from him to her would transform them both. But love was not the sort of thing you blurted out one day over oatmeal. Whenever he pictured telling her, they were lying side by side on the floating dock. Her mouth would be a few inches from his, and it would take all of his will to speak his part looking into her eyes instead of at her mouth, which he desperately wanted to kiss. Their bodies would be nearly touching, and when the wind picked up and she shuddered, he would pull her into his arms and cover her body with his. They would swim back together feeling that something between them had been decided.

The date of their departure from White Pine Camp grew near and still he was waiting for the right time, the right moment. Something had changed between Ed and Gayle—they were more droll and affectionate with each other—and this development, while generally improving the atmosphere in the cabin, limited Gene's opportunity to be alone with Maida. Soon there was only one day left. That settled it—their last day would have to be *the* day. Except that on that day Maida developed a heat rash on her arms and her legs. She scratched at it and complained about it, declaring it repellent and ugly, in addition to itchy. When Ed told her she was being silly, she snapped,

"*I'm* being silly?" Gayle offered to go into town for some oint-
ment but Maida refused, appearing to draw strength from her
crankiness, as if to be justified in her misery was better than
experiencing relief. Then whatever magic her obstinacy had
worked for her dissipated, and she was left as despondent as before. When Gene offered to bring her a glass of orange juice she
pantomimed retching, and when he lay down next to her to rub
her back she grew silent and morose.

Ed said they should leave her alone. It was their last day and
if she wanted to spend it in agony that was her choice, but the
rest of them didn't have to go along with it. He, for one, was
going for a swim.

"Leave me," Maida said to Gene, after Ed and Gayle were gone.
"I'd do the same." But he stayed with her, and she slept fitfully on
the couch. Once it sounded like she was crying. He lay on the floor
next to her, eye level with a box of Scrabble taped at the corners
and a thick book called *Trees of the Northeast* tabbed like a dictio-
nary, and as he listened to her sad little whimpering, he was filled
with an unfamiliar fear. It was the fear that whatever ailed her
wasn't in his capacity to heal. It was the fear that as long as she suffered from some unnamable pain, her unhappiness would be his.

He pushed aside the thought, recognizing it as yet another
form of delay. He was looking for a reason not to tell her, for
a way to make the things he felt seem less real than the things
other people felt. *So say it,* he told himself. *First thing when she
opens her eyes—just say it.*

Maida sat up, groggy and rubbing her eyes. Gene blurted the
words, and for a moment, her hands stopped moving. She held
her fists over her eyes, then lowered them. "Really?" she said.

They didn't talk about it, because just then Ed and Gayle,
hair damp from the lake, returned.

"Everything all right in here?" said Ed, adopting the stern but loving manner of a father who hoped to find that his cantankerous children had made peace in his absence. "Good, good," he said, without waiting for a response. He bent over and kissed each of them on the head, Gene first, surprisingly, and then Maida.

They left White Pine Camp the next day and for Gene a period of interminable uncertainty ensued. He didn't see Maida for days and yet she was more present in his mind than if she was chained to his wrist. All day long his body did certain things, while his mind lived an independent life: *Will she or won't she?* In his dreams at night, he didn't have a body. He was just an awareness flying over the entire Earth, a watery expanse of blues and greens so gorgeous it would make you weep. But wherever he looked there was no place to land, nothing solid, so he had no choice but to continue to fly. In the morning, he felt more tired than before he'd gone to bed.

At first it seemed she *had* to give him an answer, that he had left her with a question. But as the days passed and he didn't hear from her, it occurred to him that maybe she didn't know she was supposed to answer him. Maybe she thought that if he desired her enough, he would present himself again. He didn't know how it worked.

He went to Ed's and found the apartment in a sad state of barrenness. The reams of books had been culled. One small box had been sent on to Michigan and the rest were going to Ed's younger brother, who was starting at Bowdoin in the fall. The large-format camera had been traded in for something smaller, the flash umbrella put out on the street. Most of the paintings had been given away and the lone remaining chair had a broken spindle. He and Ed stood in front of the small table in the kitchen. In its center sat a cracked clay bowl containing a handful of pistachios.

"I told Maida I love her."

"Pistachio?" Ed held out the bowl.

"No, thanks. I told Maida I love her," he said again.

Ed took a pistachio for himself and set the bowl back down. "How did that go?"

"She didn't say much."

"What did she say?"

"She said, 'Really?'"

"Better that than nothing at all."

There was a silence in which all that could be heard was the nut cracking between Ed's teeth.

"What am I supposed to do now?" Gene said.

"Have you talked to her?"

"When would I have talked to her? I only see her when she's with you."

"You call her, Gene. You *call* her. She probably needs some time to sort things out in her head."

"But if she loves me she would have said it when I said it," Gene said.

"Look, you don't want a parrot," Ed said. He tossed a pistachio into the air and caught it in his mouth. "Don't expect her to say it back right away, unless all you're looking for is a girl who's going to affirm everything you say."

"But Gayle affirms."

"That's different. I don't need the affirmation, so I can ignore it." He patted Gene on the arm. "Don't worry, Maida will show up sooner or later. They usually come back, even when they don't intend to."

"If you know something," Gene said, "you've got to tell me.

You've *got* to. If I knew something about Gayle I would never keep it from you. Like if Gayle was crazy about another guy I would tell you right away."

"That would certainly be an interesting twist. If Gayle was crazy about someone else but engaged to me—"

"Of course she isn't! Wait—are you...?"

"We're getting married," Ed said, with no particular inflection.

For a second, Gene felt that something had been stolen from him.

"It was brewing all summer," Ed said. "You knew that."

Gene wasn't sure that he did. "But how did it happen...?" he said. "What did you say to her? What did *she* say?"

"It started off the same way as usual," Ed said. "With a fight. And I was getting so bored of fighting—I really didn't have the passion for it anymore—that one day I turned to her and said, 'If you like me so much why don't you come live with me in Michigan.' And she says, 'Are you asking me to marry you, Ed Donnelly?' And I say, 'I think we both know what I said.' And she starts to cry and says, 'But I can't live with you unless we're married! You know that!' And I say, 'Nothing in the world is preventing you from moving to Michigan. The Germans have been doing it for years.' And she says, 'You know I can't. If it was up to me I would do it tomorrow, but you know my family—you know they need a piece of paper.' 'All you need is a piece of paper and you'll do it?' 'Yes.' 'Fine,' I say. 'Fine?' 'Yes, we'll get a piece of paper.' 'Really?' 'We'll get ten pieces of paper if you like.' 'Oh, don't make a joke of it, not now, not when no one has ever asked me to marry them before!' Then she jumps on me and throws her arms around my neck and heaves once like she's going to sob, and just as I begin to think *What have*

I done? she perks up and then it's over and we're not arguing anymore." He explained they would have the ceremony at City Hall that week, then a proper wedding the next summer. "You know," he said wryly, "for the *families*." He and Gayle would leave for Michigan the day after the ceremony. "Oh, come on," Ed said. "Don't be so morose. We're coming back, just as soon as I collect that other piece of paper."

"You don't know that," said Gene, who was experiencing a foretaste of loss for this defining era of his life. "You don't know what it will be like there."

"Sure I do," Ed said. "There'll be college football and snow and nice leafy trees. But I don't like football and we have the rest of that stuff here. Anyway, you're acting like I'm going off to China. Don't forget I'll still have some time off in the summer, at least until residency. We'll go to the lake—you'll see."

"But it won't be the same."

"I hope not. God, that would be tedious. Maybe you'll even have a girlfriend by then."

At the time, Gene thought this would be the end of the four-way friendship. And while the memory of it would never be lost, he pictured his life progressing on a different, smaller register after that, unable to compete with this time when their freedoms were greater than their responsibilities. In the future that he imagined, he would be aware of the absent others living out their own lives, and some part of him would feel sad that such a rich confluence of friendships had come apart just as it was beginning to flourish.

But he was wrong. With Ed and Gayle gone to Michigan, he and Maida now had something new in common, which was the gloomy loss of their friends. Maida never directly acknowledged the conversation they'd had on their last day at

White Pine Camp, but she began to invite Gene to be her companion at social gatherings where her father was present. Mr. Halloran had many business acquaintances throughout New Hampshire in the construction industry, and Maida was often called upon to make an appearance at their gatherings, though there was rarely anyone in the room she wanted to talk to and her father had an embarrassing tendency to remark to his colleagues that he'd found his daughter a job to save her reputation, which she had almost succeeded in ruining at college. There was nothing Maida liked about attending these parties except that it kept her father sending her a check every month to supplement her wages.

The first time Gene met Maida's father, Mr. Halloran shook his hand and said, "You're not very tall, are you?" He then proceeded to hand Gene a beer, which he drank gratefully in silence. "You're haven't grown much since the last time, have you?" Mr. Halloran said the next time Gene saw him, and in private Maida explained that relatively speaking, this was a compliment, because it indicated her father could find no other obvious objectionable feature in Gene. "You're quiet, you're pleasant-looking, and you're kind to me," Maida said, and Gene wasn't sure if she meant that as a good thing. But since it seemed he had been brought along to play the part of her boyfriend, he took liberties with the role, draping his arm around her shoulders and calling her back to him when she had traveled across the room. Far from discouraging him, she teased him, beckoning him with a tilt of her hips or a sultry pout. Yet whenever they stepped outside, the bright, ordinary light of day would shrink his ambitions, and he would fall back on making small talk, the easiest form of which was speculating about how Ed and Gayle were doing in Michigan.

On one such day, when they were sitting together on a bench outside a tavern, Maida sighed and said, "We exist without them, you know." Then without any warning she unceremoniously placed her hand on his groin.

That was, he supposed, their official beginning, but in truth once he had become her actual boyfriend instead of the convenient stand-in, it seemed that they had already been together for a very long time. When they wrote to tell Ed and Gayle, they received in return a letter with a single word written in the middle of the page:

FINALLY!!!

They didn't bother to explain the nuances to Maida's father. It only would have introduced confusion—for all he knew, they had been together all along. Though perhaps her father did sense some deepening in their affections, because Mr. Halloran's attitude toward Gene shifted from one of mere tolerance to restless paternalistic concern. He began taking Gene aside to lecture him about the special combination of qualities necessary to succeed in the world of business, qualities he himself had been naturally blessed with, and which Gene would have to work uncommonly hard to develop if he hoped to see any success at the leather-importing company where he'd gotten a job after graduation.

Then, just when it began to seem his life had become almost respectfully dull, Ed and Gayle returned to New Hampshire for the wedding party they owed their families. The celebration was held on a private estate, and while Ed and Gayle were cutting the cake, Gene rowed Maida to the middle of the pond and asked her to marry him. Saying nothing, she began stripping off her finery, and he wondered if this was her way of saying yes, rewarding him with what he desired. But as soon as she was wearing only her bra and underwear, she climbed over the side of the boat and dropped into the water. He found her behavior puzzling, possibly even insulting, and he waited for what seemed like an eternity for her to resurface. When she finally popped up, he helped her back into the boat and wiped the slimy vegetal scum off her face with his tie. He thought for certain she would reject him. But then she said yes, she would marry him, and she was sorry about ruining his tie.

That summer the four friends went to the lake just as Ed said they would. Everyone was in a celebratory mood, and they drank to one another's good fortune, and then they drank a little bit extra. Ed and Gayle returned to Ann Arbor, and Gene began to think seriously about how he was going to support his bride-to-be and the family they hoped to have. He was convinced that the key to making good money was running one's own company. When he learned that the owner of the shoe store in Colton was looking for someone to buy it so that he could retire, Gene sent his future father-in-law a business proposal appended to a request for a loan. Mr. Halloran wouldn't even consider it until Gene and Maida were married, so although they had originally hoped to be wed at the height of summer, they rushed ahead with a church ceremony and a small backyard reception in the chilly spring of 1955. At the end of the reception, just before he and Maida departed for the Sandpiper Inn, Mr. Halloran handed him an envelope containing a signed check.

Gene purchased the shoe business and moved his bride into their first apartment, a third-floor walk-up in Colton with a stove but no oven and a bathtub squeezed into a space so narrow that you had to sit sideways on the toilet. The years that followed were busy and exhausting as they tried to grow the business and establish the rhythms of their marriage.

But there were always summers at the lake. Every year Gene closed the shop for two weeks, and Maida often stayed on longer after he returned to Colton. The summer Ed graduated medical school Gayle was six months pregnant, and the next year she and Ed brought baby Brian to White Pine Camp. Then Maida was pregnant, and the next summer the Ashes brought an infant. It continued like that, with each year introducing some new development in the families that inducted them into a life in common centered around their children.

Because really—summers at Fisher Lake belonged to children. Each day the valley filled with their delighted cries ricocheting off the mountains, as all around the lake little bodies hurled themselves off piers, docks, and canoes. The boats with their snarling engines cut from one side of the lake to the other, making the large, rocking wakes that the older children loved to dive beneath holding their noses. In the evenings sandy towels were rattled from open windows and there were halfhearted attempts at bathing and grooming the littlest ones. Then the children with their drying hair and sweet-smelling necks would be pulled onto the laps of adults, who had gathered on the deck at the back of the cabin with their wine and gin and beer to watch the mirror of the lake relinquish its light. "Look," someone might say to a babbling baby, as if she too might see and later remember the spectacular progression of the light, the retraction of gold from the water that was like a purple shade being pulled across it just beneath the surface.

There were, of course, the occasional notes of disharmony. Gene recalled the summer that Ed was reading *Anna Karenina,* and how he fell under what Gene and Gayle called the "Tolstoy spell." That summer Ed couldn't stop telling everyone what a genius Tolstoy was and how this was a book everybody had to read because it contained all of life: the unsolvable arguments of husbands and wives, the regretful necessity of politics, long gorgeous passages on the natural world, a man clinging to life in a sickroom, the confused motives of people in love. He lugged it around everywhere and while the others were playing board games or untangling fishing lines or erecting a teepee for the children, he was sitting off to the side reading. Or there was the summer he carved *broken knowledge* into a piece of white pine, plying away at it with a spoon gouge and chisel. From the rustic look of the board you somehow expected it to say *God bless this house* or *home sweet home*, but it said only *broken knowledge*. When they needed a fourth for the kayaks or a sixth for croquet, they couldn't count on Ed because Ed had Broken Knowledge. When the carving was finished Gayle hung it in the bathroom, and after that anyone who spent any time on the toilet was forced to contemplate the enigmatic outpouring of Ed's philosophical soul.

But mostly it was the vision of peace at White Pine Camp that prevailed. Their little beach, scrappy and enduring, the sand prickly and alive on their feet from the hulls of broken pine needles. The women and the lovely figures they cut coming out of the water, the beads of water clinging to their clean skin like magnets of light. The hum of young and old voices carried across the valley, and the glimmer of iron-colored water glimpsed through the trees. It was all right there before them, a prayer to human ordinariness that was nevertheless transfiguring.

With Ed's residency complete, the Donnellys moved back to Colton. Ed established a family medical practice in town, Gene had his store, and now in addition to summers together, the families began the everyday enmeshing of their everyday lives.

It was a good life, this life they had, and whenever Gene found himself wanting something to improve it (more time away from the store, more money, more recognition), these desires seemed petty. He was afraid to ask for too much—afraid that, according to the hidden demands of a universe striving for some degree of equilibrium, wanting too much would compromise what he already had. But sometimes you were lucky and got what you wanted anyway.

Even now, in his grief, he knew that. He knew he had been lucky in the things that mattered most.

3.

DARY WAS ENAMORED with the idea of holding the memorial at St. Mary's, the church where Gene and Maida had been married. They had never compelled her to attend religious school or holiday masses, and probably because of this their daughter found churches charming and quaint, as if their association with religion was merely a curious and incidental part of the historical record. She had gotten the idea that Maida's family's ancestral church would make a picturesque setting for her mother's memorial, and Gene had to remind her that according to an agreement between him and Maida, the Ashes' wedding was to be their last day in church.

Dary's second choice for the memorial was Walden, the private college where Maida had worked in the day-care center for over thirty years and where she had arguably spent most of her adult life. Once Dary was in high school it wasn't unusual for Maida to stay on campus after the end of her workday to partake in the life of the college, where every week it seemed a different luminary in his field was delivering a talk, or a newly restored film was playing at the campus theater. Sometimes

Maida invited Gene and sometimes she didn't, and sometimes he came along and sometimes he stayed home. He was never especially comfortable on the campus—he felt like a hanger-on, illicitly cleaving to a time of life that was no longer his to enjoy—and his discomfort increased the older he became. So while it would have been easy to hold the memorial at Walden—all that remained was to sign the papers and put down a deposit—it was a bad fit. The few memorials he'd attended there over the years had been for professors who, having played a substantial role in the life of the college, had developed a nearly cultlike following among the students. Maida's contribution was no less than theirs, but her instruments had been alphabet blocks and coloring books. She would have been embarrassed by the idea of the large quadrangle filling up with guests to pay homage to her.

With out-of-town guests confirmed, Gene saw that he had already lost an argument with Dary about the scope of the memorial. Now it was a matter of exercising what little power of his remained. At the beginning of his daughter's visit, he had put forth several venues as countersuggestions to the church: the local Elks Lodge where he had an in with an old classmate; a respectable pub where the sandwiches were named after the founders of Colton's cotton mills; the veterans' hall, which had the advantage of being right at the center of town, not far from the office he'd maintained after his store had closed. But when, after their beach day, they visited many of these venues together, Dary found a reason to dismiss each one of them. "This has a Grim Factor of eighty-nine," she would say. Or later, when they had returned to the house, "You can smell the staleness of that place all the way from here."

So they were back to the beginning. Only the beginning had

become a kind of midpoint, because the failure of one option nudged forward the likelihood of the church.

"What about St. Mary's?" Dary said, as if this was the first time the idea had occurred to her.

They were standing on the steps of the veterans' hall, where they had just met with the staff, a contingent of shrunken old women smoking cigarettes they ashed into coffee cups.

"Your mother made me promise we wouldn't go back there," Gene said.

"I never heard her say that."

"It happened before you were born."

"You always make it sound like every important decision happened before I was born." She let out a small, impatient sigh. "It was Mémère, wasn't it? She was the reason you didn't go back there."

It was true that his mother had made the wedding difficult. She had been a devoted parishioner of St. Charles back when there were separate Catholic churches to keep the Irish and the French from mixing. In that sense his mother's ideas of propriety had hardened a million years ago, in an era when the birth of a baby to a French mother and an Irish father or vice versa was recorded in the register as "mixed race." By 1955, when he and Maida wanted to get married, it seemed like those days had been over for half a century, but they still weren't for some people. For Gene's mother the spiritual distance between St. Charles and St. Mary's was as great as the distance between a Protestant and a Jew. All her life she maintained it was a sign of divine favor that the bells of St. Charles rang a half second before the bells of St. Mary's. She didn't express outright objection to Gene and Maida's nuptials, but she publicized her dismay by suggesting that they had chosen St. Mary's in order to cause her shame.

And yet his mother wasn't the reason they hadn't gone back to the church. It was something sillier, really. On their honeymoon, cloistered in the Pelican's Nest, they had discovered that neither of them had actually wanted to marry in the church and that in trying to please each other, they had discarded their own true feelings. At first when they recognized this, they anguished over having marred what otherwise might have been a perfect day. But soon enough they found themselves laughing about the whole incident, and in unity they turned against the force that had betrayed them, vowing to keep the church out of their lives.

"It wasn't your grandma's fault," Gene said.

"Why didn't you ever take me to church?" Dary said.

"We thought you could become a decent person without it. Which you did. You're mostly perfect, except—"

"—I forgot to get married."

"I wasn't going to say that."

"What were you going to say?"

"I was going to say, You're mostly perfect, you just have terrible ideas for a memorial."

"You don't really think that."

"That you're mostly perfect? I do. But let's think about what your mother liked."

"She liked her job," Dary said. "She liked Walden."

"She liked peonies," Gene said. "For her there was nothing prettier than white peonies in a vase."

"She also liked shucking corn, but that doesn't mean we should have the service in a barn."

"Well, it's not the worst idea," Gene said. "She loved visiting that farm in Hampton Falls, the one where you pick your own apples and get a horse-drawn hayride."

"It wasn't because of the apples."

"It's the only place with Fujis. She was very hard on American apples. Unfairly so, I thought."

"Bobby Jaeger owns that orchard."

"Who's Bobby Jaeger?"

"Mom's first boyfriend."

"Not true. I was her first boyfriend. Aside from some bozo in college who made the mistake of telling her that he had to end things because he loved her too much."

"Yeah, Bobby Jaeger."

"No, somebody else. An art-history doofus."

"Well, why did he end it if he loved her so much?"

"She never told me."

There was a brief pause.

"Peonies," he said. "That's what we should get."

That evening he sat down at the computer, which he still thought of as Dary's because she had set it up for him and Maida in a corner of the living room. In the beginning he forgot his password regularly and would call her in the middle of the day asking her to remind him what it was. Having tired of this, on her next trip she taped to the side of the monitor a sticky note with his username and password written in her hand. He knew the password now but still consulted the sticky note automatically, a step that in some way confirmed for him once again that with this supposedly private act of logging into his AOL account, he was entering an indefinite world that belonged more to her than to him.

His early forays on the internet had been limited to responding to the emails his daughter sent him and occasionally reading the sensationalistic but nevertheless impossible-to-ignore news stories that appeared on his home page. (He wondered if this was something Dary could tell from the settings—that he clicked on articles such as "Nude Man Accidentally Tasers Self" or "Beano Bandit Apprehended.") When Dary realized how little he was using the computer she tried to help him, but the only thing that really stuck with him from her tutorials was this idea that you could ask the internet a question, any question, and it would give you not just one answer but dozens. He found this oddly reassuring because it suggested that somewhere on the other side of the internet connection, back in the human realm, somebody—and possibly a lot of somebodies—had the same semiprivate question that was more comfortable to send through a filtering layer of inhuman data.

Now he typed into the oracle field: "How to write a eulogy." It was nice, or at least nonjudgmental, he supposed, that the internet assumed nothing about your existing abilities. Maybe you were a human willing to exert some effort, or maybe you were a half-automaton who needed to pass himself off as acceptably human. If he hadn't wanted to write the eulogy there were plentiful options: premade templates, preselected themes, inspirational quotations, mournful yet triumphant poems. He was looking for something else, something that wouldn't give him the shape of the thought, but that would tell him how to begin a process of thinking about the unthinkable.

The most reasonable site he found had been created by an entity who called herself "the Lady in Black." She said that writing a eulogy was "a personal journey of gathering memories." She suggested collecting personal items that belonged to the deceased, and "spending time with them until they speak to you—not literally, of course!" Following the Lady in Black's suggestion, he got up from the computer and went upstairs to the bedroom to find these items.

He opened the top drawer of Maida's dresser. She had never bothered to match up her socks, mixing them loose among her underwear and bras, and her pantyhose often ended up stretched beyond use or tangled in a knot. How many times had she and Gene been late for some event because on the way she had made him stop at the drugstore to buy a new pair? She would wriggle into it standing beside the car right there in the parking lot, while Gene would lower himself in the front seat, hoping nobody they knew saw them. When she was alive her tendency to make them late had never ceased to frustrate him, but now he looked upon her disorganization with peculiar fondness. Suddenly everything that was hers—the coins that had once been in her pocket, the hour and minute she had last set her alarm—was overburdened with significance. In some mad inversion of time, grieving his wife's death resembled falling in love.

He examined her lipsticks, black and silver tubes of brilliant color worn down to various states of concavity, each one offering a negative image of the curvature of her mouth. How he loved her mouth! He'd loved all of her physicality—her hair blonded by the sun, her eyes guarded by dark eyebrows taunting you to try to ignore her—but he loved her mouth especially, its full lower lip with the slight droop on its underside even when she smiled. He touched the tube of the most worn-down lipstick lightly to his own lip: it tasted of the soapiness of his wife's made-up mouth. It was the taste of her saying he wasn't allowed to kiss her because she had just finished her face and it was the taste of him ignoring this and kissing her anyway.

It occurred to him that maybe the Lady in Black hadn't foreseen that for certain people, this matter of choosing one or two special items would be next to impossible. Say, if you had lived in a house with someone for more than forty years, and in that house everywhere you turned you confronted evidence of another person's sensibility. Had he ever picked out a toaster? Given his opinion on the style of an armoire? It seemed that everything they owned was an expression of her taste, right down to the living room furniture that had been an anniversary present from her parents, the couch with the curved wooden back and matching armchairs all the color of a drowned olive, the low, sledlike wooden coffee table, the wheeled cart for the television. How could he choose among these things?

Don't worry about choosing "the most important thing." Whatever you choose will have meaning. It is said that meaning is the mother of memory.

Her shoes were beautiful expensive items, most of them ordered by him from specialty catalogs that were customarily sent to women living in Hyannis and Boston and New York. On the day a new season's catalog arrived at his store he would make a mental note of what he intended to get her, because her appearance was a reflection of his professional integrity and the wife of a shoe man deserved footwear as fine as the women in cities. He had kept her closet filled with pieces made as carefully as art: horse-hide booties with elegant stitching along the cap; sandals whose buckles disappeared beneath the genius of their design; pointy-toed slip-ons cut from a single piece of calfskin.

He found a nightgown he'd bought for her years earlier, a frilly, pretty length of buttercream silky fabric with lace finishing across the bosom and around the armholes. It had been expensive at a time when there had been no money for indulgences, which was exactly why he had bought it (this was what the credit card was for). It was only a little slip of fabric—the cost per square inch enormous—but you couldn't put a price on reinvigorating love. Maida was embarrassed when he brought it home in its tissue paper and glossy white box. She asked him to take it back, but he told her it had already been paid for and it couldn't be returned.

Why had he bought the nightgown? In the beginning of the marriage every time he wanted to do something frisky in the bedroom, he had the disturbing feeling that his mother was aware of these particular kinds of thoughts even in their most incipient form. It was like she was sitting in a mechanical room somewhere back in the Old Country, just waiting beside a machine that would spit out the ticker-tape evidence of his fornicating mind. What else had she ruined for him, with her brand of faith that drew its energy from a general suspicion of the pleasures of the body? When he couldn't have been more than eleven years old, he and the little girl who lived next door had danced cheek-to-cheek to "Stardust" in the living room, and when his mother caught them they had to write a letter to the priest telling him everything. After that Gene was forbidden to play with the little girl, though sometimes at bedtime after his mother had recited a prayer over him and left him, he would climb out of his covers and flash the light in his room. Then he and the girl would send through each other's windows paper airplanes on which they had written secret notes. He could still hear his mother reciting the prayer over his body: "I beg of Thee to give him love for the virtue of holy mortification, by which he may chastise his rebellious sense, and cross his self-love. At the same time I beg Thee to give him holy purity of the body, and the grace to resist all bad temptations..." So strong was this feeling of her as a witness to his innermost sexual self that it had persisted for years after she had died.

Not that he and Maida had talked about this. There was an unspoken agreement between them that they would not go out of their way to make each other uncomfortable. He never told her about the image of his mother with the ticker-tape machine; to have told her would have made her suffer in an inner drama she was helpless to alter. It would have also given the image a greater power over him than it already had. Which wasn't to say he and his wife didn't converse about sex. They conversed plenty, they just did it mostly without talking.

(But this was not the sort of thing you could write about in a eulogy.)

A photo of the deceased will be your helper in this process.
Take a special photo along with you on your personal journey.

There were hardly any photos of her in the house. The upstairs hallway connecting the bedrooms was a veritable photo gallery of Dary, but the few of Maida had been taken long ago on formal occasions, like the one of them on their wedding day, standing on the brick steps of St. Mary's next to the handicap rail. Maida had never been shy about proclaiming her dislike of having her photo taken; "I already know what I look like, thank you very much," she would say, and send him off with his still-shuttered camera. When they first became a couple, he asked for a photo of her as a child. "That's just kooky," she said. But she allowed him to take from her room in her parents' house an ink-and-watercolor portrait of her and her sisters. It had been made by a man who fancied himself an artist and was hopelessly in love with the second-eldest Halloran girl. In the portrait the three young women sat nestled on a grassy hillside like doves, their faces forever preserved in expressions of charming modesty, their hair pinned back in rose-colored bows that matched the rose-colored buttons on their white pinafores. It was all made up, Maida said— they had never sat together on a hill, and they certainly had never worn silly outfits like that. But for Gene the fictional elements didn't detract from the powerful feeling they evoked.

Take these precious items somewhere quiet, somewhere free of distraction, where you can hear the stories they have to tell you.

The house had three bedrooms, one larger than the other two, and the two smaller rooms next to each other. One of these was Dary's old room, the other a guest room, and both contained identical desks. It was a narrow wood-and-metal model, sparse and tidy and not particularly functional except as a resting place for keys or wallets. It had been added to Dary's room after she moved to California, and he supposed it accomplished what Maida had wanted, which was to convert a teenager's bedroom into a neutral space for additional guests. Afterward he went into the room with the cordless phone and shut the door behind him and pressed the "MEM" button followed by the number 1, which connected him to Dary, who was mildly startled to hear from him because he didn't call very often. Without assigning blame, he informed her that there had been some changes to her room, that her mother had made further changes, and though he didn't want to get involved, he also felt it was Dary's right to know her room didn't look much like her room anymore. To which she unsentimentally replied: "But it *isn't* mine."

He set himself up at the desk in the room where Annie was staying, bringing along with him the items he'd collected for the sake of the eulogy. He studied the photo of him and Maida taken on their wedding day. His eyes had the hooded, puffy quality that they did after a bad night's sleep. His pants were too big and his hair overworked by a comb, but there was something he liked about his appearance, a pose of confidence, a weary declaration of manhood. His arm was around Maida's waist and her nose and chin were raised slightly in the air, as if just before the photo was snapped she had heard someone calling her name.

He understood this was an image of him and his wife, but he didn't entirely recognize the people. At least he didn't quite recognize the couple they became, not the one that had stayed together for forty-nine years. He couldn't help searching anyway for visual clues that would hint at the narrative that would become their lives, and he was conscious of his unhelpful effort to assign the slightest meaning to everything, not only their expressions and the relative position of their bodies but also the pigeon in the corner gorging itself on an unexpected cascade of rice, and the distended clouds above the church's portico, and also the particular cast of the light tinged both gray and yellow, slightly more gray in the open space of the sky and slightly more yellow on their faces. The truth was that what had been photographed that day was lost to him. He couldn't remember any of it in his body—not standing on the steps, not putting his arm around Maida, not the sensory experience that accompanied being able to say for the first time in his head, *My wife, my wife, my wife.* In the end his memory wasn't spurred by the photograph, it was simply identical to the photograph, its details and limitations.

He set it aside.

Someone had placed a bud vase with a single hydrangea on the corner of the desk. He recognized it as a bloom from his own garden. Someone had done this, but of course, *someone* meant Gayle. She had made up the beds in the two guest rooms the day before Dary and Annie arrived, and he saw now that she had also placed a little dish of chocolate mints in silver foil on the dresser, alongside a drinking glass turned upside down in a cupcake liner. He tilted the vase toward the light. The water was leafless, colorless, and clean. So Gayle had been by the house to refresh the rooms since his daughter and granddaughter had arrived, and she had done this without telling him or asking anything from him. He wondered why she had done it, why she had done all the small, private, benevolent acts for him that he would never find out about in his lifetime, his knowledge of them only accidental and sporadic, when he happened to catch her before she was able to disappear. What had made these unrequited gestures throughout their lives acceptable to both of them, acceptable to give and receive without explicit acknowledgment? Just thinking of it circulated a warmth through his chest, and he didn't know why contemplating this unanswerable question should kindle his mind, when by comparison the task of writing about Maida seemed impossibly onerous.

He supposed it had something to do with regret. The way that with a living person the imagination still had liberty, but with the dead, everything was finite. Whatever happened between you and the deceased could no longer occupy the present or the future, so you were confined to the rigid facts of the past, which were recorded somewhere and not subject to reformation. Not that he especially felt any regret about his marriage. He didn't regret any of it, not even the lapse someone more superficial might think he was supposed to.

Actually it bolstered him to think of it, though it was so ancient he was almost embarrassed that it still meant something to him. This was at White Pine Camp more than forty years ago, when Maida's heat rash had returned and she refused to nurse Dary, who was crying and flailing in the portable crib, her little body turning the disturbing color of water after beets have been boiled in it. "What's going on here?" he said, and Maida said she couldn't feed the baby because her skin was on fire. "What do you mean, *can't feed the baby?*" he said. "A mechanical problem?" And she said, "Oh Christ, Gene, just go to the store and get me a box of lime popsicles, all right?"

Maybe if she had just asked for popsicles without specifying a flavor he wouldn't have reacted with the same intensity, but the fact that she could demand lime popsicles but was somehow unable or unwilling to feed her child provoked him to rage. What kind of mother was so derelict with a helpless creature she had birthed from her own body? Possibly he said this out loud and possibly he said it only in his head—he could no longer remember—but either way, it was very loud, so that even if he hadn't spoken it, she had seen it in his face, and she had called him a shithead and told him to go fuck himself. In his rage he was too upset to handle the baby, so Ed put her in the car and left to drive around.

It was one of the few times he heard Gayle say anything unkind about anyone. Maida was upstairs in the bedroom, cloistered in her misery, and Gene was sitting on the deck trying to collect himself. He was getting drunk on gin and watching a diaper-clad Brian in the playpen pull himself up to standing and fall down and pull himself up again and fall down again, when Gayle put her arms around him from behind and said, "She's a real bitch sometimes, isn't she."

He turned and grabbed her then, grabbed her and kissed her, a full sloppy kiss with her warm mass pressed against him, and her tongue tasted of his tongue, of salt and juniper, and she kissed him back. When they parted he felt a light-headed desperate urge to protect himself and his family, which in the craziness of the moment transposed itself in his mind in such a way that his instinct was to pack up Gayle and Brian in the car and drive as quickly as possible as far away as they could. But when he went to lift Brian from the playpen and Brian began to wail, the sound of that wail, sharp and alien, pierced the unreality that had seized him.

Before long Ed returned and transferred the sleeping baby, still in her bassinet, just inside the door, where they would be able to hear her if she woke up. Then he and Gayle and Gene arranged their chairs together on the deck and, without any acrimony, continued to drink and to dunk the lime popsicles Ed had brought back into their gin, as they discussed whether or not they ought to organize a fishing excursion before the end of the week.

Gene and Gayle had never talked about the kiss. He had never told anybody about it and he saw no reason to. They had never kissed like that again. And when he thought of the consequence of it, of what had been born out of it, it wasn't sexual or romantic love. It was a deeper loyalty—not just to each other, oddly, but to their spouses. It was almost as if the whole experience, the airing of all those young hot feelings—his wife's childishness and his own whipped-up anger and Gayle's complicity—had happened with the express purpose, hidden to them at the time, of helping each of them bend more pliantly toward the lives they already had. It all presented itself so clearly to him now.

He studied the photograph of their wedding day once more, but the elements were still the same and still retained their sealed quality. The original way he had encountered them was impossible to recover. Something definite had been lost. This was his feeling: *something definite was lost.* He wrote it down and counted the words. It was the closest he'd come to articulating something he knew to be true. Was there such a thing as a four-word eulogy? Perhaps he could launch the trend, relieving mourners from having to falsify an order in their mind that couldn't possibly exist under the circumstances.

Perhaps—but then he doubted it.

When he looked at his watch he saw that more than an hour had passed since he'd sat down. The number of words on the page was still four. He decided he would have to go to his office if he was going to get anything done.

4.

THE FOLLOWING MORNING he walked into town, a short walk that took him by the abandoned mill. It was a massive fortress of brick four stories high and several blocks long, barred with an iron gate that remained locked, at the top of which was an empty armature where an iron bell used to hang before it was stolen. The window glass, what was left of it, was the color of old milk. The fate of the building was regularly debated in cycles that coincided with city elections, but the only repairs the voters could agree on were the ones that kept the smokestacks from shearing off into the river or collapsing the street.

Colton's downtown was faring only slightly better. There were vacant lots and empty storefronts, but the bars always had customers and the Save Mart carried two brands of instant coffee. Each spring large pots of white, purple, and pink geraniums appeared on the sidewalk and they were lush and exultant for a few weeks, after which they were used informally as ashtrays and receptacles for trash. A few of the nicest old buildings with intricate brickwork and extra-tall windows had been touched up by new tenants.

A new business had moved into his old store the previous spring. It was a mystery to him how it survived, selling its oddball collection of bits and strings: tiny, spidery succulents, scissors with cast-iron handles made to look like twigs, leather bracelets, diminutive wooden spoons, and household matches in little bell-shaped jars. He'd run into the proprietress half a dozen times in the street, she with her large, broad forehead and widely set eyes that somehow made her look both innocent and dangerous, and each time she'd tried to wrangle him into the store for a cup of tea, cheerfully assuring him that he would always be welcome there. During one of these uncomfortable meetings she had thrust a delicate jarred succulent into his hand. He tried to give it back, claiming a black thumb, but she insisted that the little plant, which was already lacking soil, needed no more than a drop of water now and again. "I believe in you," she said. The last time he'd come into town, he and Annie had gone inside to look at a necklace she wanted, a scanty thing of string and chicken feathers and a small metallic charm that she claimed was the same one worn by someone named Sugar Dakota, whom she referred to as "only like the best singer to have ever lived."

He climbed a dark stairway in the building next door where the buff-colored carpet smelled of cat pee and stale tobacco and was rucked with trapped pockets of air. Three flights up, on a small triangular stair that passed for a landing, he unlocked a door. The top of the door was cut on a slant at a severe angle to accommodate some hidden structural aspect of the roof. He gave it a good shove, forcing it over the carpet.

It had been a sore point between him and Maida, his keeping an office after his store closed. When she brought it up, it was always in the context of money: why were they continuing to pay for him to have an office when the business had closed and there were rooms sitting empty at home? Whenever they had the argument, he thought, it was both about the money and not about the money. On the one hand, she'd always kept an eye on their money. Possibly because he'd accepted that loan from her father, or possibly out of habit, since in the early days of the business she had helped him by keeping the books. He still had a wonderful image of her sitting on the floor beside his desk with her stockinged legs tucked beneath her and the crown of her head catching the late-afternoon light as she bent over the accounts. It had never failed to surprise him when out of the depths of this serene repose she looked up with a slightly cross expression, explaining that they would have to restructure their debt or finally give up cash-basis accounting.

Working together, they'd shared a sense of purpose that in some way they'd never been able to fully recapture. Before long they had Dary, who kept Maida occupied at all hours of the day and sometimes at night too. And then just when it seemed the baby was getting more self-sufficient, Maida began to talk about getting a job. Initially he was against it; he didn't like the idea of her working when Dary was so young. But she didn't want to stay home all day with the baby, and he didn't know how to make her want what she didn't want herself. When she got the job at Walden he told himself it was just an experiment. Of course the experiment had lasted over thirty years, and during that time his attitude had changed. He came to respect the advantages of her employment: the health care, the paid vacations, the retirement fund.

So money was part of it, but it didn't account for why his keeping the office galled her so much. If only he had been able to explain to her why he needed it. But then he couldn't, because the truth skimmed too close to his ego. There was a period of time when Maida hadn't retired yet but his store was gone and then where was he supposed to go during the day? He couldn't stay home for all those hours, rearranging the cupboards. It wasn't good for a person, it wasn't right for the brain to be cooped up all day pretending to invent engrossing problems and solutions in domesticity. He was accustomed to having a place of his own, a place apart and in communication with some timeless unaging version of himself, where the mundane concerns of his life fell away and he could rediscover himself as a fundamentally reflective creature. Even during the best and busiest years of the store there had been afternoons slow enough that the high school boy he'd hired could manage by himself, giving Gene time to think. This was the most useful thing he'd learned from the poetry class in college, and he'd found it in a footnote about one of the poets, a life-insurance man. He found this man's poetry almost willfully unintelligible, but he was nevertheless affected by something he had recommended, namely, an hour or two of thinking, *pure thinking,* each day, even if you found yourself "staggered" at first by the confusion and aimlessness of your thoughts.

There was something to this. In a protected solitude there was no one to judge the directions his mind pursued, no one to call this detour a productive one and that one a waste. Leaving behind the desire to please, the desire to be right, he observed how the mind eventually calmed itself with its own wildness, and how the further out of bounds it drifted, the more settled it grew. These idle, motiveless hours in his office were the one part of his life that belonged to him entirely because they were separate from his identity as a husband, father, and provider. The pleasure he derived from this freedom was contingent on not being responsible to anyone else in the world.

He turned the lights on. A grown person could stand comfortably where he was near the door, but as you traveled toward the outer wall, the roof drew closer to the floor and made the space beneath it largely unusable except for storage. This oddity suited him; in addition to keeping the rent low, it provided an annex for the boxes he was planning to sort through when he found the time. They were filled with useful things: shoelaces, seasonal decorations, women's toe stockings, tins of off-black shoe polish, half-filled notebooks and notepads, wholesale catalogs spanning four decades, and unsold inventory in the form of men's and women's shoes made in U.S. factories that didn't exist anymore.

Of the 212 steps in the manufacturing process, he could speak knowledgeably about most of them—how the tanned hides were cut with metal dies, or the vamps punched for laces, or the shoes tacked to wooden lasts, or the outer soles stitched to welts, or the heels nailed and stitched to the soles, or the soles trimmed, or the edge of the soles pounded with hot irons, or the soles sanded, or the uppers waxed and polished. He'd gotten a great deal of satisfaction out of showing his customers how to identify a quality product—to gently scratch an outer sole with a thumbnail to test how deeply the leather had been tanned, or to remove an insole to examine how the shoe had been constructed, always looking for stitching in two directions (the top and the bottom) and whether the crossed threads lay flat in the groove of the sole.

He hadn't seen it coming, the shift in attitude in his customers. The new customers came into the store already knowing what they wanted and grabbed directly from his displays. They appeared hassled when he suggested beginning with an accurate measurement, and they regarded with suspicion his attempts to engage them in friendly conversation, as if they feared becoming a victim of a scam. He was baffled to discover his expertise treated as irrelevant when clearly it wasn't, judging by the number of people who asked to try on dress shoes in the size of their athletic trainers. He would kneel in silence as an impatient customer pressed the toe of the shoe and declared that it fit properly, when it was plain to see that the ball of his foot didn't match up with the widest part of the shoe. Or he would listen to a woman who had a high instep insist she didn't need the wider width. These same people complained openly, bitterly about his prices. They demanded discounts he couldn't give them, citing prices online he couldn't believe existed. How did they expect him to live? He had to pay for the same things as everyone else. Groceries, prescriptions, property taxes, the cars. When he thought of these customers buying shoes at three in the morning in darkened rooms glowing sickly blue, he imagined their sense of triumph and happiness having created a world that successfully circumvented people like him.

He removed a blank notepad from the drawer of his desk and found the pen he liked to use, a black ballpoint with a little gold kiwi bird on it—a gift from a distributor. He had not gotten rid of the large paper calendar from 1998 tucked snugly at the corners into its vinyl case lying on his desktop. On the corner of his desk was a pair of tan calfskin half-brogues that had been ingeniously constructed; each toe was slightly more recurved on the inner vamp than the outer, so that in spite of the asymmetry of the toe medallion, one half of the shoe appeared to mirror the other. If at times he found himself wondering what he'd been up to all those years—what it had all been for, the effort to run the store and keep the business afloat—he could turn one of those shoes over in his hand and remind himself he had given people the opportunity to own a piece of American craftsmanship they could use.

He rubbed the toe as he did when he needed something extra, luck or a little self-trust, whatever would temporarily silence the doubting voice within that often suggested, as it did now, that his mind was not the right instrument for his life. Because the truth was that he still had no idea what to put into the eulogy. On the one hand, he had his feelings, private and chaotic, and on the other, there was the eulogy, public and requiring an intelligent summing up, a coherence the feelings did not lend themselves to. He might attempt some approximate projection, most likely flawed, of what Maida might have wanted said about her, but that also seemed wrong. Was he simply to report his feelings? And if so, this demonstration—who was it for? Was it meant to console others or himself? It seemed unlikely that any public expression of feeling could relieve his or anyone else's grief.

What was familiar in all of this was the sense of futility. His father had been dead for more than sixty years and still he remained an impenetrable figure. Years after his death, Gene's mother would recall some characteristic of his that corresponded to nothing of what Gene remembered about him, and he found himself wondering if his own memories were false. How was it that his mother spoke of his father's selfishness and laziness when Gene remembered eccentric generosity and propulsive enthusiasm? Even after the tannery cut his father's hours and there was never enough money, it was just like his father to come home with some unusual bounty: a whole sack of warm pumpernickel loaves still in their crimped paper jackets; a pair of wooden tennis rackets with square heads and string sharp as wire; a record player in a grooved walnut box with an Artie Shaw record already inside. When Gene thought of his father it was of his restless pleasure tangling with his finds—frying up the bread with butter and onions for supper, or racing into the street to hit a tennis ball with Gene, or carrying the record player on his shoulder over to the neighbors' house after dinner. But because Gene's mother had lived longer, her version of his father competed against all the others with an outsize power, either augmenting a distance that had always existed between the boy and the man or else creating that imagined distance, which had the same effect.

It made him wonder about the life span of relationships, about when they were allowed to be declared over and dead. Was it never? Did they go on until everyone with a memory of the person was dead? That seemed too long. Already for most of his life he'd had two fathers—the living father and the dead one. Now he feared it would be the same with Maida: not one, but two. People he didn't know were writing notes to him about episodes from Maida's past, and at least as far as he could tell they did so because the news of her death awakened long-dormant feelings and memories they felt a duty to record and transmit. Some of their stories were charming and some were appalling (one high school friend had written about an accident with a home-bikini-wax kit), but even the least of them aroused in him a strange mixture of gratitude and possessiveness, a relief to be learning what had been previously unknown and a despair that he couldn't touch these parts of her, that they remained sealed in the past as other people's memories.

There was a knock at the door, followed by a groan of physical effort. The door opened, scraping over the carpet. Annie did a silly promenade into the room, twirled, then assumed a still pose in front of his desk with her chin slightly raised in the air and her eyes cast down. He felt he was being asked to notice her beauty and that he couldn't help noticing it. She had velvety dark lashes and a high pale forehead and slender shoulders that poked through the wavy tangles of her hair, giving her the appearance of a minor goddess, a sculpture you might find peering out of an alcove at the back of a vine-thick garden. She was more beautiful than her mother had been at her age, and it left him wondering, as it often did, who was responsible for her face.

He would probably never get used to the idea that his daughter knew more about the sperm donor's taste in music (he was fond of the Eagles) than his face, the likeness of which Dary had never seen. When Gene learned this, it had appalled him, though he'd had no shortage of grounds on which to raise objections to his daughter's decision. It had taken him a long time to recognize that the more he expressed his discomfort, the less Dary would disclose to him. Maida had encouraged him to focus on the future, the one in which she prudently anticipated that he would want to have a good relationship with his grandchild—an unlikely outcome if he alienated his child in the process of her becoming a mother. How grateful he was to Maida, then and now, not because she had magically smoothed over his differences with Dary, but rather because the future his wife had helped him envision had in fact arrived. He loved his grand-daughter more than he thought possible. Sometimes it was easier to love a grandchild than a child.

He'd been in the habit of telling Annie how beautiful she was until Dary asked him to stop, or to find something else to praise besides her looks. He hadn't stopped thinking she was beautiful, but mostly he had stopped saying it.

When he asked her what she was doing that day in town, she told him she had been in the store downstairs. He asked her if she knew that was where his store used to be.

"Yeah," she said. "But then you ran out of money."

"That's not exactly how it happened."

"Mom said—"

"Did she tell you how much she used to love the store as a kid? It was a little girl's dream, all those high heels. You wouldn't know it now, but your mother used to be a dress-up girl."

Annie picked up one of the shoes from the corner of his desk. She peered inside it, sniffing a little, then quickly drew back with exaggerated disgust, though he happened to know it didn't smell of anything but the leather it had been made of. "How come you sold shoes, anyway?" she said.

"Everyone has to sell something. And my father—your great-grandfather—worked in a tannery. Do you know what that is?"

"Great-grandfather wanted you to sell shoes?"

"He died when I was just about your age. I never got the chance to ask."

"Then how come you didn't decide to do something else? Something more fun? Why didn't you make ice cream? Or work at the zoo?"

"Is that what you're going to do when you grow up?"

"I'm going to be famous."

"What for?"

"Everything."

"Like what?"

"Like the way I dress, and the music I listen to, and just *every*thing."

He noticed then that she was wearing the Sugar Dakota necklace. So she had bought it. "I hate to break it to you, Annie Moon, but you don't have a rich—family." He had almost said "father"—he had wanted to—but he caught himself in time. "You're going to have to find a way to make money."

"Famous people make *lots* of money."

"Sure, but they did something to become famous first, right?"

"Not everyone has to make money, Papa."

"You either have to make it, or you have to have it already. Trust me."

"Are you making money? Is that why you're here?"

He told her he was trying to write.

"A book?"

"No, about Nana. For the memorial."

"Still?"

After she was gone he felt dissatisfied with himself for not having given her a better answer about his work, about why the shoe business and not something else. He believed it fell to parents and grandparents to create the impression that events didn't arrange themselves according to arbitrary forces, at least not completely, and that labor directed in a purposeful fashion would be rewarded with desirable outcomes. He felt a responsibility to demonstrate to his grand-daughter that his life had had a purpose and that this purpose was inseparable from his life as he had lived it. He didn't always perceive this to be true—sometimes, in fact, he longed for an alternate life whose main attractive quality was simply that it was different from everything he knew—but in his everyday sort of life, the one in which he felt it was a matter of good faith and character and citizenship to be reconciled to the life he had, he told himself that his path reflected only what his path could have been, and that it was inherently meaningful in spite of his inability to fully artic-ulate the meaning.

But somehow, with Annie there, he had been less certain that the signs he'd followed as a young man had pointed unambiguously in this one direction. A slight shift in circum-stances might have made for an entirely different life. What if Ed had changed his mind about introducing him to Maida? What if he hadn't married her? What sort of career might he have pursued then? Without the loan from Maida's father, he never would have been able to open the store. But without a wife or child to support, he also might have chosen an entirely different path.

It was a game he played with himself—how far could he go, how different could his life become—before he said *Stop* and withdrew, reversing out of the discomfort he had caused him-self. At this juncture another part of his mind took over, one that was genially affirming to the choices he had made and which, in its own conservative way, returned him once again to a known, secure world.

He didn't really believe any of it had been arbitrary. It couldn't have been.

He hadn't misspoken to Annie when he'd mentioned his father. Not that he would ever claim, in any kind of one-to-one correlation, that he had sold shoes because his father had worked in a tannery. The truth was that he didn't really know his father and his father hadn't lived long enough to see who Gene became. Still, the heft of his father's truncated life intruded on the reality of Gene's own. That was perhaps what he had failed to convey to Annie, who was too young to comprehend how the person missing in her life might shape it anyway.

When he got home there was a condolence card for him and several items for Dary, who was having her mail forwarded to the house for the duration of her stay. One of these was a newsletter for Annie's school, and he glanced at it on his way into the house. There was a profile of an alumnus who made his living from juggling and origami (something about the "and" made it particularly funny to Gene—not juggling or origami, but both) and an event for parents with the author of a book called *Raising Children in a Rainbow World*. At the back, in the announcements, he found notices about group meetings for adoptive parents, Single Mothers by Choice, and the East Bay Queer Book Club. He wondered if this culture was part of what had drawn Dary to the school in the first place—the hope that it might attract other parents like her, women who had chosen to have children without men.

"Do queer people read different books than other people? Is that why they have their own book club?"

Dary was on his computer in the living room. "You know, sometimes it's not so good to think out loud," she said.

"I'm serious," he said. "It's a serious question."

She asked if any mail had come for her.

"Why is it nobody tells me anything? If there's such a thing as a book club based on who you like to have sex with, I want to know why. How come there isn't a book club for men who like women?"

She extended her hand for the stack of mail that was in his hand.

"Oh, look," he said. "Something from Walden." Before Dary could reach for it, he opened the envelope and saw that it was a contract. "What's this?" he said.

"Oh," she said, and told him that on Tuesday she had signed the papers to hold the memorial there.

He counted backward in his mind. "But that was the day we looked at the veterans' hall."

"You had a lot on your mind."

"I don't understand. They let you sign the papers without putting down a deposit?"

"I put down the deposit. Of course."

"But that's my job."

"Dad, this is why I'm here. You have to let me take some things off your plate."

He wouldn't have said that he didn't trust his daughter, but some part of him didn't trust her. How else could he explain what he did later that evening when she was in the backyard watering the climbing hydrangea? There was nothing wrong with the tin that Maida's ashes had arrived in except that it looked a little cheap, with the pattern of acanthus leaves on the lid already wearing away. The empty canister of instant coffee he switched the ashes to and then hid behind a box of seldom-used cornmeal was not an upgrade. He didn't try to justify to himself why he was doing it, he just did it. The acanthus tin (filled with cornmeal for weight) was back in its original position on the sideboard in the dining room by the time Dary turned off the water a few minutes later.

5.

THE ORIGINAL PORCH on the Ashes' house had been too narrow.
For years Maida had wanted to redo it, but whenever they talked
about it they always discovered a reason to spend the money
on something else, an outcome that secretly pleased Gene. His
cautious attitude toward altering the house resulted in part
from his having observed the way renovation could be used as
a stimulant, introducing false excitement, or worse, become an
addiction that required a steadily increasing supply of money.

The Donnellys' unflagging interest in upgrading their own
house was evident not only in the regular turnover of rooms,
appliances, insulating materials, and monitoring systems, but
also in the relationship with their contractor. They spoke of him
in a rather startling, proprietary way, as if he were a fond part of
their household while at the same time of a decidedly lower order, like a live-in servant or a nanny. At parties or gatherings of
well-to-do people, Ed sometimes offered to loan out their contractor for other people's projects, as if the man himself didn't
need to be consulted in this.

The story of how, in the end, the Ashes' porch got renovated went something like this: the previous year Maida went to Ed and said she wanted a new porch, and the next day Ed got the contractor involved. The two men discussed some ideas, after which the contractor went away and made a rough set of drawings, which were eventually presented to Gene under misleading circumstances. The Donnellys had invited the Ashes over ostensibly to cast a tie-breaking vote on the color of their new kitchen tile, but it happened on this same evening that the porch drawings were sitting out near the tile samples and the contractor was on hand to explain his designs.

Gene saw that there was nothing to be gained by fighting the new porch. His main contribution was simply to advance the idea that he would save them money by building it himself. For a minute or two, the others indulged this proposal as a serious gesture, which is to say, they acknowledged Gene's wish to be able to build something himself. But then the conversation proceeded with the Donnellys figuring out when the contractor could step away from his duties at their house in order to be free to work at the Ashes'.

So Ed's contractor built the porch Maida wanted, a wide porch with long floor beams that ran parallel to the front of the house and met in a pretty diagonal pattern at the corners. The pale exterior of the house was repainted a blazing blue, a color Gene had only ever seen on the bathroom walls of a show house. The new porch (white, like the trim) was now wide enough for furniture. The contractor built some custom benches out of ash and finished them with a natural-looking stain. They were attractive, no question, but if Gene was by himself, he preferred to sit on the steps leading to the yard, where he would not have to look at the unnecessary project on which they had spent a great deal of money perhaps just so they

81

could be the type of people who spent a great deal of money on frivolous things.

Not everyone shared this opinion, of course. The renovation was exactly what Maida wanted. And whenever Ed came over he made a point of remarking on his satisfaction, which once included him pulling away one of the benches from the wall, turning it over to examine the underside. With a murmur of approval at the handiwork, he said, "Yup, that's my guy."

On the morning of the camping trip, when Ed arrived to pick up Annie and Gene informed him that she wasn't yet ready, Ed said that he would wait outside and Gene felt an obligation to wait with him. The day was already warm, too warm for the early hour. The air smelled of the river, the brackish water gulping for rot along the boats' hulls, the dead fish parts scumming the banks with their ripeness. They sat on one of the benches and Ed gazed up into the eaves of the porch once again, as if his estimation of the work might be different this time. "I'm glad she got what she wanted," he said.

I'm glad she got what she wanted. Gene repeated the words in his head.

"You can't say it's not an improvement," Ed said.

"It's something," Gene said.

The silence between them that ensued was neither completely comfortable nor uncomfortable. In general Gene found his relationships with men to be trickier than with women. It was unclear who was to inquire about whom or if the aim was something else entirely, like the ability to withstand discomfort at close range without adopting the behavior of a threatened creature. In his life his friendships with men had mostly proved tenuous. The connection depended on the immediacy of shared circumstances and as soon as the circumstances changed, the connection dissolved. His friendship with Ed had been the exception, though if they were honest with themselves, their dim view before the children were born was that kids were going to ruin their social lives, especially the friendships. But the children had turned out to be what had kept them together, and early on the parents had discovered there were forms of support and wisdom a grown-up could offer to a child who wasn't his own. Gayle and Ed had taken a special interest in Dary, Maida was especially fond of Colin and Michael, and Gene had a particular affinity for Brian.

Gene supposed his preference for Brian was partly due to the fact that Brian had never had the social confidence of his younger brothers. He was the lanky ten-year-old reading his father's copy of *War of the Worlds* in the back seat of the parked car, feet against the window, while Gene and Ed went into the store to buy fishing rods. When Brian was fifteen he told everyone he wanted to build airplanes, and sure enough he went to engineering school, where he studied aeronautics. His junior year he met Allison, the daughter of a commercial pilot, and they married as soon as he graduated and then moved to Florida, where he'd gotten a job working for an aeronautics company. Housing was cheap at the time and Brian figured out that if they bought a small house, improved it, sold it, and did this twice, they could afford the large house they really wanted in less than a decade. So he and Allison moved into a bungalow and did exactly that. They had two gifted children, twins who were now teenagers: a boy they had twice sent to soccer camp in Moldavia during summers because the Moldavians took their youth sport training more seriously than Americans, and a girl taking private lessons in music composition from a retired symphony conductor.

It had never made much sense to Gene why Ed couldn't get along with such a smart and successful son. When Gene asked Ed about this once, Ed corrected him and said he got along with Brian as well as Brian did with anyone; it was just that getting along with Brian was difficult because Brian was uptight. After that Gene felt a tribal, paternal duty to like Brian even more in compensation for the lack of interest he must have perceived from his father.

Now Gene said, "How's Brian? How many houses does he own these days?"

"He may not own any soon," Ed replied. He told Gene that Allison was filing for divorce.

The news caught Gene by surprise. To him the marriage had always appeared uniform—in a good way—across its various areas of aspiration. Brian and Allison were the kind of people who said what they were going to do and did it, whether it was in the plans they made for their real estate holdings or the way they went about raising their children. They'd had more success in these areas than many parents, and if *they* couldn't stay together, he didn't know how anyone else would manage. A rift of sadness opened inside him, sadness and also a strange sense of guilt, because in his own life he had experienced a joy that was repeatedly demonstrating its unavailability to the next generation. He'd been married for forty-nine years. How many people currently living or not yet born would achieve that in their lifetime? The guilt was related to a sense of personal failure: some set of skills or values had not been successfully transferred to the children they had raised. It was as if no one had told them there was a difference between courtship, in which the smallest misstep might bring about a sudden and absolute ending, and marriage, which was meant to absorb these missteps and grow more durable because of them. Hadn't they heard? Marriage wasn't inoculation against conflict.

"Allison finally figured it out," Ed said. "She realized Brian was on the hook to pay for the kids whether they stayed married or not."

"Maybe it's just a threat to get what she wants," Gene said.

"What she wants, is to get out of the marriage."

"That's just a thing people say when they're angry. It's like a chew toy. You chew it, but you don't actually swallow it."

"So Brian should call her a liar?"

"Look, if a patient comes to you and he's dying, do you say, 'Too bad, bud, better luck next time,' or do you do everything you can to save him?"

"We patch him up."

"Well, there's your answer."

"But they die anyway. Eventually."

"All right, but in the meantime you make an effort. You would stay awake for a week if you thought you could save somebody that way."

"I don't know that I would. Anymore. After you do that sort of thing once, you're tired. You realize pretty fast the only way you can keep going is if you hold something back. You can't just give away all of yourself, even if it means someone will probably die."

"You're just being humble."

"I don't believe in being humble. Humility's just a covert form of arrogance."

"You would do your best."

"Maybe," he said. "But no one gets all of you."

"If this were Brian's third or fourth marriage, then sure, maybe the thing to do would be to walk away. But he's still young."

"His mistake is he's telling Allison she can't leave him because it'll ruin his life. I told him he should tell her his life has never been better."

"Women like a man to fight for them occasionally," Gene said. "It renews their interest in romance."

"I'm talking about *marriage*. If Brian knew what was good for him, he'd recognize that it's over and start thinking about the rest of his life. That's what Allison's doing."

"But it isn't finished until one of them dies," Gene protested. "Even then, it still isn't over. Children are forever."

A new silver station wagon slowed in front of the house and pulled to the curb.

"Speaking of," Ed said, standing up. "Colin's going to be hanging around this weekend while we have his kids."

Ed met his son in the street and the two tall men hugged, a double hug that involved switching the position of their arms halfway through. As they approached the house they were both smiling, Colin's smile a more effusive and optimistic version of his father's, and the two of them with their thin lips and broad smooth foreheads.

When Colin was twenty-two and his college peers were vying for jobs in business and consulting, he had signed up for the Peace Corps and spent two years in Senegal. His decision gave his parents something to tell people at parties that eclipsed most of the other things people tended to say about their offspring, a situation that seemed to please Ed and Gayle. Colin's life hadn't looked terribly different from that of his peers since he'd returned to the States—he'd gone back to school for an executive MBA and become a respectably paid CFO at a nonprofit in Boston, where he worked long hours and had a 401(k) like everyone else—but Ed was proud of him in a way that always seemed brand-new and at the same time rooted in this past when Colin had been a scared but brave young man teaching entrepreneurship classes to village women old enough to be his mother. Ed was proud of Michael too, though that was a little bit different, since Michael worked in finance and in general Ed disdained the overt pursuit of money. But Michael had gotten his first job on Wall Street almost accidentally, when his AA sponsor connected him to someone sympathetic to his situation, and Michael's struggle to get sober had provided just enough sordid counterbalance for Ed's taste to make his youngest son's moneyed New York lifestyle more acceptable to him.

Colin kissed Gene on one cheek and then another, a ritualized greeting Gene found somewhat excessive and which he had always explained in his own mind as a residue of those years Colin had been a foreigner. A hug followed, and before Colin could undertake the double hug, Gene detached himself.

"Wow," Colin said, gesturing to the house. "You really went to town."

"It was all Maida."

At the mention of her, Colin took Gene by both elbows and looked into his face with a softness that Gene found intolerable. "She was one of a kind," Colin said. "She never tried to sell you on any of that fake stuff other people did. You know, once when I was a kid I told her that when I was sleeping a monster sometimes stole my face and put on my clothes and went around doing really bad things to other people, only I could never tell anyone, because of course they'd think it was me. And she said, 'Oh, I wonder if we've got the same monster.' I'll never forget that. Another parent would have told me it was all just a dream and not to think about it anymore. Justine and I talk about it all the time. Because *we* are those parents, telling our kids not to worry. But Maida understood how to talk to children. My mom tries, but—"

"Your mother is a saint," Gene said. "Believe me."

Annie appeared on the porch wearing a large humped back-pack that slued noticeably to the left.

"Honey, look who showed up here," Gene said. "It's Uncle Colin."

"Hello, Anna-banana," Colin said. "God, I can't believe how much they grow when they're away from you."

Dary stood in the doorway with a camera. "They grow extra when you can't see them. They're sneaky like that."

"Come here, rascal," Ed said.

Annie came slowly, carefully down the stairs. When she reached them Ed began to fix the alignment of her backpack, tightening some straps and loosening others. "How does that feel?" he asked.

"Heavy."

"It's going to be heavy, no way around that." He adjusted the straps some more, until gradually the mountain of blue nylon found its center on her back. "How's that?"

"I'm still alive, I guess."

Ed squeezed her head affectionately. "That's my girl."

6.

WHILE GENE WAITED for Dr. Fornier, he regarded himself in the mirror above the sink. He no longer felt much connection to his body, this broad frame his granddaughter still occasionally jumped on without warning. The curvature of his belly was as pronounced as it had been for most of his life, but this flesh was strange to him now, the remnant of some other life before Maida's death in which each food had a distinct flavor that he could taste and sometimes even craved, and eating and drinking were more than just required daily actions for nutrient delivery. He brought his hands to his face. It felt oddly lumpy, a homemade mask of a face.

There was a sharp double rap on the door and then Dr. Fornier entered. After the usual greetings the official business began, with Dr. Fornier asking a cascade of questions:

"Sleep?"

"I don't need much."

"How many hours a night?"

"Consecutive hours?"

Dr. Fornier made a note. "Any problems with walking, balance, or locomotion since I last saw you?"

"Not that I know of."

Dr. Fornier placed his notes on his knee and began to discourse about the foot, that sudden locus of peril in age, of ingrown nails, unresolved dampness, subterranean warts, protuberant spurs, ulcerous sores, and unwelcome odors. "Foot health," he concluded, as if he had just finished taxonomizing a new condition that would forever bear the distinguished imprint of his biography and name. "Any problems?"

"Not that I know of."

"That's the difficulty, isn't it? We get a little older, the feet seem farther away." He said this with plaintive delicacy, as if he was speaking with authority on the subject not from education or training but from the despondency that comes from having experienced the situation firsthand. But Dr. Fornier was younger than Gene by at least a decade.

He touched one of Gene's toes. Could he identify which toe it was without looking? At that moment Gene hated Dr. Fornier. This hatred bolted through his body and joined up with an old hatred left over from his last visit with the doctor, when Dr. Fornier had examined the ankle that sometimes rolled. During that appointment the doctor had made him demonstrate how he would use a cane if he was to use a cane, a question that was a) completely irrelevant, since he would never use a cane and b) infinitely insulting, since only a moron could fail to use a cane properly. Throughout this humiliating exercise Dr. Fornier's aspect had been at once supervisory and congratulatory, as if Gene was a child and Dr. Fornier his parent.

"How about any disturbances in mood, diet, or exercise?"

"No, thank you," Gene said.

"Still a sense of humor," Dr. Fornier noted approvingly and actually wrote something down. "How about this—why do you think your daughter wanted you to come in today?"

Gene gazed at the ceiling as if he might find the answer written up there. "My wife passed away."

Dr. Fornier looked up from his notes. "Yes," he said. "I remember. How are you doing with that? Is there anything I can do to help things along?" Dr. Fornier studied him for a moment the way a person takes one last look at something complex in the moment before he translates it to something simple and apprehensible. "Let's get you feeling like yourself again, Eugene," he said with brisk confidence. He removed a small notepad from a drawer and began scribbling. "I'm giving you something to help you go to sleep and something to wake you up, so to speak." He ripped off a page and handed it to Gene. "You let me know how it goes, okay?"

Dary met him downstairs in the pharmacy. She was wearing what he thought of as one of her draperies. There was hardly any distinction in her appearance between her public and private lives: at home or out in the world she wore the same formless tops that looked like the idea of a shirt before it had been cut, and the same stretchy leggings favored by babies and eleven-year-olds— anyone, in other words, who might spontaneously wish to curl up on the floor for a nap. Her style of dress had never passed through that succession of phases seen in some professional women where as their rank advanced they got dowdy, but Dary had also missed being stunning. In the totality of a life it was a minor loss, except for when you considered that you could never predict whom you might meet running an errand.

There was no line to drop off the prescription. Within ten minutes his name was called. There was a line, however, to pick it up: several customers waited behind a piece of grungy yellow tape meant to extend privacy to the person receiving instructions at the window. Dary offered to wait in line for him, but the idea of her collecting the prescription on his behalf embarrassed him. He couldn't prevent her from noticing signs of his body's failure, but that didn't mean she needed to receive material proof of it. He wondered why it was inherently humiliating to acknowledge the body's decline. Why did the glitches seem to reflect negatively on him, as if he had done something blameworthy? It made no sense, no more than the pride some people took in their uninterrupted good health. And yet his shame was real and present.

At last the pharmacist called for him. From a white paper bag she removed two plastic vials, one containing blue pills and the other containing white pills. She asked him if he had taken either of these medications before, and he said he wasn't sure. She explained that the first medication was a sleeping aid. The second was for erectile dysfunction.

"But I didn't order that," he whispered fiercely across the counter.

"There's nothing to be ashamed of," she said. "We get much younger men asking for it all the time."

"But there's been a mistake."

"Would you like to see the script?"

He heard his daughter's voice behind him: "Is everything all right, Dad?"

"Fine, fine," he said, and he felt he was saying this not only for his daughter's benefit but also for everyone else in the room who could hear them. He paid for the medications in a hurry and swept the paper bag off the counter.

"What happened?" Dary said. "Was it a problem with the insurance?"

"They never give you the generics unless you ask for them."

"I hate that," she said.

He took one of the two sleeping pills he was allotted that night before he went to bed. It had the strange effect of making him tired but not sleepy. It didn't stop him from thinking; it just made the thoughts revolve in a slower circle, as if there was more friction along the rails. An hour passed, then another, and still his body exerted itself against the medicine, unwilling to surrender to the mental wool. It had to be very late—he couldn't hear a single car, not even a distant one—but he was afraid to look at the clock.

His daughter was talking on the phone in another room, her low modulated murmur occasionally interrupted by a mournful laugh. And it came to him once again that she hadn't been with her mother when she died. She hadn't been with her mother because Maida hadn't been sick and wasn't supposed to die. She had gone in for a knee replacement. The knee was successfully replaced and she was discharged, and none of them knew that three days later she would die of a blood clot. He wondered what difference it made that Dary had missed those final days, whether she felt the ache of having been excluded from something monumental or the gratitude of having been spared something terrible.

In the past when he thought of his own death, he and it had moved toward each other at a synchronous pace: death was coming for him in the likely guise of illness or disease, and he would use his remaining weeks or months or years to prepare himself for its arrival. Not that he would be ready when it arrived, but that its signal to him would allow him to access some intensity of being that, although it couldn't solve the main problem, would rapidly dissolve the old difficulties in the rest of his life. Cancer Time—that was really what he was picturing, that the end of his life would unfold on something like Cancer Time, where there was of course not enough time for all that one might want to say and do, but still *some* time, and a heightened sense of it at that. Maida's death, the arbitrary brutal swiftness of it, had changed all that. Cancer Time if you were lucky, but maybe not.

Why hadn't he been able to tell Dary what had happened at the pharmacy? Why did some ancient habit make him shy with her? Getting the erectile drugs by mistake—that was funny, wasn't it? Couldn't they laugh about that? Right now they could be staying up late making each other laugh.

The next evening at dinnertime Dary microwaved something in a paper towel and ate it out of her hand on the way up to her room. He imagined her sitting down at the desk to write a letter to the person she had been talking to on the phone at night: *Dear X, The air in the East is dim, and my father is an old man.* Or she was efficiently composing her mother's eulogy, taking down as if by dictation the sentences that appeared fully formed in her head. He anticipated hers would be tendentious and smart; it would be unlike her to miss an opportunity for controversy. Maybe in her rendering Maida would be a victim, a woman tragically besieged by the needs of other people's children. Maybe she would try to pin the blame for this on him, turning him into her mother's lifelong oppressor. By the time she finished delivering her remarks it might be possible to believe that her parents, these two people called Gene and Maida, had never once sat together with their legs entangled on a couch, or gone for pizza, or made love.

Gayle and Esther Prince would also speak at the memorial, and four eulogies seemed like plenty to him. But it had nearly been five. Dary had invited Ed to speak too, and he'd initially agreed. Later on, though, he changed his mind, explaining that Gayle would speak for both of them. It was a decision that seemed in everyone's best interest, since Ed was not exactly known for his concision.

Gene wondered what Gayle and Esther would say about Maida and what they would say about him. Gayle could be relied upon for simplicity and sincerity. She would be soothing and sanguine, a postage stamp of feeling. Esther was more difficult to predict. She and Maida had lived together at Bates and had remained friends after Maida dropped out and Esther went on to get a master's in Boston. As long as Gene had known Esther she'd had hair the same shade of platinum and the same tiny waist. Her nostrils were pinched to slits and her forehead was large enough for someone to write a message on it, but somehow these extremes didn't diminish her attractiveness. She was the kind of woman both men and women referred to as striking, and he supposed she had gotten used to being beautiful and felt she had to maintain her good looks the same way some people maintained a mustache or a hair braid as a signature of personality. In her twenties, when Gene first met her, men were always following her around trying to talk to her, and rather than pretending it was a nuisance for the sake of other girls' feelings, she used to laugh about the hangers-on and speak of them as if they were appendages she had a right to encourage or discourage as capriciously as it suited her. She'd never married but traveled sometimes with a man she referred to simply as "the Greek." More than once Gene had gotten the feeling that whatever interest Esther showed him was merely a courtesy to Maida, a formal accommodation that for her fell somewhere between an annoyance and a joke. He, in turn, found her vain and self-approving, which neutralized for him the enticements of her beauty.

Just as he was thinking about her, his body did something strange.

There.

And there again.

What had started out as an almost pleasant sensation grew frightening. Something in his chest—his heart?—began to seize. He gripped his chest, pressing his hands to the seizing thing. He could hardly breathe.

Eventually the sensation passed.

When he felt sure it wouldn't happen again, he got up and knocked on Dary's door.

"What is it?" she said, her tone cordial but nevertheless indicating that he was interrupting her.

"Just checking to see if you're still there," he said through the door.

"Still here."

"Okay. Me too."

And that was all.

He paused before the photos of her in the hall. The youth soccer diptych with her on one side kneeling in the grass, and on the other, the full team assembled in their yellow-and-maroon jerseys. The school pictures with their vaguely cosmic marbled-gray backgrounds, an awkward triangular shape cut out of her bangs in one, a missing tooth dramatized with the tip of her tongue in another, and the rest unfolding somewhere along this spectrum of changing hairstyles and orthodontics. He had always thought of these images as describing a progression that was deeply personal and unique to her. But now it occurred to him that the images could belong to nearly anyone's childhood, and that the passage of time made them almost generic.

Years and years ago he and Maida had talked about how the best way to parent a child was probably to do it impersonally: on the one hand, to take nothing of the child's wretched behavior as a reflection of your own worth, and on the other, to take nothing of the child's sweetness as a measure of your success. But this was not quite being honest. Because there was nothing less impersonal than sowing your genes and all of the muck they carried into a new human being. It was hard not to want your child to turn out a certain way, especially if in the desired scenario she brought you happiness.

He knocked on her door again.

"What is it?"

"Is it too hot? You can open the window."

"Already open."

"It didn't get stuck?"

"Just write it, okay, Dad?"

He went downstairs and watched a little news and checked his email. There was nothing new in his inbox but he reexamined the messages anyway, the ones he had kept provisionally because he couldn't decide whether to officially keep them or discard them. This time, as in all previous times, he didn't find any new reason to make this distinction. He clicked on a news story about an Ohio couple, tourists in Hawaii, who had fallen backward off a cliff while having their photo taken.

After a while he went back upstairs, to Annie's room, where the items of her clothing that she hadn't packed for the camping trip were scattered across the floor. He wondered whether she was having fun with Ed and Gayle and their grandchildren. He hoped so. Though at the same time he also hoped for an invisible parameter on that fun, one that included missing him a little.

Dary was on the phone again. He listened through the wall. She had canted her voice low so that her words thrummed together in a way that made them sound more like dull music than units of meaning. From this continuous murmuring a complete phrase sometimes lifted itself just barely out of the thrumming—

It isn't a question of being willing...

That's easy to say when you've escaped...

It just doesn't enter the equation for him...

He opened the window and stuck his head out. The heat buzzed in his ears, insectile and electric. There were two blooming buttonbushes in the yard below, buoyant, springy shrubs with broad leaves of green topped with pale orbs of flowers. Moths feeding at the pale blooms lifted and rearranged, lifted and rearranged, in coordinated adjustment to the breeze. He leaned farther out over the ledge, wrapping his ankle around the arm of the desk chair for counterbalance. "All right," he heard her say. "Okay. You too." And then he presumed she hung up, because she suddenly appeared in the window and sat down at the desk.

He ducked back into Annie's room, still close enough to

her that they could have had a conversation through the open windows. On the desk, next to a stack of blank pages, the sheet on which he'd written "Something definite was lost" was sitting where he'd left it. Nothing had been added to it, not even a tiny desecrating doodle, which he found some-how disappointing. He began folding up the page, his hands executing the familiar folds without the intercession of his brain.

When he was finished, he leaned out the window, testing his angle. Then he thought about how stupid it would be to meet his death sending a paper airplane into a room, and how his daughter would never forgive him if he died falling into the yard. He drew back inside.

He aimed and shot at the closest buttonbush. His aim was good and the colorless moths rose into the air and hung motionless for a second. Then some unseen signal passed among them, and in the same instant, they were drawn back to the dark bush. It was a kind of ordinary magic. He hoped Dary had seen it.

He wondered how he and his daughter had arrived at this moment, traveling their separate trajectories of grief. Had it taken a long time—the length of her life—or just one instance? When had she decided that she no longer belonged in his world? There was a photo of her, in which she couldn't have been more than three, at a UNH football game wearing a Wildcats T-shirt that hung past her knees. When the time came for her to think about college, he'd hoped she would apply there, but by then she had already determined that she wanted to go out of state. She also didn't apply to Walden, where her mother's employment would have meant deeply discounted tu-ition. Instead, the colleges that had captivated Dary looked like temples. There were phrases about truth and light carved into their stone lintels and pediments. These institutions asked their freshmen not to worry about planning a career, instead encouraging them to offer themselves up to an experience. He was concerned that the kind of education she would receive at a place like that wouldn't prepare her for the world she actually had to live in, and he tried to convey this to her without being dismissive of her interest. But evidently he was too successful in his light-handed approach. When a small, private liberal arts school in Massachusetts offered Dary a spot, she happily accepted it.

In college while other girls went to courtyard dances and dorm-room parties, Dary bustled around with a small group of friends who earned their distinction by haranguing the administration. Writing petitions and staging demonstrations, they struck against the school's health clinic, the dining services, and a hallowed college ritual in which, every spring at the center of the newly seeded quadrangle, a crop of willing freshman girls was invited to compete in a drinking contest in which the penalty for losing was taking off their shirts. In their most well-known complaint, Dary and her peers protested that the women's athletic facilities were inferior to the men's, and at the height of the rancor four young women, each wearing the uniform of one of the women's sports teams, stripped on the steps of the President's Office, a stunt that landed them in the national news. It was bewildering to Gene why taking off your clothes in one circumstance could be so objectionable and in another a righteous mode of protest. An acquaintance remarked that if *his* child had behaved the same way, she could expect to foot the bill for the rest of her schooling. But when the bills from the college arrived, Gene dutifully paid them with funds from the thirty-year loan he had taken out for that purpose.

College was the time when Dary began to see a therapist. Why she voluntarily chose to undergo this was baffling to Gene. She was an accomplished person who was doing well. She hadn't been abused, neglected, or otherwise stunted—to the contrary, he and Maida had tried to give her every opportunity they hadn't had, even when that had meant mortgaging their lives. Dary used to refer to the therapist by her first name with a frequency that made him uncomfortable; it was as if the woman became a part of their family interactions. Once when Dary was visiting during a winter break, Gene asked her why she felt it was necessary to see a therapist. She demurred and when he persisted, she said it was free through the university health plan, an idea he found absurd when he considered that it was his thirty-year loan that was financing this free care.

He now wondered if those were the years he'd lost her.

The breeze lifted a piece of paper on the edge of the desk. He grabbed for it, but he wasn't quick enough. The breeze carried the paper out over the yard, where it descended past the buttonbush and the moths and came to rest on the lawn. When the breeze came again, rather than resisting it, Gene moved the stack onto the windowsill and allowed the pages to be whisked out. The breeze played with them, tilting them in the air, then pitched them into the bushes or onto the dark lawn. When it wasn't strong enough to take what remained of the stack, he pushed the pages off the sill.

The door of Dary's room opened. There was the sound of unhurried feet on the stairs. His daughter appeared in the yard. She was wearing the same dark shirt and white shorts she had been wearing all day. She walked a little ways through the littered yard and then paused to look up at his window. He perceived an attitude of imposed calm. She picked up one of the blank pages and held it toward the porch light. After a moment, she crumpled it and let it fall back to the lawn. She picked up another page, and it received the same treatment. Then she disappeared around the side of the house.

When she returned, she was carrying a rake, which she used to begin cleaning up the yard, dragging the loose pages to a central point in the middle of the lawn. His eyes went to the paper airplane lying at the base of the buttonbush. It was raked up and added to the pile of debris.

His daughter seemed to regard so much of what she did for him as an inevitable inconvenience, demanding completion but not inquiry. Was it all just so ordinary to her, raking paper from the lawn of her father's house at night? It would be, he supposed, if she was eager to return to a private life, a life that didn't include him. She was dutiful but not the least bit curious. It seemed his curiosity about her far surpassed her interest in him.

But what did he actually know about his daughter? He could tell you all about her golden retriever, Hoolie. Hoolie was housebroken, even though he'd had a number of accidents, which Dary called "setbacks." The dog suffered from separation anxiety when he was left alone during the day, so Dary had made a recording of her and Annie talking and they played it on a continuous loop when they were out of the house. A big breakthrough had come when the dog trainer taught them to use Hoolie's name only in a loving way, so he felt "emotionally connected." Hoolie was charming and funny and neurotic and sometimes, listening to Dary talk about him, Gene felt himself starting to believe what was not possible—that is, that a dog had a personality as complex and interesting as a human's.

Had she ever been in love? The question was almost too awful to ask. He remembered some men—there had been times when a man's name was mentioned, an explanation for the way she would get to an airport, or how she would carry a desk up a flight of stairs. Maybe these men had meant something to her. Maybe she had left behind a ward of bruised hearts. He hoped so. He wanted her to have every possibility in love.

He and Maida had often lain awake in bed talking about Dary and what her life would be like. The choices she made worried them not because the decisions in themselves were necessarily frightening, but because she would bear the consequences alone. He wasn't so antiquated to think that a family could be assembled in only one order, the order in which lovers became spouses and then parents, but he thought it was its own kind of stubborn backwardness not to acknowledge that this was the way it happened a lot of the time. If a person was arrestingly beautiful or boundlessly wealthy or gifted with exceptional talent, it seemed somewhat easier to transcend this order. But for everyone else, for the ordinary and merely regular, the order couldn't be disregarded as completely irrelevant. He worried that by raising a fatherless child Dary had imprinted her life with an odd tattoo that prevented her from blending into a normalcy that wasn't desirable simply because it was considered normal, but because it had brought a great many people the most genuine happiness they could point to in their lives. He worried she had traded her happiness for her independence, or had confused them as interchangeable. But this was only speculation.

He realized then that the feeling he had was of missing his daughter. He missed the parts of her he didn't know.

7.

THE FOLLOWING EVENING, when Dary was out having dinner with Colin Donnelly, Gene went into her room. He didn't intend to imitate her eulogy or borrow from it in any way, he just wanted to see how she had gone about it.

A pale grayish light from the street fell across the desk, illuminating a piece of paper. He went toward it.

"Looking for something?"

His hand flew to his chest.

Dary clicked on a small lamp by the bed, where she lay on top of the covers wearing the clothes she had gone out in.

He frowned. "I thought you were out."

"I was. I'm back."

"Did you and Colin get a chance to catch up?"

She raised herself up on her elbows. "You know, it's not really fair, the things we already know about each other. It's like I have institutional memory for a person. I can remember how when he was eleven or twelve he thought his private parts were really something special, a unique set, and he would completely freak out if someone accidentally opened the bathroom door while he was taking a piss. It's hard to catch up with someone like that, when I already have the feeling of knowing too much. We mostly talked about his brothers. Michael had a surgery to make his chin more defined."

"That's none of my business," Gene said.

He noticed a bottle of gin, still mostly full but with the cap off, on the floor by the bed, and Dary asked him if he wanted a drink. She swung her legs around the side of the bed and sat up, then looked around her feet. "You seen my glass?"

There was no glass. "The glasses are downstairs," he said.

"Doesn't matter," she said. She picked up the bottle and drank from it. "Tastes the same."

"Hold on, hold on." He went to the bathroom and returned with his rinsing glass, which he handed to her.

"You're not gonna have one?" she said. She poured gin into the glass.

"I've got work to do. The eulogy."

"Still?"

He turned to leave.

"Hey, wait." With surprising quickness she downed the gin and set the empty glass beside her feet. "Why don't you try it out on me?" she said. "Whatever you're thinking?"

He demurred.

"Oh, c'mon—you can try, can't you?" She leaned down and poured herself another drink. "You don't want one?"

"We don't usually drink upstairs."

"You want me to go downstairs?"

He sighed, relented, and held out his hand for the glass, which she filled.

"What do you think they're doing right now?" she said, falling back on the bed.

"Who?"

"The campers. Annie. Ed and Gayle. Colin's kids."

"I think they're asleep. I think their feet hurt and they're snoring."

"I think they're having fun," she said. She hummed something to herself, a tune he didn't recognize. Then her head popped up and she looked at him with fresh interest. "Hey. How come we never went camping? When I was little?"

He took a small, tidy sip of the gin. "I didn't realize you were interested in camping."

"Well, how was I supposed to know if I didn't know what camping was? Isn't that, like, the job of a parent? To show their kid everything...everything interesting there is to do?"

The implication of her question—that in some way he had failed to do his job as a parent—irked him, though he tried to cover it by drinking more of the gin. "I don't know what to tell you," he said. "I didn't spend much time camping as a kid myself. Plenty of time in the outdoors, sure, but not camping. That takes a lot of gear."

"You didn't take me camping because of...gear?"

"I didn't know you wanted to go."

She was quiet but he could sense her wakefulness, the collision of subjects in her mind.

"What are you thinking about?" he said.

"Oh, just Hoolie. We've never been away from him this long."

Then she lapsed into silence again, and he found himself wanting to say, *Now* what are you thinking? *Now* what are you thinking? *Now* what? But he didn't say anything.

"I'm really grateful for Hoolie," she said. "Dogs are so amazing. It's like they can sense everything you're thinking one second before you walk into the room, and then they know whether now's the time to play or just lie at your feet. It's so— so *un*human. I sometimes wonder what it would be like to meet a human that was like a dog."

"Do you ever meet any humans?" he said, hoping to pose the question in a neutral sort of way. "Out in your neck of the woods?"

"I meet people all the time."

"Oh, I'm glad. I'm glad you're—trying."

She made a face of displeasure. "It's not like a transcendent way of being, you know, always making an effort."

"Is that what I said?"

"I'm just pointing out that sometimes there's a value to giving up."

He wanted to ask her what she had already given up. Love? The hope of companionship? Some other dream? Or if he was especially daring, he would ask her about sex—whether she'd experienced the satisfaction of it within the context of a loving relationship. But he still had to write the eulogy—and besides, he didn't know if he was prepared to hear her answers. He felt he would be content to skip over the talking part if there was another way to learn this information. These were not the sorts of topics he himself had ever talked about with a parent or grown-up, and he couldn't imagine how it would be anything but uncomfortable for both parties. He said only: "I hope you're not giving up."

"I'm here, aren't I?" she said.

He held out his glass, and she refilled it. Since she'd arrived, it was the closest they'd come to a moment of tenderness.

When he came downstairs in the morning, the back door was wide open. Dary was outside, drinking coffee at the glass table in the backyard. He had one moment of pure discomfort when he thought she might have discovered her mother's ashes. But then he remembered that his daughter didn't drink instant coffee, only the freshly ground kind.

He found his slippers and went out to join her. It was silly, but he tended to forget about the backyard unless someone reminded him it was there. Neither he nor Maida had been particularly diligent gardeners. The climbing hydrangea was slowly pulling the fence to the ground. Once a year the redbud tree exploded in pink flowers that seemed to float on the air rather than be attached to the tree itself. Then the flowers disappeared and the leaves turned green and scraggly, and he and Maida would find themselves wondering if it made sense to keep such an ugly tree alive. But it was all talk. They never did anything without input from Gayle, because Gayle knew about green things and seemed to care about theirs in spite of their neglect. She was still coming by once a week to cut back the hydrangeas, giant lacy blooms that snowed their petals everywhere.

Dary was wearing a long shirt that left her legs bare; he supposed she had slept in it. There was something about her appearance—the bare legs, the way her hand trembled when she raised her cup to her lips—that made her appear a more fragile version of herself.

"Is your offer still good?" he said, sitting down. He explained he could use some help with the eulogy after all.

She shaded her eyes with her hands. "You want me to write it for you?"

"Just help me get started."

She frowned as if he was asking for both too much and too little. "No birds," she said. "No butterflies. No winged aspect of nature of any kind. None of those supposedly uplifting symbols of nature's renewal, okay?"

"Have those been retired?"

"Have you been to a funeral lately?"

"But your mother loved nature," he said. "She had great respect for nature."

"If you believe what people say," Dary said, "every woman who ever lived has had a tender and overwhelming respect for *some*thing. Better yet, for some *vulnerable* and *helpless* thing."

"And what's wrong with that?" he said. "For goodness' sake, your mother spent her life taking care of kids."

"I just wonder why she wasted so much time on other people's lives."

He bristled. "She never saw it like that."

"But at the end of the day, when it was all over, what did she have for herself?"

He couldn't recall his daughter speaking to him so directly before, and it made him wonder whether she had been more in the habit of speaking this way with her mother. Maybe Dary's habitual reserve with him had not been the direct result of the relationship between the two of them, but rather of the way the relationship had been governed by the presence of a third body, like a moon. "I can't say I understand what you're asking," he said.

Dary gripped her cup with both hands. "I'm saying, what did she get in return for—for everything she did? What came back to *her*? Was it all just heartfelt thank-yous and nice Christmas cards at the end of the year?"

"Now you're just making everything sound small."

"Then explain to me how it isn't."

A pair of nuthatches dove into the redbud and the leaves

quivered with their invisible play. Then the birds shot out again, disturbances in the air.

"There was dignity in her work," he said. "Self-respect. Knowing she had done her part." He paused. "History depends on people like that."

"That's so corny, Dad! That's like saying the man who invented the lightbulb and the maid who brought him his dinner accomplished the same thing."

"Well, how are we to know?" he said. "Maybe it was a good meal that inspired him." As soon as he said it, he sensed the weakness in the argument, but still he hoped it would get past Dary.

"We *know*," Dary said, "because we have the name of the man who invented the lightbulb, and we don't know anything about the maid. She's not interesting to us."

"Being interesting wasn't high on your mother's priorities. It wasn't important to her."

Dary shivered. "I don't know why that crushes me," she said. "But it does."

"She was happy," he said. "That's enough. Happiness justifies itself."

"What did she have to be so happy about? There was nothing she could point to and say, 'I've made this, built this, envisioned this.' She didn't have anything."

"Or maybe," he said, "she had everything that matters: family, love, security. You may not believe it, but not all happiness has to begin as struggle and misery to become genuine. It doesn't always have to be earned. Sometimes it just happens."

8.

IT WAS DARK by the time he arrived at the Sandpiper Inn but he wanted to see the water anyway. The boardwalk behind the main building was illuminated sporadically by lights sunk in the brush, and he waited for his eyes to adjust to the dark. Many of the boards were no longer in their proper place, some having settled beneath the level surface and some having risen up, warped and twisted. He was wary of tripping or falling. But after a minute or two, he realized that his eyes were not going to adjust any more than they had. The fact was, he no longer saw well in the dark.

He walked past several cottages, their curtains drawn. After the last cottage, there were no more lights, and the night seemed to drop in around him more fully, penetrating everything except the moon itself. The dark opened his other senses. A strong fishy smell permeated everywhere, probably a fish with its insides torn open and discarded by a gull. His nose picked up the pungent, coastal plant that smelled strongly of semen, though he didn't know which plant it was. In the dark every sprouted thing seemed to exhale a slightly sour, tangy smell.

He passed the hulking shape of a dumpster and knew he had to be close. The boardwalk made a sharp turn and what he thought was the fence, a humped black mound dividing the soft gray sea grass from the sky, rose up before him. It seemed taller than he remembered it. He drew closer and saw that his impression wasn't wrong; brambles now buried it. He remembered there being a latched gate somewhere, but when he stuck his hands into the brambles to find it, the briars snagged his clothing and dug scratches along his arms. He scanned up and down the barricade for where the gate might be, a place where the briars had been cut back, but in the dark the overgrown mound stretched on without end.

It seemed a long time before he reached the lit section of the boardwalk again. The smell of the ravaged fish was still putrid in his mouth. At last he saw the cottages, their angled roofs pitched against the stars. A slight breeze rustled the sea grass, a sound like the swish of a woman's dress. There was a low murmur of voices: a woman's laugh, a man's reply.

No light came from the Pelican's Nest and when he tried the door it was unlocked. The switch above the sink clicked with precision but didn't illuminate the bulb. He turned on the faucet and drank the water from his cupped hands. It was cold and felt good against his skin, raw from the briars. There was a towel wrapped around the pipe beneath the sink and he removed it and soaked it in cold water in the basin. Then he plunged his nicked hands inside the cold towel and wore it like a mitten.

He lay across the bed on top of the bedspread. Moon shadows of trees outside fell against the pine-board walls. The bedspread was tinged a bluish white, its pattern of roses transformed to a lunar landscape. He had forgotten about the particular luster of a seaward moon. How when a moon hung over the ocean they were not separate entities, but a third element fused from their continuous correspondence. The planks of the cottage walls appeared fastened together by this faint glow.

Forty-nine years ago he had come here with his new wife, and in three days he was to give a eulogy for her because she had died.

What could he say about this? He could say he loved her, but others believed they felt the same. He could say she had spoiled him with her care, but that was dwarfed by all that had passed between them. He could say that his life would never be the same, but even this felt wrong, because his life didn't feel like a circumstance that belonged to him anymore.

He thought of the last time they had been here together, during their second year of marriage. Maida had suggested it, a weekend alone together after two difficult weeks at White Pine Camp when they had been woken up each night by a fussing Brian Donnelly. Gene was initially against going back; he was afraid the sweet memories of their honeymoon would get mixed up with ordinary life. But Maida called ahead anyway, and when she learned the Pelican's Nest was available, this decided it for her.

The trip didn't start out auspiciously. Thunderstorms buckled the sky the afternoon they arrived. The sound in the frail little cabin was as if the sky above them was made of glass and someone was kicking it in. In the brief moments of quiet the glass would be replaced—only to be savagely kicked in once more. The heat was terrible. It layered in around them, a fog they couldn't see but could taste with their skin. Maida said she could feel a rash coming on, the tiny hot pinpricks hammering within her cells. He tried to get her to eat something but she wasn't interested in food. Sleep was all she cared for—sleep if he could just find a way to keep her pillow cool. He brought her washcloths drenched in cold water and switched them out whenever they warmed to the temperature of the air. His fingers pruned down to ridgy buds that lost their feeling. Once he returned from the bathroom with a fresh washcloth to discover her asleep. He lay down beside her, half-expecting her to wake up at any moment and at least say good night.

She slept straight through to the morning.

When she woke up, she was scratching herself in bleary fatigue. He had barely slept at all and was on the verge of proposing they go home when Maida stretched her arms above her head and announced she was hungry. He took her to a diner where she ordered a double stack of banana pancakes with two eggs and a side order of bacon and proceeded to eat through the food with methodical urgency. The more she recovered, the freer he felt to be annoyed with her. Why had she brought him on vacation only to treat him like she might have been happier alone? He thought it, but couldn't bring himself to say it. Illness trapped you that way, dissolving your valid claims against the sick one. This was why he hated sickness in everyone but himself.

In the end it turned out for the best that he hadn't said anything. Because when there was nothing more to eat, Maida began to talk. There was a digressive and confusing preamble, but gradually her thoughts organized themselves in a single, clear, unambivalent declaration: she wanted him to make her a baby.

"When?" he said.

"Now."

Sometimes she had a way of looking at him that left him feeling at once giddy and insecure. It was the impression at times that her interest in him was a guise for something else. But if his wife demanded that he ravish her, what else could he do?

He smiled now, thinking of it after so many years. He'd done just what she asked. He took her back to the Pelican's Nest and loved her until she told him to stop.

A month later, they learned she was pregnant. It was such a happy time. He hadn't anticipated the scope of his own happiness.

He knew he understood something about his wife that few people did. She might be moody, she might be demanding, but she was rarely this way out of a purely selfish motive. Her moods, her demands—they always served an end, and though you might not see it at the time—though you didn't know it yet—just possibly she was giving you the very thing you wanted. She was one of the most selfless people he had ever known, and she was better than other selfless people because she never insisted on her selflessness as an identity. There was never any sanctimony with her, none of the humorlessness of pathological do-gooders. He had been lucky. She had married him, and that had made him the husband of someone genuinely good.

He rolled across the bedspread with its lunar roses and reached into the drawer of the bedside table, where he found a pencil and a small pad of paper bearing the Sandpiper logo. Dawn was still several hours away. He had all that time to write. But now that he was finally getting started, he didn't think he would need it. The change in his mind from having nothing to say to having something was complete. Before long, he could hardly comprehend within himself why it had once seemed so difficult to write a few words about the person he loved.

9.

GENE ARRIVED WITH Dary and Annie at the college's quadrangle to find a scene already in progress. The women, many
wearing large straw hats in dark colors, were monitoring the
lawn for the new arrivals, inspecting them for information
about their relationship to the deceased. The men, some in suits
with handkerchiefs protruding from their pockets, tended to
drift to the outskirts of the women. The most elderly guests had
found refuge in the shade of a large beech tree that had some
importance to the college that Gene could no longer remember. This failure of memory both saddened him (Maida had told
him why it was important) and relieved him (his mind was freed
from responsibility for a fact that had never meant much of anything to him). Nearby a large white tent sheltered a table of
refreshments—plastic cups of sparkling lemonade, strawberries
impaled on toothpicks, butter cookies with jam centers. Dary
left his side to circulate among the guests, and Annie ran off and
piled four cookies on a plate.

He felt adrift in the milling, waiting crowd. He knew more
people there than anyone else, yet he couldn't think of anyone

he wanted to talk to. The mere idea of struggling to find a neutral topic—or, failing that, talking about present difficulties—
exhausted him. He had already had all of those conversations
and they hadn't led anywhere.

Michael Donnelly was there with his wife and son. Michael
had met his wife, who was a good deal older than him, in his
building a few years after he'd gotten sober. Luke, their son, was
probably five or six by now, but Gene was always confused because Luke was a big guy who looked like he might be older.
Michael and his wife still lived in the same building—Michael
had bought the apartment next to his and merged the adjoining
properties—and though Gene had never seen it, he remembered
there was a gym with a steam room in the basement, because at
the time Michael had told him about it, Gene had never heard
of anything like that.

Colin was there but his wife was not. For a moment, feeling
sorry for himself, Gene latched onto Justine's absence, constru-
ing it as an insult. Then he remembered that Justine had been
sent to Sudan to help coordinate a food program, and she was
extremely sorry she would miss the memorial. She had sent a
warm note saying exactly this. Colin had brought his children:
the two little girls who, with their long, thin faces, already
looked like their mother; and the older boy, Max, who presum-
ably still had an impressive and slightly irritating vocabulary
that belied his eleven years. (The last time Gene had asked Max
how he was doing, Max replied he was "feeling insouciant.")

When Michael saw Gene he approached with a vigorousness
that translated as excitement, though just before the two men
met, his stride changed abruptly and he almost stumbled, as if
in that moment he remembered why they were meeting. His
chin was indeed more defined and it would have made him more

handsome, except that for some reason the smoothness of the skin in that region didn't seem to integrate completely with the rest of his face.

"You're looking well," Gene said, taking Michael's hand.

Colin spotted them and descended with his alternating kisses. The three men had a conversation about what Gene had done that morning, as if it mattered greatly whether he had eaten his oatmeal with or without peach jam and whether he had glanced at the newspaper or merely carried it inside.

"Where's Brian?" Gene asked.

Colin, who was quite a bit taller than Gene, lowered his head slightly, taking what appeared to be extra care to move centrally into Gene's visual space. "He wanted to be here," Colin said. "He really did. He tried to make it happen."

"But his wife's a whore," Michael added.

Colin grimaced. His expression toward his brother, in which disappointment and disgust mingled, seemed to say, *Why do you always do the thing I tell you not to?* Then he appeared to dismiss his brother altogether, and turning to Gene, he rearranged his face into a mask of pleasantness. "Did I tell you Justine and I bought a townhouse? There's an extra bedroom in the attic. Anytime you want a vacation, you let us know. The room's all yours."

Before long Gayle sailed up to them in a nimbus of strong perfume and pulled Gene into a bosomy hug. "You found the monkeys," she said. With a tender, doting murmur, she inspected Gene's appearance. His chin was marred with an invisible smudge, which she erased with a good rubbing. She straightened his tie, then took his arm and shepherded him across the lawn to the rows of chairs. She deposited him in the seat next to hers at the front and assured him they would start momentarily; they were just going to wait a few more minutes to see if Esther would arrive. Her flight from New York had been delayed and she was coming from the airport.

Ed approached with a bottle of water for Gene.

"I'm too nervous," Gene said.

Ed stowed the bottle at Gene's feet and said it would be there for him later. Then together they stared at the garland of white peonies strung across the podium.

"Gayle?" Gene said.

"I told her they looked a little bridal, but—" Ed shrugged to suggest this was the extent of his powers.

Dary, looking slightly overwhelmed but happy, made her way over to them and took a seat next to Gene. She asked him how he was feeling.

"This wasn't my idea," he said.

"You're a good sport anyway."

He didn't think this was particularly true, but the remark temporarily quieted some of his internal opposition.

Annie was playing with the youngest children, picking them up in turn and whirling them around. When Dary called her over to join them, she came with a little girl, a child who belonged to one of Dary's friends from high school. Gene expected that she would return the child to the mother, but when Gayle said it was time to get started, Annie sat down with the child on her lap.

Gene took his place behind the podium and avoided looking at the faces. Sweat shimmered in the seams of his fingers as he unfolded his pages. There was no temptation to speak extemporaneously. He began by saying that Maida was a natural mother, born to it. Natural with all children, whether they belonged to her or not. He spoke of her more than thirty years at the day care. How she had lived to see children whose diapers she'd changed graduate from the college with honors and go on to get important positions in the government and at companies. How it never would have occurred to her to take offense when these same men and women, returning to campus for reunions or an alumni award, didn't remember her. She never wasted time wondering if the things she did were the right things, she just did them with fortitude and patience. He recalled a scene from the middle of their marriage when on a beautiful summer day they had walked together through a familiar wood that had been charred by a fire earlier that year. The wood was favored for nesting by a particular owl that built her nest year after year in the same white pine previously inhabited by woodpeckers. With some hunting they found the tree but it was no longer living; it was just a blackened pole sharpened to a crude point at the top. And yet the owl had returned to it and made its nest in the same chiseled-out cavity. He had found this tremendously moving, but Maida seemed to take it for granted. Now he could say she was a bit like that owl—as stubborn and as steady, and with as little inclination for regret.

His voice died away and he heard from the assembled crowd what perhaps had been beneath his speech all along: a cautious, respectful silence. It was over, and he felt the relief of knowing that something wearying had been carried off with just enough elegance and propriety. A compression that he hadn't known was there was released at the base of his spine. He was a little taller and looser in his body when he returned to his seat.

Dary smiled at him in a way that made him uncertain of her pleasure.

"Well?" he said.

"It was different," she said.

He didn't know whether she meant it was different from hers or from what she expected, and whether she viewed this favorably or not. But she bowed her head closer to his, and this seemed to signal, if not her endorsement, at least not her complete disapproval.

Gayle spoke next. She talked of the enduring connection between the two families, how at the cry of a child from the bathroom not one of them thought to inquire whose child needed his bottom wiped. She read a passage from *The Velveteen Rabbit*. ("Once you are Real you can't become unreal again. It lasts for always.") Tears moistened her eyes and she went on. It was this continuing on, rather than the tears, that moved him. She felt such responsibility to him. When she returned to her seat, he squeezed her hand as if to say they had accomplished something together.

There was a pause in the proceedings as a new effort was made to locate Esther. An inquiry went out into the crowd and came back with the information that she still hadn't arrived. Gene was surprised to feel a pang of distress on her behalf. He imagined how awful it would be to miss your oldest friend's memorial, and especially to be *aware* you were missing it as you sat helplessly in traffic. But another part of him was perfectly placid; it wouldn't break his heart if she failed to turn up in time. Either way, there was nothing to be done about it. They had to proceed.

Dary's face glowed with muted rosiness above the podium. She smiled at various people in the crowd, her eyes not scanning past them but alighting on individual faces, now nodding at some acquaintance in the rear, now smiling at the child on Annie's lap. If he didn't know the reason they were gathered, he might have thought she was enjoying herself. The crowd certainly seemed to be enjoying her. You could feel the way she was winning people to her with her smile, with this long expressive pause that resisted lurching directly into speech. She was inciting some connection, real or imagined, and she didn't seem to feel any shame about it.

"We've heard a lot today about Maida as a wife and mother and friend," she began. "But one question I've been thinking about since her death is what she was like when she wasn't taking care of anyone." There was a perceptible shift, a slight resettling in the crowd. "It isn't an easy question to answer," she went on, "because her life didn't allow for much solitude. It may be the closest thing she had was the two weeks of summer we spent every year with the Donnellys at Fisher Lake. Now I know what you're thinking: that's not much solitude at all. But consider for a moment she'd been sprung from her house. She was in someone else's home, on borrowed time. And I imagine this temporary—and, let it also be said, imaginary—freedom was the nearest thing to solitude for many women of her generation..."

A part of his mind slumped at the phrase "women of her generation." It was like a tic his daughter had, this constant need to reimagine the past in a language that would have been unintelligible in the context in which it transpired. He wondered what she would say about him and the marriage. She went on for some time with her political inventions of solitude and freedom and something else made-up that she called "the deep yearning to be cast as yourself in your life." It hardly seemed like she was talking about her mother, about a real, specific person. It was all an abstraction. And as she continued and as he failed to hear himself mentioned, it dawned on him that she was going to skip over him. She was going to skip over her own father, who not incidentally had been married to her mother for forty-nine years.

It was cruel, this exclusion of him. What had he done to deserve it?

Dary must have seen Esther arrive as she was speaking because when she finished her remarks she called Esther's name and coaxed her up to the podium. Esther affected a flustered air, but she looked as put-together as ever (still the platinum hair, still the tiny waist). She and Dary hugged on the platform, and as Dary made her way back to her seat, her smile said, *How lucky we are to have such a person in our midst!* She took her place beside Gene once again, and her smile toward him was softer and sweeter than the smile she had given him before. She seemed to be experiencing the same burst of lightness and freedom that he had felt once his eulogy was over. But one of them had spoken more truthfully than the other.

Esther began her remarks with an apology. She said she had collected many wonderful stories from Maida's college friends, and she had hoped to share them. But having arrived so late, she would have time for only one, which she had decided as she sat in traffic would be the story of how Maida met Reginald Hay, the handsome ("too handsome, really") professor whose book on Renaissance painting Maida had helped to write. Hay was demanding and arrogant, which Esther supposed was exactly how newly minted thirty-two-year-old professors ought to be when they were fresh back from a fellowship at the American Academy in Rome. His lecture on Botticelli's *Primavera* was known to draw students out of other classes for the day, all of them piling into the crowded auditorium where they sat on the floor and in the aisles, as Esther and Maida did one day in the spring of 1951. Hay stood before an image of the *Primavera* projected above the stage, and when the lights went down he noted the half-lidded eyes of the women and their peasant necks and stiff arms and sallow skin. For the next seventy-five minutes he proceeded to lecture on his theory of why a painter as adroit as Botticelli would choose to give the women features that typically wouldn't be considered sensual or appealing.

"When the lights came up," Esther said, "Maida raised her hand. She told him it was a pretty good lecture, only he'd forgotten to say which traits supposedly made women sexy. 'Not sexy,' Hay chided. 'Sensual.' 'So you maintain they're unrelated?' Maida said. By then there was a palpable charge between them—the room had gone totally silent—and I remember thinking, *Well, he's either going to make her life hell after this or he's going to fall in love with her.* We all know how *that* story goes. But what's important to *this* story is what Maida said as we were walking out of the auditorium. She was a little ruffled, a little irritated, I could tell, and when I asked if she was okay, she said, 'I don't know what the big deal is about a person's looks anyway. Everyone knows the brain is the most sexual organ we've got, but everyone goes around trying to cover it up. Don't you wonder what it would be like to take our clothes off our brains?' That's when I realized this person wasn't at all ordinary, and I should probably pay attention to her if I wanted to learn something about life. Which I did."

Esther paused momentarily as if she might go on, but instead she collected her notes, shuffled them together, and left the podium.

TWO

TWO

10.

IN THE FALL he met three people Dary had interviewed by telephone, all of whom expressed interest in a part-time position to help a recently widowed man with miscellaneous errands and chores. The first of the three candidates was a boy right out of college, an energetic young man with an interest in land stewardship and something called eco-development. He told Gene he cooked only one dish, a bean macaroni, but that everyone who had ever eaten it had asked for it again. Gene liked him at once, but felt it would be unfair to hire him. Anyone could see it wasn't this young man's destiny to spend his days taking care of an older man.

The second person was a woman in her thirties, a mother of three, who had managed a restaurant before having her kids. He liked her well enough but was reluctant to hire her, fearing a mother with young children would have trouble making the job a priority.

The third person, who was the closest to him in age, seemed most promising. Having worked a number of different jobs as a cashier and before that in a salon, Adele said she was ready for a change. She was pretty in a plain sort of way, with overcast blue eyes and an appealing fullness in her face. The simplicity of her appearance—no long fingernails, no hair doodads, no mounds of necklaces—pleased him. She didn't object to working the occasional evening or indicate other demands on her time. He had the impression she lived alone, except for the two old dogs she had mentioned, and it appealed to him to have someone who might be available during off-hours if he needed her. When he offered her the job, she said she could start right away.

He wondered what Maida would have thought of her. Probably she would have pitied her a little, finding her too transparent in her need for someone like Gene, someone who had the means to make a job for another person in his home and would feel a degree of responsibility for her. Gene himself felt unresolved about having this help, but Dary believed it would make his life easier.

On her first day Adele showed up in the same outfit she had interviewed in, a plain white V-neck tee of the kind that sold three-to-a-pack at the Food & Drug, and blue jeans that had some elastic in the waist. Once inside, she changed out of her canvas sneakers into a pair of slip-on rubber sandals, the type that people were encouraged to wear in public showers to prevent the spread of germs. He wondered if the outfit was a kind of uniform for her.

She was eager to see the house. This was what he hoped to delay, having not kept up with the housekeeping. When he suggested they sit down together first, she made a little noise of compliance and then stalked off while he was setting out the fig cookies he had been saving for this purpose. When he found her in the living room there was a strange look of satisfaction on her face, an expression that didn't diminish as he followed her from room to room. Plates crusted over with the previous night's dinner, unmated socks strewn at the base of the washing machine, worms of toothpaste that had calcified along the bowl of the sink—all of these she confronted with a remarkable lack of judgment, as if they were familiar landmarks that helped her to understand where she was headed. When she opened his refrigerator and saw the half-eaten can of tuna fish and the unwrapped block of Emmental, the only comment she made was that she liked the same cheese.

She offered to go to the store for him and when she came back she prepared food by the pound, a lasagna with seedy green and yellow squashes, and vegetables washed and diced and frozen in small sealed bags equivalent to a serving, so that all he would have to do later was empty a bag into a bowl he could microwave. She threw out shriveled apples and a blackened banana; took all the silverware out of the silverware tray and wiped out the little brown shavings of crud; and dusted in the living room, including the computer and the TV, which had odd dust-collecting vents built into their sides that had convinced him they weren't really meant to be cleaned. At three o'clock, her hour of departure, she changed back into her sneakers and left the rubber sandals sitting by the front door.

Dary called that evening to find out how the first day had gone.

"You don't have to worry about me," he said. "I'm not an invalid." He was still raw about not appearing in her eulogy. He hadn't brought it up with her—he didn't want to bicker about what couldn't be changed—but some part of him insisted he continued to have a right to those sore feelings.

"Look, if you didn't like her," Dary said, "I'll repost the ad."

He said he liked her well enough. "But I still think I could manage on my own. And besides, I have Gayle."

"We talked about this already," Dary said. "Gayle has a life."

Part of his resistance to accepting help was that he didn't want to become a manager. He had managed various employees at his store over the years, many of them teenagers in high school, and by the time he had them thoroughly trained, they tended to quit on him. He didn't want to invest the energy in grooming someone to help around the house if in a month's time she was going to disappear.

But of course, an adult woman was nothing like a teenage boy. Gene had found that most women, once they were inside a house—it didn't matter if they had never been inside it before—instinctually seemed to know where everything went and how it was all to be coordinated. As when after the memorial some guests had come back to the house to continue to visit with the family, and a small group of women led by Gayle had produced trays of miniature sandwiches and plates of cookies and pastries and carafes of hot and cold tea from the kitchen and afterward had packaged up all the leftovers and sent people home with the ones the Ashes couldn't possibly eat in the next few days and labeled the rest for the refrigerator and washed the plates and drained and stored the carafes back in the dining-room cabinets and found the unlikely drawer where the good teaspoons were kept and rubbed them dry with a soft cloth that didn't mark and then stashed them away. Whatever that special transmission was that women received to know their way assuredly and unobtrusively around another person's house, Adele had gotten it too.

He had figured it would take her about a month before her

presence was more of a help to him than a hindrance, but within her first week, she managed to detect several sources of annoyance in his life and frictionlessly remove them. She collected his mail and presorted it for him, saving him from encountering the junk, and she noticed the clogged strainer basket in the sink and replaced it. The oven rack too small for the oven had puzzled him, but she figured out it was an accessory to the microwave. When she was tossing out expired items in his pantry, she found the canister of instant coffee containing Maida's ashes. Another person might have neglected to open the can, or having opened it, simply thrown it out. But without making a remark, Adele wiped down the outside of the can and returned it to its original spot at the back of the shelf. Not knowing for sure if she had recognized what she saw, Gene felt an obligation to explain. But as soon as he began to say something, she cut him off. "You won't catch me snooping," she said. "For all I care, you can run around in a dress pretending you're Miss America." They agreed she would work three days a week, and by the end of the first week he found himself forgetting she was his employee, because she had so little in common with the people who had worked for him in the past.

On the days she didn't come to see him he found himself storing up things he could tell her, little things that didn't seem worthy of existing in his mind for his own benefit or entertainment, though as soon as he imagined himself telling them to her they seemed exciting and interesting. He found her easy to talk to, partly because she could listen for long stretches without needing to assert her own opinion, and partly because she didn't know any of the people he talked about. If he portrayed his daughter as self-serving, Adele accepted this version of Dary without challenging him. And if he said his wife had made the best strawberry-rhubarb pie in New Hampshire, she didn't doubt this was true.

One day, when she informed him he had received a letter from Esther Prince, Gene asked her if she would read it to him. He explained that he had written the woman, his wife's old college roommate, a letter after his wife's memorial, and he expected this was her response. He didn't know why it helped to hear the letter in Adele's voice, but it did. When she finished, there was just one part he wanted to hear again:

> I'm sorry you felt disappointed with my remarks. That was not my aim, and I am genuinely sorry for my role in that, if any. But life is full of disappointment. I assumed you of all people would know that.

He tried to remember what exactly he'd written in his letter, but that was almost two months ago. Of course he remembered the gist of it. He had made it plain he doubted the things Esther had spoken of in her eulogy had happened in the way she had related them. He didn't spell out all of this in the letter, but Esther was no twit and she would have gotten the idea. Sending the letter was probably foolish, because Esther would never admit to being a liar. But there was a deeper problem the letter couldn't solve, which was that Esther had caused Maida's college crush, the art-history doofus, to become irrevocably mixed up in Gene's mind with the superstar professor Esther had spoken about. The art-history doofus had never been young or handsome or tenured in Gene's conception of him, suggesting they were separate people. But then how many men had Maida known intimately at Bates? Why had she told Gene that Gene was her first real boyfriend? No matter how he tried to explain away Esther's lies, his questions persisted with their own stubborness.

"Does she have the hots for you or something?" Adele said, examining the envelope.

"Esther? No way." He paused. "Why?"

"I thought maybe you had a girlfriend."

"Not that I know of," he said, with some embarrassment about the question. And then, because he thought the door had been opened, he added, "What about you? A boyfriend?"

"Oh, not me."

She asked him what he wanted her to do with the letter and he told her to throw it away. He assumed that she wouldn't—that she would put it somewhere inconspicuous, giving him the opportunity to decide about it later—but he was wrong. She threw it in the trash, and as if sensing this might not be enough, she tied off the trash bag and walked it outside to the bin. The simplicity of their communication—he asked her to do something, and she did it— thrilled him. It made him oddly aware of the way in which, in marriage, the sent message was rarely received without a layer of interpretation.

She didn't talk much about herself but he felt no less close to her because of this. He felt that her not wishing to discuss the details of her life expressed how she viewed her life more than any words. Instead she amused him with stories about her dogs, two old rescue greyhounds that had suffered a ravaging life at the races. She said they were the ugliest dogs you'd ever seen, and she showed him a picture: loose folds of skin where their muscles had atrophied and small wiry eyes in snouty heads. They were always causing trouble, stinking up the bedroom with their awful flatulence, or costing her $400 in antibiotics. She was unequivocal about their nuisance and yet you could tell she would never get rid of them. Once when he asked her why she kept them, she replied, "If I don't, who will?"

He learned about her son in a roundabout manner. One day Gene received a phone call and a gruff, impertinent voice said, "Is she there?"

"Who?" Gene said.

"Who do you think? Put her on."

Gene told the person he had the wrong number.

"God, you're a selfish bastard," the voice said. "You tell her she still has to pay me for the baby."

It turned out that Adele's thirty-seven-year-old son was living with her, and so was the son's nineteen-year-old girl-friend, who was seven months pregnant. The son didn't have a job and Adele had agreed to pay for the girlfriend's prenatal care—"paying for the baby" was apparently paying for a visit to the obstetrician. Gene was too polite to inquire into the rest of the family's financial arrangements, but from the way Adele spoke of the situation, he got the impression she was supporting the couple.

Occasionally something would remind him that there was a deceptive quality to their intimacy, because three times a week she dropped into his life from nowhere and withdrew just as abruptly. Sometimes, when she wasn't working, he examined her rubber sandals. Her feet were considerably larger than Maida's, both longer and broader, and she clearly overpronated. Maida would never have worn shoes like that, except possibly for a costume in which she was aping the frumpy version of herself she would never become. At times the sandals seemed to underscore the fragility of the happiness he was constructing. What was he thinking? He and Adele hardly knew each other.

Once, wanting to hear that she liked coming to see him, he

asked what her favorite out of all of her jobs had been. She thought about it for a moment and then said it was the one she'd had before working for him, a domestic position with a man who had multiple sclerosis. This was news to Gene; he had thought he was her first. He asked her what was so good about that job.

"Well, he was depressed when I went to work for him," she said.

"Some people would quit."

"It made it easy," she said. "Depressed people know what they want—they'd like to feel better. But they don't actually expect any real improvement. They're reasonable."

She told him that when she had worked for the man with MS she had occasionally rubbed and oiled his wife's feet as the man looked on and gave her pointers, because this was something he had once done in the marriage and now couldn't do. Gene had never had his feet touched like this by anyone, not even his wife. It sounded demeaning. But from the way Adele spoke of her relationship with her former client and his wife, it was apparent she didn't find anything odd about the situation. This was maybe the first indication to him that there was something loose in her, something not quite fixed in its proper place, a flash of what he had glimpsed in her relationship with her son. It worried him a little, this part of her that could be taken advantage of by someone inclined to exploit her unusual temperament.

Sometimes he tried to resist her kindness toward him on principle, to show her she didn't have to do anything out of the ordinary for him. When she offered to bake him a pie to take to the Donnellys' for Thanksgiving, he told her not to bother, since the main benefit so far of being a widower was that whenever he was invited anywhere, people emphasized he didn't have to bring anything. Losing a spouse, and perhaps particularly a wife, appeared to be a temporary excuse for social irresponsibility. But having proved to himself his ability to resist Adele, he then relented and said it would be fine after all if she made him a pie. What kind of pie did he want? she asked. Any kind she felt like making, he said, though he found apple pie too much dominated by cinnamon and considered blackberries better suited to summer, while pumpkin pie was too much like sweet potato and pears were better for tarts.

"Strawberry-rhubarb, then?" she said.

"If that's what you like."

Whenever he found himself thinking of Adele, a voice inside him asked whether there was anything improper in his feelings toward her. The possibility made him uncomfortable. But the discomfort always yielded to a vigorous internal affirmation of his devotion to Maida, which was the same as his devotion to things exactly as they had been before she died. Then, having confirmed the appropriate feelings, he would allow himself to acknowledge that he derived some mysterious, benign pleasure from Adele.

Thanksgiving morning Adele stopped by to deliver the pie, a gleaming pouf of pastry with deep pockets of berry. It occurred to him then, in a way it hadn't before, that she had made a choice to spend her holiday doing something extra for him. It gave him a jolt of esteem, restoring him to a sense of himself as someone worthy of such a gesture, and it awakened in him a curiosity for what this effort meant. He bowed before her and her creation and said, "I serve the mistress of sweet things," because those were the first words that popped into his head.

She laughed a startled laugh, and he asked her if she wanted to come inside to sample her handiwork. She made a face that scolded him for threatening to slice up the pie before it arrived at its intended destination, but he could tell that beneath the scolding she was pleased that he was pleased.

Just then something made her reach out and graze the back of his neck with her hand. "Your hair's gotten long," she said.

He blushed and instinctively touched the spot where her hand had been. "I guess I'll have to grow paws to justify it," he said.

"Oh?" she said. "Are you more of a wolf or a bear?"

A thrill passed through him—she was playing along. "Just some creature that howls at the moon," he said.

"Do you really?"

"Would it scare you if I did?"

"Oh, it takes a lot more than that to make me afraid." She raised her eyebrows and looked askance, perhaps trying to look tough, but then she smiled anyway, as if she couldn't help it. She offered to trim his hair before he went over to the Donnellys'.

They set up a chair on the linoleum floor in the laundry room. She wrapped him in an old sheet and pinned it at the neck with two clothespins. Beneath the sink, there was a spray bottle containing diluted vinegar. She emptied it and filled it with water.

She said, "It's not my fault if you smell like a pickle all day."

Before dampening his hair she ran her hands up and down the back of his head as if she was at once measuring the quantity of the hair and trying to coax the individual hairs to lie in the same direction. It was a shock to his system. When was the last time he had been touched, really touched?

She sprayed down his head and began to snip. The warmth of her fingers against his scalp alternated with the scissors dashing across his head, and he found himself anticipating the return of her hand. Every now and then she adjusted the angle of his head using a light touch along his jaw. It was this, more than anything, that made him feel how severed from human touch he had been. When you didn't have a lover, no one ever touched your face.

When she was done, she made him look in the hand mirror. She put her face over his shoulder near his face, as if someone was preparing to take their photograph.

"Nice," he said.

"Handsome."

11.

AT THE DONNELLYS', before the meal, Ed insisted on showing Gene the new gas fireplace that had been installed since he'd last been there, as if it wasn't right for there to be any changes to the house without Gene knowing about them. The fireplace was bigger than its predecessor, and Gene remarked on this, complimenting the installation. But it wasn't enough that he was admiring. Ed made him flick the switch that produced the pumpkin flames that flickered over the pile of artificial logs.

After some talk of the fireplace (the models the Donnellys could have gotten but didn't and why this one was paramount), Gene and Ed went into the kitchen to find some wine. Gayle filled their glasses and then informed them they had to get out of the kitchen because they would only be in her way. It was a pretense—Ed was a skilled cook—but years ago the Donnellys had decided this would be one of their standard performances in the presence of guests: Ed playing the role of the barbarous, untrained husband and Gayle playing the savior of the civilized party. The roles had been this way for so long that Gene sometimes found himself believing them. It was almost as if his retreat to the study with Ed was a thoughtful escape to make Gayle's life easier.

Gene remembered when the study had been Brian's bedroom and Ed's designated personal area just a long folding table in the basement. Then Brian had grown up and an interior designer was brought in to advise the Donnellys on converting the bedroom to a study. As this room was resettled other rooms became ripe for renewal, and eventually it would be this room's turn to be refreshed once more. The funny thing was that there was hardly any need for any of these improvements. The Donnellys had thought of everything already: recessed lighting, dimmer switches, a laundry station, built-ins for shoes, cookbooks, spices, and jewelry. If there was a junk drawer in the house Gene had never found it. The only misstep he had spied was a toilet in the guest bathroom that flushed by pulling the handle up instead of pressing it down, and it made him secretly happy every time he discovered it again.

In the study, a new model of an older type of wood ladder provided access to the heights of the bookshelves, which contained a treasury of literature and history: novels, poetry, dramas, natural histories, biographies, political treatises. Interleaved here and there among the books were souvenirs of the Donnellys' travels: African wood nesting bowls, a small jade Buddha, a bamboo ladle. For one of Ed's birthdays Gayle had framed photographs he had taken over the years at Fisher Lake—a picnic table strewn with spent lobster claws and discarded lemon halves; strange clumps of wet laundry clinging to the line; the back of Gayle's head against a blurry white sky. It was a room that felt like the culmination of a life, and Gene alternated between finding it repugnant and desirable.

Ed explained that soon he might be spending more time

in his study. When he sold his practice the previous year, he had negotiated to remain in control of all aspects of the medical side, with the buyer, Integrated Health, assuming responsibility for billing, insurance, and other nonmedical aspects. But the reality was turning out to be somewhat different. Ed said he felt under pressure to see more patients and spend less time with them, to order more expensive tests and prescribe more drugs. He had always employed an office manager—he'd hired her twenty-six years ago and now she was the grandmother of nine—but Integrated had slashed the payroll, insinuating her responsibilities could be absorbed by the nurses. Ed told Gene he'd been left no choice but to take money from Integrated's side of the business to keep his office manager.

"Does Integrated know about that?" Gene asked.

Ed shrugged, releasing himself from responsibility. "They're the ones making everyone unhappy."

It was a bad situation, not easily remedied, and Gene felt the difficulty of Ed's position. At the same time, he marveled at the bewilderment Ed expressed in finding himself in this predicament. It was as if nothing in his life had prepared him to cede control.

Before long, Gayle called them to the table. Gene had assumed Brian wouldn't make the trip from Florida, but he'd hoped he might see Colin or Michael. But Colin was spending Thanksgiving with Justine's parents, and Michael had flown his family to Hawaii. As Gene and Ed and Gayle took their seats at the table, Gayle seemed a touch melancholy about all the empty chairs. But Ed chided her, saying they didn't have a right to complain, since they would be seeing Colin and Michael and their children at Christmas.

Gayle had made her traditional spread. In addition to the turkey, buttery and golden, there was a mound of stuffing lumpy with raisins, cranberry sauce with flecks of orange zest, garlic-roasted green beans, and bouffant mashed potatoes. A peculiar aspect of Gayle's hospitality was that once she had called people to the table and urged them to start eating, she would often disappear, slipping off to the kitchen. She would reappear a minute or two later bearing some dish that had refused to declare itself ready on time, and then she would sit down for a while, but her presence was never really permanent. A knife that would cut the meat more quickly, or a jar of rosemary salt that someone had brought them from France, or a saucer to keep the gravy from dripping onto the tablecloth would call her away, and she would disappear and return again. Gene didn't mind it anymore. There was something almost touching about it, how she hadn't given up perfecting what she had already perfected. But it clearly bothered Ed. The crease in his forehead deepened with each new trip she made to the kitchen.

That evening a good deal of time was spent talking about the children, which was their way of talking about themselves without expending the energy to do it in a purposeful way. Gene found himself repeating something Dary had told him in a phone call that morning about how the dog had been given a bone and carried it happily into the yard. Then he heard himself and loathed himself and loathed all of them, speaking of their children and animals as if their own lives were devoid of immediacy and vibrancy.

He missed Maida in that moment and longed for his companion. He wanted her beside him, wearing her wry expression as some new feature of the Donnellys' well-appointed dining room was pointed out, or for her to reach over and put her hand in his lap under the table after she'd had two glasses of wine and grew bored with the talk. These were not the gestures of high romance that anyone dreamed about when they got married, yet they cohered in one of the most underrated experiences of having a spouse: the way you provided clandestine cover to each other in the midst of the company of others, the small private gestures toward your society of two, shielding both of you from the strain of performing the rituals of polite company. It was a tacit lifelong vow Gene and Maida had made to each other, and he felt a desolation and something sharper too, something like anger, that Maida had abandoned this responsibility to him. But of course it was absurd, this sharp feeling, this bitterness. It hardly lasted, and the purer ache of missing her took over again soon enough.

The three of them were conspicuously not talking about Maida, as if the subject was a circle drawn on the floor they had all agreed not to step into. There was nothing hidden about the circle, it was in plain view, and Gene understood that nothing and no one was preventing him from stepping into the circle, he could do it at any time. But the unspoken collusion made him fear that by speaking he could ruin something that belonged to all of them, though he couldn't have said what it was.

The telephone rang and Gayle got up to answer it. While she was gone, Ed asked Gene whether Dary was planning to return to Colton for Christmas as usual. Gene wasn't aware of any reason why she would deviate from the tradition, but he acknowledged he had no idea what his daughter's plans were. After this there was a brief silence between them, in which they listened to the rain that was beginning to fall.

Gayle returned to tell Ed that Brian was on the phone, and Ed got up and left Gene and Gayle sitting before their half-eaten meals.

"Your hair looks good," she said. "Are you doing something new to it?"

"It's just shorter."

"Well, you look better," she said, a confiding note in her voice. She lowered her eyes. "You're looking better every day."

Ed returned to the table and announced that Brian's soon-to-be ex was dating someone new.

"What a nightmare," Gene said.

"He's totally fixated on finding out who the guy is," Ed said. "He's got bills to pay, he's got two kids who are depressed as hell that their parents are splitting up, and all he can talk about is Allison sleeping with some guy who isn't him. He's obsessed. It's a disease."

For a moment Gayle looked ashamed, as if she was the one to blame. But she couldn't remain dour for long; she brightened as she told them how, while looking for the holiday decorations in the basement, she had come upon a trove of old photos from their summers at Fisher Lake. "There's the cutest one of Brian sitting on his training potty on the deck, looking across the lake like he's the king of it all. Imagine that—a potty with a lake view!"

"He was always the smart one," Gene said.

"We used gummy bears to train him. I always said, 'It's not a bribe, it's a reward.'"

"You knew what you were doing," Gene said.

"Don't you remember, honey?" Gayle said, turning to Ed. "Don't you remember Brian carrying his little potty onto the deck?"

"I believe you."

"You don't remember? It was so funny!"

"Then I'm sure it was."

"But you don't remember how it used to make us laugh?"

"I guess my mind's somewhere else." He said it flatly, unapologetically, and there was something almost cruel in his indifference to Gayle's enthusiasm. The implication seemed to be that if she insisted on prattling, it was her fault if his mind wandered off. "I was just thinking about the day Maida swam across the lake."

There was a brief silence. Then Gayle said, "I never did understand why anybody would do that. Whenever I'm in the water for more than ten minutes, I get so cold I can't feel any part of my face except my tongue."

"The tongue isn't part of the face," Ed said.

"Well, you know what I mean. You have to be a little cuckoo to spend so much time in the water."

"Plenty of people do it," Ed said. "They're all cuckoos?"

"I can't think of anyone who did it besides Maida."

"What's her name—the Olympian, Amory Johnson—she used to go all the way across *and* back for training."

"Amory Johnson looks like a man! How would you like to smooch a woman like that? No, don't answer that. But she does look like a man."

A decades-old image of Amory Johnson flashed into Gene's mind. It was true: with her short hair, waistless slab of torso, and hulking shoulders, she was sexless and androgynous. "Whatever happened to Amory Johnson?" he said. "You don't hear much about her these days. I wonder what life was like after all those medals."

Ed reminded them of the controversy over naming the swimming pool after her.

"I never understood that," Gayle said. "Was it something political? You know how I go deaf when it's politics."

Ed explained that people hadn't liked it when she came out of retirement while her son was still an infant. As he spoke, elaborating the nature of the controversy, a slight hint of color rose in his face and his speech became animated. For every declaration he made, he looked to Gayle for a corresponding ripple of appreciation. Her expression said that it was her delight to furnish this to him, her delight and also her usefulness to him.

"Subconsciously it all comes down to breast-feeding," Ed said. "People don't want public evidence it's taking place, but they also feel it's a problem if mothers aren't doing it."

"*I* breast-fed," Gayle said. "I breast-fed each of my babies for a whole year."

"Of course you did," Ed said. "You're my wife."

"But what happened with the pool?" Gene said.

"Oh, she got it. But the plaque was very small."

"Only a man needs his name on a very big thing," Gayle said.

"Gene doesn't need a plaque," Ed said. "Isn't that right?"

The rain was still coming down when he left. The low places in the road were swollen with water, and every now and then he drove through one and it seemed to lift his car like a boat. The wind had picked up and it drove the rain against the windshield. It bent the trees on the side of the road into snarls, which snapped open with sudden violence the moment the wind passed. When he came around a curve in the road, his car planed over the water and the tail swerved back and forth. He tried to correct this by wrenching the wheel in the opposite direction, but the car began to spin. He let go of the wheel. The car scraped against the curb and eventually came to a stop. Gene grabbed the keys and pulled them out of the ignition. He sat in the dark, his heart rapping against his chest. His hands were shaking, nearly crawling in his lap. He waited until his heart slowed. Then, with trembling hands, he drove the rest of the way home.

He was still agitated when he got to the house—surprised to be alive and also terrified not to be. In truth, he didn't understand why he was still alive, not when there were so many stupid, easy ways to die. He drank a cup of cocoa, thinking it would calm him. He could feel the sugar in the cocoa mix eating away at the enamel on his teeth, but he drank another cup, thinking the second would wash away the feeling of the first. He brushed his teeth and put on his nightclothes. By the time he got under the covers, his heart was hammering again and he was wide awake.

He hadn't thought about the day Maida swam across the lake for a long time. It was the summer Brian's crying had kept them up at night, when everyone was a little on edge from not sleeping enough. There had been a fight the night before in front of the Donnellys. Gene thought Maida shouldn't swim the distance alone. What if she got a cramp? What if she got tired? At least she should let him row a boat beside her. It was only a few miles, she said. By the time he found a pair of oars she'd already be across. *Don't be stupid,* he almost blurted out, but instead he said, "Don't be selfish," which was perhaps closer to his real feeling. He tried to cajole some sense into her, and the argument went on for some time until Ed finally said, "Oh, leave her alone already. She's going to do what she wants and you're going to do the same."

It turned out to be a fairly apt description of what happened.

The following morning Maida slipped out of bed before Gene was awake, and when he realized she was gone, he found the oars under the house and began rowing toward her splash, which from a distance looked like a small mar on the surface of the water. It was hard work catching up to her—he was no champion rower—but he made progress, and eventually he slowed down so as not to get too close to her and minimize her sense of achievement. When at last she reached the shore and hobbled out of the water, she had no idea he was the vigilant speck in the boat. In the end, they had both gotten their way, yet he never enjoyed the memory. Some unpleasant aftertaste clung to it.

There had been countless such spats over the years: not just Maida and Gene but Ed and Gayle, each of the couples airing their differences or just failing to conceal them in front of one another. It was almost as if the presence of an audience gave voice to what might otherwise have remained unvoiced. There was something both satisfying and humiliating in this— the satisfaction of having one's grievance verified, and the humiliation of having craved that verification in the first place, while being forced to acknowledge that one's relationship suffered the same mortal dysfunction known to other people. The audience somehow heightened the sense of injury, as well as the deliciousness of the eventual repair, and in this regard the couples had shamelessly used each other, though it was a victimless kind of using.

It was strange and almost funny that while they had all gotten older, their arguments had been immured in a permanent adolescence, never developing much beyond their original themes. Ed was generally permissive in a way you might think would make everyone happy, but somehow this permissiveness

didn't reliably extend to Gayle. Gene and Gayle had both encountered its limits, and they had broad empathy for each other
as creatures who were devoted to Ed in spite of his flaws. Maida
didn't extend such a deferential welcome to Ed. She was more
liable to tell him outright when he was being an asshole. Over
the years Gene had sometimes wondered if they might have
made the better pair, in the same way that he'd wondered about
himself and Gayle. Had Ed ever considered marrying Maida?
Clearly there was feeling between them, but whatever it was, it
hadn't looked consistent over the years. Sometimes they found
each other amusing, which seemed tied to their respect for each
other, and at other times they were openly prickly, as if they had
forgotten the respect and regarded the other as essentially careless and condescending.

It was hard to know for sure why any of them had stayed in
their marriages. Was it all so wonderful? Or were they all just
lazy by default, just trying to squeeze another year out of the
connections they had formed when they were young?

This was the sort of moment when he ached for Maida. This
predicament of mind, when everything looked ordinary on the
outside but inside felt like it was coming apart; when his speculative mind went on generating one question after another,
the second meant to answer the first but in reality only taking him deeper into unknowable territory, where he began to
believe that the only way out of the situation was to find an
answer that would resolve the questions. Then Maida would
bring him back to his life. Often she brought him back through
touch, something as simple as tousling his hair or clasping his
hand. And somehow the recognition that his agitation hadn't
leaked into her and that his life was still continuing outside his
mind in a completely normal fashion allowed him to glimpse

the absurdity of his questions, and how they had at best a tenuous relationship to the actuality of living. This was the reaching of the hand of safety into the world of danger, and he couldn't do it for himself. That Maida was not available to do it for him—that she would never do it for him again—made him almost frightened of himself, the fear a sense of separateness from something stronger and more stable than himself.

He got up and took one of the sleeping pills Dr. Fornier had prescribed for him. Then it seemed that he listened for a long time to the rain blasting the side of the house. Of the many things he thought, waiting to fall asleep, one was how the pills that were supposed to defuse your mind never quite did their job when you most needed them to.

After a while, finding himself still awake, he looked at the clock. It was after midnight, too late to call anyone under ordinary circumstances. But it had not really been an ordinary kind of day, and some intuition told him that Adele would forgive him.

She was surprised to hear from him—was everything all right? Almost immediately he was embarrassed he'd called her. He told her he would see her on Monday and hung up the phone. Then, afraid he'd been rude, he called back to apologize.

She didn't sound the least bit angry. She sounded just like herself. Was he all right? she asked. He told her the truth.

When she arrived he was still in shock from having told someone the truth. She said nothing about his appearance, his bathrobe dusted with powdered chocolate and the belt trailing off to one side. He offered to make her a cup of cocoa, but she treated the suggestion as amiable nonsense. If he was too agitated to sleep, they should put their energies toward reducing his agitation.

He thought it would feel strange to have her in his bedroom. But she had been in his room many times before—to change the sheets, or vacuum, or put away his clothes—and it almost seemed natural to have her there. She lay down next to him and told him she would stay until he fell asleep.

He waited in the dark for her to change her mind. He figured that after one minute, or two minutes, or three minutes had passed she would get up quietly and leave him. But every time he checked, she was still there. Eventually he rolled toward her until his body was wedged against hers. Her skin smelled of something cooked, rice or pasta or maybe a pilaf.

He had thought that having her there would calm him, but instead a restless energy began to surge through his body. The heat of her body pressed against his stomach and thighs, stirring a faint pulsation that traveled the length of his spine and down his legs. He put his arms around her and she responded by adjusting herself against him, finding the hollow places in his own shape that she could fill with her warmth.

It had been a long time since he'd touched someone like this. The last time with Maida, perhaps a month before her death, hadn't been quite the full sexual experience. There had been tenderness, but also laziness and indecision, because they had both been drinking and weren't sure whether they had enough energy.

He knew before he touched Adele's breasts they would be good, nothing like the tubes of flesh you saw on some older women at the beach. He felt her breasts through her shirt and her flesh rolled into his hand, giving itself to him. The pulse within him that had been faint began to quicken.

She sat up abruptly.

In the darkened room, where her face wasn't visible, he didn't know what this meant. He was afraid he'd offended her, afraid she was going to tell him to stop.

But all she did was pull her shirt off over her head and un-hook her bra and toss it to the floor.

12.

WITHOUT WARNING HIS life entered a new period of happiness. Adele continued to cook and clean for him, they continued to have their lighthearted conversations, and now there was the welcome development of their physical intimacy.

At first he wouldn't allow himself to look at her in her full nakedness, because then he would be aware of what he was doing, which was looking greedily at a naked woman who wasn't his wife. Somehow he could convince himself that his hands answered to some bestial power outside his responsibility and control, but there was no deceiving himself about his eyes, which he attempted to keep downcast as he undressed her. Her feet, which were nothing special, were connected to her legs, which were connected to the recess of warmth between them, and when he had gotten this far something else took over. His heart summited in his body. His legs felt the impossibility of holding still. Everything about this bodily call-and-response told him that if he was going to continue living, there was no choice but to heed it.

In the beginning he worried he wouldn't know what to do

with her body. Early in his marriage Maida had trained him to pleasure her with his mouth and his hands, but there were long stretches when her enthusiasm for these intimacies waned, and without them her climax was never reliable. It didn't bother her but it bothered him considerably, and as he got older his own pleasure depended more on hers. At times when they were entwined he found himself doing a kind of backward math in his head, trying to figure out if an earlier conversation about whether there was enough money in the checking account or if they should change the brand of garbage bags was to blame for a bland lovemaking session. He had read once that the way to keep sex exciting was to be continually open to introducing new elements, and he wondered who these people were, the ones who after long days of working at jobs and caring for children still had the energy and creativity to show off in the bedroom. It touched on an insecurity of his to be told that such people were not fantastical but that they existed—and were perhaps in every other regard completely ordinary. Then he would remind himself it was only natural to imagine other people's sexual lives as more interesting and satisfying than your own. It was just the cry of the threatened primordial brain, and he could recognize it without automatically accepting it as truth.

Learning a new body was thrilling and surprisingly intuitive except when his mind interfered and tried to assess it: Was this time with Adele as good as the last time? Was being with Adele better than, or just different from, being with Maida? Then, sensing the dispersion of his mind, Adele would pull away from him and ask what was wrong. He was reluctant to tell her, afraid that she would mistake his preoccupation for a complaint. And it *was* a kind of complaint—at some barely perceptible level he was angry with her for so easily capturing a part of him that had only ever belonged to Maida. If she asked him again what was wrong, he ignored her and flipped her over and held her bottom in his hands and when he came he thought, *This. Is. Her. Ass.*

His understanding of women's emotions had led him to expect there might be occasional scenes and outbursts connected to the undefined nature of their relationship. But he saw nothing to indicate Adele was harboring a grievance. What was between them seemed to exist beyond mental maintenance. It was physical, unspoken, unburdened with meaning. There was no need to define it. Their source of pleasure was in each other and they could be matter-of-fact about this without a temptation to become sentimental. That he wouldn't be required to love Adele, or to support her, or to anticipate her needs—he experienced this as an utterly shocking freedom.

Sometimes he would catch himself in his contentment and wonder what had happened to his liver-eating grief. Where had it gone? Somehow it had pivoted from its quality of midnight emergency, with all the corresponding alarms, to a dull background ache he could ignore if what was before him was exciting enough. The grief he thought of himself as having wasn't the grief he seemed to have anymore. Sometimes he almost wanted the old grief back because of the way it had made his wife everywhere and near. Then he would remember its unbearable devouring quality and feel a relief at its absence that was too awful to admit. Recalling that old grief was like running into a stranger he had an affinity for. There was recognition, there was mutual regard, but the stranger and he had separate destinies to fulfill.

The only time he wasn't happy was when Adele was leaving. He came to despise Fridays at three o'clock, which in addition to being the hour of her departure was also when she expected to be paid. At the end of the first week they had spent as lovers, some part of him hoped they would have a real goodbye full of ardor and affection, and later he would figure out how to get a check to her, if a check was still what she wanted. But Adele reminded him he needed to pay her, and he lied and told her he had misplaced his checkbook. It was an idiotic thing to say to the person who kept your belongings organized. She knew exactly where his checkbook was and went off to retrieve it. And when he wrote her the check, her gratitude was genuine. It was the genuineness of it, more than anything, that made him ashamed.

After that he was determined to find a way to free their time together from the taint of money. Since Dary was reimbursing him anyway, it occurred to him she could pay Adele directly, and this was something it turned out she was happy to do.

Then in December Dary bought tickets for her and Annie to visit for two weeks at Christmas, and for three miserable days he and Adele talked of ending their liaison. They agreed it would be difficult for them to continue seeing each other when his family was visiting, and he almost convinced himself this was the natural end point of the affair.

It was a sensible proposition, but his body rebelled against it. His body hadn't forgotten the moment she had touched his face while cutting his hair, the ripple of shock it had sent along his nerves, reminding him of his isolation from other people. He would jeopardize virtually everything in his life not to experience that misery again. Of course he wouldn't give her up.

He still didn't know what he would tell Dary about the relationship. There was a part of him that wanted to tell her and believed that telling her would usher them into a closeness they'd never had before. And there was another part of him that foresaw it would be too painful to mention anything, because it would shame him to stake intimacy with his daughter on behavior she might consider a betrayal. A betrayal of her effort to do something straightforward and practical to improve his life—or worse, a betrayal of her mother.

He asked Adele what she thought he should tell Dary. It seemed appropriate, since it concerned both of them.

"Wait and see what it's like when she gets here," Adele said.

"But I want to know what you think," he said.

"Wait and see, that's what I think."

He was perplexed by how little invested she was in what was said about her, and he felt himself frowning in a paternal, disapproving way before he could stop himself.

She frowned back, a clownish mirror of his face.

He said, "Someday you'll meet my daughter and you'll know what I mean about her. What do you think of that?"

"I think you're getting ahead of yourself."

13.

THE ARRIVING FLIGHT discharged its passengers and the hall
swelled with swiftly dispersing humans. Gene waited for the
moment when from the sea of faces bobbing up and down
two of them would cohere and become the distinct faces of his
daughter and granddaughter. When he saw them he waved his
hands above his head like a ground controller guiding a taxiing
plane: Here I am; here I am.

He drew Annie into a burly hug, and as they parted, he
clasped the skinniness of her upper arms. "How did this
happen?" he said. "Don't they feed you anything at that fancy
school of yours?" His daughter he embraced lightly, patting
her in the center of her back. They looked each other over,
assessing the wear of the intervening months. Small wrinkles
crouched around Dary's eyes and mouth. Most of them probably had been there the last time he saw her, but sometimes
there seemed to be new ones and more of them, and it never
failed to shock him to rediscover he was old enough to have a
child with wrinkles.

"There you are!" a voice called out across the terminal. A man waved and began making his way toward them through the crowd. He was wearing cowboy boots, a belt with a glinty silver buckle. "Dale Elverson," the man said, sticking out his hand to Gene. "I had the good fortune of being seated next to these two special ladies on the flight."

Dale wasn't at all bad-looking. He had a wheaty shock of brown hair and his build was fit. In the chitchat that ensued he mentioned he was the owner of two houses, one in the city where he was a partner at a law firm (Gene had actually heard the name before), and another in the country, where he joked he was paying "an arm and a leg for everything to be inconvenient." Gene laughed at this, not because he knew anything about this particular feeling but because he could see Dale was just trying to be friendly.

As the talk wound down, Dale took out his card and suggested Dary call him sometime.

"The thing is—" Dary said, a weary note in her voice. "I'm not here for very long."

"Well, the next time, then," Dale said, continuing to extend his card.

"The thing is," she said, "I don't want to give the impression that I'm interested when I'm not."

"Oh, you don't mean that," Dale said in an upbeat tone, and looked to Gene, appearing confident that Gene would share his opinion.

"Why not take the card?" Gene said to Dary.

"See?" Dale said. "You don't know what you're missing. You could be making a big mistake."

Gene waited for Dary to say something that would save Dale from rejection, but she only shouldered her bag and draped her arm over Annie and, in that same weary tone, said she was ready to go home. And because Gene couldn't let Dale go on like that, waiting for a better answer, Gene took his card and thanked him and invited him to drop in on them in Colton sometime.

In the car on the way home, Annie fell asleep in the back seat, and Gene struggled to keep afloat a conversation with Dary. Whatever he asked her about—the food on the flight, the weather in California, the arrangements for Hoolie—she obliged him with a response, but then allowed the conversation to die out. There was something vaguely punitive about her silence, as if she expected him to intuit why she was feeling sour.

There was some congestion on the interstate, inexplicable sections where cars that had been going seventy miles an hour slowed abruptly and then seemed to progress only by nudging one another forward. "Do you ever wonder where all these people are going?" he said, trying yet again. He turned his head to glance at the person in the neighboring car and asked Dary where she thought the man was going.

"Dad—" she said. "You're making me nervous. Would you please watch the road?"

"I am."

"Exclusively," she said.

"Then you look at him."

She twisted in her seat. After a moment she said, "On his way to visit his girlfriend in prison."

"No."

"Okay, wow. To pick out a kitten? Is that better?"

"Does he look nice?" Gene said.

"How am I supposed to know?"

"You get a feel for these things."

"Maybe *you* do."

"Just try."

"Look, if this is some kind of test—"

"Who's he getting the kitten for?"

"I don't know. His mother."

"Why her? Why not—"

"Because his mother accepts him. Everyone else thinks he has to be improved, but his mother just loves him."

Gene paused, unsure of how to respond to this. "All right," he said finally. "Does he get the kitten?"

"I don't see why not. It's hardly plutonium."

"Look, anything could happen. C'mon. For the next minute you have perfect vision into the future."

"I don't know," she said helplessly.

"Yes you do. It's up to you."

There was a long pause.

"Dary?"

"Please," she said. "Please let's stop."

"Why can't we ever have a little fun?" he said. "Why are you so opposed to fun?"

He pulled off for gas in Newburyport. As he filled the tank he observed her sitting motionless in the front seat. A car trembling with bass pulled up on the other side of the pump and two young couples spilled out of it with the restless energy of people who have been confined for too long. Despite the chill in the air the young women were bare-armed, and as they waited for the tank to fill, they warmed themselves by wrapping the arms of their boyfriends around them, as if the young men had been put on earth precisely for this consolation. For an instant his daughter's unhappiness surged in her face. He wondered then if she was one of those people who subsist on misery. Usually such people thought they had suffered worse than anyone else—they clung to a wretched childhood, they hardened it into a story of deprivation they could live over and over again. But Dary's childhood hadn't been anything like that.

How had she become this person? And why was she so difficult to understand? His whole life he had been waiting for them to like each other. When she was a child, he thought for certain it would happen when she became an adult. When she was an adult, he thought for certain it would happen when she became a parent. But it hadn't happened, at least not in the way he had imagined it would.

And the longer it took, the more he disbelieved in the possibility, until he'd become somewhat irritable about this wasted opportunity. Someone might even call him an irritable old man. But the smug young people who casually threw that phrase around didn't stop to consider that maybe there was a good reason to be irritable toward the end of your life, having withstood a measure of disappointment that was not really fathomable to people who believed they still had enough time to reverse events that didn't favor them. When you thought about it, it was amazing that everyone over seventy wasn't perpetually irritated. It wasn't a pleasant feeling to sense that possibility itself was limited. And it was especially not pleasant when you harbored a perhaps silly but nonetheless honest delusion that once in a while loving someone should be enough to get what you want. Of course love was not enough—it was never enough—but now it was too late for him to adopt a new delusion. He had no choice but to go on feeling everything contained in the warped bundle above his heart: sorrow, fear, regret, diminished hope, irritation, disappointment. Maybe disappointment most of all.

What was it Esther had written?

I assumed you of all people would know.

14.

WHEN PEOPLE SAID that Christmas was a special time of year, he agreed with them, and not just out of politeness but because he sincerely believed it. He understood that some people (including the Donnellys in years past) viewed the holidays as a time to escape someplace warm, where they could avoid the winter fervor that made otherwise normal people spend a month's salary on colored lights for the front of the house or three days baking and delivering goody bags filled with angel-shaped cookies. But this shameless enthusiasm was the very thing that made him love the people who were swept up by it. Why go to Puerto Rico and miss the one time of year when people everywhere embraced silly, timeworn rituals? For a brief moment, you could pretend kindness was universal and generosity contagious.

He didn't particularly care what their own family traditions were, as long as they stuck with them. It was the sticking-with-it that seemed to be the antidote to seasonal despair—the whole point was familial togetherness. It didn't matter if one year you were in the mood and another you weren't.

Every year when Dary was young, he would take her to the White Mountains to cut down a tree, a daylong excursion that involved the novelty of eating all of their meals out of the house. The Ashes also made a ritual of wrapping presents in misleading packages, elaborate ruses that might involve padding mounds of newspaper around a cassette-tape player and girding the newspaper with masking tape, so that the finished package looked more like a papier-mâché basketball than an electronic device. After the presents were laid out under the tree and the bounty had been documented, he took Dary to the Three Hearths Inn for peppermint hot chocolate, where they sat in a cozy room with other children dressed up for the special occasion, little boys in flannel vests and church loafers and little girls in ruffle-edged dresses and patent leather Mary Janes.

He had always been a little nervous around Dary when she was young, but somehow that nervousness hadn't gotten in the way. The first time he took her to the White Mountains to cut down a tree was also their first trip without Maida, and he worried he might do something stupid to jeopardize his daughter's safety and well-being. He thought of a certain class of fathers as being innately, almost fatefully, careless of children, and while he mentally maligned these men, he also sometimes feared he might be one. But the trip had gone fine. His child had evoked in him a desire to be a better father than he was, someone more playful, more ingenious, more fun. On the car ride up he stuck Cheerios in his nostrils and sang "Deck the Halls," changing the words so that "boughs of holly" became "cows and French fries," which to his amazement had the desired effect: his daughter squealed with laughter and made him sing it again. When it came time to pick out a tree, he told her the secret to choosing the one to take home was to find the one that smelled the loneliest. Her eyes widened as he said this, and then she went around using her tiny mittened hands to clap various branches to her nose. On the way home they stopped at a roadside restaurant and posed together for a photo imitating the giant wooden bear making a fierce clawed gesture over the parking lot. And when he looked into the future, he thought that for years they would still be visiting these stations of love, only Dary would be taller and possibly wearing braces and he would be slightly more tired and there would be gray in his hair.

He still remembered the end of those times. One year she asked him why they drove all the way to the White Mountains when they could buy the same kind of tree from the Boy Scouts, who maintained a seasonal tree lot across from the bank. Because she was only nine and because he hadn't perceived the seriousness of her question, he repeated what had often been said to him as a child, which was that sometimes you did things a certain way because that's how they had always been done. The expression on her little face after he said this showed alarm. It was as if the trust she'd had in him suddenly fell away and she saw him not as her father but as a regular person. For the first time, it seemed to occur to her that other Ashe family traditions might be arbitrary, and if arbitrary, then also maybe not mandatory. That year he found himself at the Three Hearths Inn drinking a peppermint hot chocolate by himself, surrounded by little girls in black velvet dresses, none of whom was his.

Then in one of those strange turns that life makes, doubling back as it dogs forward, Dary inadvertently revived the family traditions by starting to bring his granddaughter to Colton for Christmas. Annie proved herself a willing, malleable companion for holiday pastimes. Under his tutelage she became expert at rolling paperback books into poster tubes before wrapping them and eating two whole maple-frosted eclairs at the Three Hearths Inn. And since he was no longer in any shape to be cutting down trees, they had added a new tradition of going as a family to the children's museum, where Annie loved the replica of a whale.

But this year Annie was bleary and sluggish in the mornings, rising late and then squinting at everything with a slightly tense expression. After her morning shower an hour would often elapse before she emerged from the steamed-up bathroom, and if he asked her what had taken her so long, she looked startled and then replied, "Oh, nothing." If he asked her if she wanted to go to the Three Hearths Inn, she wasn't hungry, though twenty minutes later she was likely to be begging her mother to order a pizza. "Eat a piece of fruit," her mother said, and this induced a look of horror on Annie's face, as if only two options were left to her in the world—pizza or starvation—and her mother had consigned her to the dire one. She tepidly investigated a banana, and with some noises of protest made a drawn-out performance of peeling it, grimacing at the brown spots. But when the telephone rang, the performance was immediately abandoned and suddenly she had no time to finish the banana or a sentence.

The caller was often one of Ed and Gayle's grandchildren, up from Boston or New York, visiting for the holidays. Annie had always been encouraged to think of them as cousins, and in the past Gene had been under the impression that she found these alliances fostered by adults to be inauthentic and tiresome. She often referred to Colin's son as "Fangnose" and Michael's son as "Smelly Luke." She was friendlier with Colin's daughters, at least since the camping trip, though she hadn't mentioned them once she returned to California and began school. But now the cousins consumed her thoughts and she was anxious to know what they were doing when she wasn't with them, and whether they were having any fun without her, and whether her absence had been adequately noticed and mourned. It amazed him she had time to miss them since she saw them every day, leaving her almost no time for him.

Once when she returned to the house after having been out all morning and he asked her where she'd been, she said she'd been helping to pick out a present.

"Nice of you to help your mother," he said.

"Oh, it wasn't Mom. Max couldn't figure out what to get his sister."

"Colin's kid? 'Fangnose'? That Max?" Her impassive face told him he was right. "I thought you loathed the guy."

"I don't *loathe* anyone, Grandpa."

"Loathe is *dislike*."

"I know what it means. Or, whatever, I get it."

"This is the first time I've heard you refer to Max by his real name. All this time it's been 'Fangnose this' and 'Fangnose that.'"

"Well, I don't call him that anymore."

He was surprised by the amount of independence she was given—the way she would be permitted, for instance, to go over to the Donnellys' for the whole day and not return until after dark. He tried to remember the age at which your child stopped requiring a babysitter and *became* the babysitter. With Dary, he had been shocked by the proximity of the two roles: one day your child was being put to bed by the neighbor girl and the next your baby was putting someone else's infant to bed.

This was when he felt Maida's absence. Not when he would have expected it, in the moments that were preloaded for sentimental grief, as when they decorated the tree or wrapped presents together, but instead when he was overcome by a feeling of not knowing something he had once known. Maida would have been able to tell him how old girls were when they became babysitters. And she also would have had something smart to say to Dary about her attitude toward Annie's independence. Not a sharp remark but rather a discerning one, which would have disabused his daughter of her illusion that no one but she had any relevant experience in how to raise a child.

Gene often wondered what was being lost to his granddaughter because her relation to the world was overseen by one person. It wasn't that he thought of Dary as a bad parent, but it somehow seemed unfair to Annie to have so much power over her concentrated in a single person, a person who like everyone else had flaws and deficits that cried out for counterbalance. He didn't understand why Dary didn't seek that counterbalance by marrying someone who could become a parent to Annie, just as he didn't understand why she refused to acknowledge that Annie's biological father was a person of consequence in their lives. Somewhere in the world there was a man who had given as much of his human material to Annie as Dary had, and the undeniable fact of his existence had a bearing on their lives that couldn't be discarded simply because he was an inconvenient figure in Dary's mythology of herself.

One evening Annie returned to the house rosy and animated. There was a brightness in her eyes, an uptick in her speech. Twice she mentioned Max's name, though what she said about him amounted to very little, as if she wanted both to highlight their connection and depict its ordinariness. When Gene asked her what they had been doing earlier, she said, "Oh, nothing," and abruptly fell silent. Then she gathered her belongings and ran up to her room.

When Dary and Gene were alone, he asked her if she had noticed anything unusual about Annie's recent behavior.

"It's great, isn't it?" she said. "Once you let them out of school, they feel so free."

The next day he retrieved Dale Elverson's card and dialed his number. Dale's phone manner, courtly and self-assured, confirmed Gene's instincts that if anyone could help, it would be somebody like him, a person who had an important law firm's name printed on his card. When Gene asked whether, hypothetically speaking, it would be possible to identify the paternity of a child based on privately held records at one Pacific Family Center in Berkeley, California, Dale didn't treat the request as bizarre. He merely replied that it wouldn't be easy to do, because such facilities were set up to prevent it. Still, for someone clever enough, he suggested there was a way around everything, and he said he would be happy to look into it for Gene.

His separation from Adele revealed something remarkable, which was that she had made his body into a different sort of body than he had known during the last decade of his marriage. He and Maida had always had a sex life, but it had been erratic. Sometimes they made love every other day for a week, and then a whole month might pass before Maida appeared interested in being touched again. In their twenties and early thirties, he had attributed this to their tension around children—he had wanted more, and Maida had vacillated between not wanting more and simply feeling uncertain, especially because her work at the day care consumed much of the energy a new baby would have required. She had been pregnant one other time, at thirty-two, and after she miscarried at eleven-and-a-half weeks, she became more certain she was finished having children. After that their sex life became more regular, but in the last decade their lovemaking seemed to drop off once again. He had more or less viewed that development as evidence of the regrettable but unstoppable slowing down of the physical aspect of existence, which was not always or often aligned with one's inner desires. It seemed no amount of will or persuasion could alter this slowing down, and the best he could do was to try to quiet his indignant mind. But a week without Adele showed him otherwise. More than once he woke up in the middle of the night in a froth, heat emanating from his skin and his chest covered with sweat, and the thought of the way he touched her and she allowed herself to be touched sent him rolling onto his hands with a groan.

He called her every other day, sneaking up to his room to whisper into the phone. He didn't enjoy deceiving Dary, but he also didn't blame himself for this. His happiness subscribed to a logic of its own, a logic that freed him from the constraint of explaining his behavior. What was between him and Adele was as pure as the physical tenderness between them, he reasoned, so a lie in service of it wasn't really a lie. And if someone pressed him to give a name to their connection he would have called it love—the first pulse of an awakening love. But of course it couldn't be, because it hadn't been long enough since Maida had passed away.

The sneakiness required to make his conversations with Adele possible, the fear of being caught by his daughter, the tremulous, exhausting suspense of being parted from the person he longed to see—all this combined in him to produce a volatile, emotional state that overflowed at the first sound of Adele's voice and was amplified by the contrast with her preoccupied manner, which he assumed was the result of her increasingly demanding family situation. Because her son didn't have a job and his girlfriend wasn't speaking to her own mother, Adele was the chief person planning for the arrival of the baby. There were the myriad items to be acquired—diapers, bottles, clothes—and then the question of how to find the money to pay for these things.

"Don't worry," Gene said. "We'll find a way."

The language of his mind already speculated in the idiom of *we,* and the same infatuation responsible for replacing *I* with *we* prompted him to freely and unself-consciously imagine the new shape his life might take. He had never met the unpleasant son or his girlfriend, yet he listened to Adele discuss her changing family with the delectable terror of a man being given a vision of his future. It was entirely possible that what was hers would become his and what was his would become hers. Did he really want an infant in the house? Did he want to encounter the bare-chested son in the hallway on his way to bed, wafting the smell of cigarettes after a night of partying? Would Adele let him keep his office? Would they have separate accounts, or joint?

He reminded himself it might be a long time before any of it happened.

His attitude toward Adele's accommodation of her family was split down the middle. On the one hand he admired her generosity and forbearance. He was quite sure he couldn't be attracted to a woman who didn't embody these qualities to a greater degree than he could imagine adopting them himself. That was part of attraction—attraction was aspirational—and it was important for the women he admired to exceed him in this respect, enhancing his stature and giving him a bright mark to aim for if one day he decided he wanted to improve himself. But rushing against all of this was an opposing desire, stronger and more torrential, that Adele's loyalty and generosity not be wasted on the feckless son who would never appreciate her efforts, when instead these same qualities of hers might nourish Gene.

Dary had asked about the relationship only once. The two of them were in the bank to speak with someone about adding her name to his accounts. The waiting area was adjacent to the tinted glass cubicle of the banker they were waiting to see, and on the exterior of one of the walls was a promotional calendar for that same bank featuring a photo of a white-haired couple laughing together on a bench. Somehow without words you implicitly understood they had been married half a century and had planned prudently for the long happy retirement they were now living out together. Gene couldn't help feeling the wrongness of his situation, the strange reversal of having his child become a custodian for him. If Maida was alive, she would still be managing their accounts. The only proper situation was one in which the two of them were waiting for the banker together, the same way the white-haired couple was waiting for more happiness and wealth on the bench. He missed Maida terribly in that moment, though the feeling was reduced by a sense of embarrassment: it seemed a shabby way to miss his wife, to be summoning her in his mind for her transactional competence. And it depressed him to recognize the way you missed someone was subject to degradation like everything else, so that while at first what you missed was a transcendent union with the person, later sometimes you just wished she was still managing your money.

The calendar with the retired couple showed the wrong

month. He got up and flipped the page. When he sat back down, Dary asked him how it was working out with Adele.

"We enjoy each other," he said.

"So it isn't all torture and humiliation?" There were the first stirrings of a triumphal smile on his daughter's face.

"Not—no."

"You look forward to her visits?"

"It's a change of pace," he allowed.

"Ah," she said, and now the triumphal smile was openly arrayed on her face. "You recall how not so long ago, you went on and on about how I was trying to constrain your life?"

He didn't think he'd gone on and on. "I'm not complaining," he said.

"You have a pretty sweet deal."

He resented the way she made it sound like the world was doing him a favor. "It's not all torture and humiliation for *her* either, you know. Some people actually think your father is good company."

"Good for you," she said. "Good for you for making a friend."

"She is," he said. "She's a very good friend."

15.

HE WENT WITH Annie and Dary to the children's museum on Christmas Eve, the last possible day before it closed for the holidays, a trip that might not have happened at all if Gayle hadn't called to say that Brian was unexpectedly driving north and would be arriving the next day. She was sorry to have to send Annie home but hoped they would understand she had to put the house together.

Annie showed little interest in her old friend, the replica of the whale, a minke with a glum, downturned mouth and faded patches on its tuxedo-coloring where children had worn away the hue with the oils from their hands. The one exhibit he thought for certain would bore her, the aerodynamics lab, turned out to be the one in which she wanted to spend all her time. It wasn't really an exhibit at all but a workshop where children built so-called flying ships out of foam blocks of different colors, cranked them twenty feet into the rafters on a conveyor belt, and launched them into the air with the ostensible purpose of discovering the mechanics of flight, though the potential to have your ship collide with another person's head seemed as much of the allure as the engineering experience. The lab was in a bright, airy renovated space with exposed air ducts painted the same bright orange as the low stools tucked under the gleaming workbench, and there was a tall glass door that opened onto a central courtyard. None of it matched the dingy, huddled brick building that was the rest of the museum.

He was struck by how many fathers were in the lab. Some were sweetly and energetically collaborating with their children while others were simply building their own flying ships. It was an astonishing male zone of production in the middle of the museum, which was otherwise reliably a society of women, the mothers and grandmothers and babysitters pushing around strollers filled with discarded outerwear and piled-up water bottles. He wondered if the fathers had been sent here by their wives in some like-minded effort to manage the boredom and unease of men stuck at home with children during the holidays.

He was having his own version of anxiety about Christmas, the day itself. If he found himself missing Adele on the holiday, he could remind himself he would see her again, and the disagreeable feeling would be mitigated. But if he missed Maida, there would only be misery.

"Oh, cheer up, Dad," Dary said.

He wondered if he looked a little like the whale, as faded and as glum.

"We're here because of you," she said. "Remember?"

We're here because of you.

At first, in the fog of his melancholy, the words took on an almost mystical meaning. They sounded monumental and loving. The next moment, though, he was irritated by them.

It sounded like his daughter was indirectly blaming him for something.

They got Annie established at the workbench and she began to build her model. He and Dary stood next to a framed poster on the wall that declared success isn't success unless you've failed, a motto that annoyed him because it had almost certainly been penned by a resoundingly successful person.

He asked Dary if she was aware Brian Donnelly designed real-life flying ships. "He would fit right in here, don't you think?"

"It's creepy to come here without kids."

"Brian *loves* his kids. Did I mention he's getting divorced?"

"Yup. Twice."

While Annie was building her flying ship he stepped out into the courtyard. Though it hadn't snowed yet, the cold had an edge of ice, and he tugged his scarf higher around his neck and his ears. There was another bundled-up man out there, his hands deep in the pockets of his caramel-colored coat, with only a strip of his face visible between the cream scarf hiding his mouth and a matching hat pulled over his brow. Gene joined him to look out over the half-frozen river, sluggish and gray. The land for the museum had been donated by the city some thirty years earlier in one of its attempts to revitalize the old industrial district, and Gene was perhaps one of a few people who recalled that the tannery where his father worked had been there on the other side of the river. You could just make out where the pits had been; the earth had filled itself back in over the years but not completely, leaving sunken patches of ground littered with dead leaves, windblown plastic bags, and other debris.

The man gave a slight nod of his head, which might have been a greeting or just his reaction to finding his solitude intruded upon. He pulled his scarf away from his mouth, and gestured to the land in front of them. "It's a shame, isn't it?" he said. He was young but tired-looking, his skin pale and his lips pale and eyes pale too. "Why don't they do anything with it?"

"Someday they might," Gene said.

"The museum could be twice as big. Then they could dump this whale and get a bigger one. Have you seen the one in New York? Now *that's* a whale."

"I don't mind this one," Gene said.

The man looked troubled, deeply so, as if Gene had said he didn't mind child slavery or something awful like that. He pulled his scarf back over his mouth and returned to his sullen contemplation.

Gene didn't remember when the tannery had finally closed, only that his father was dead by then. He didn't know what had happened to the other men who worked there, whether they had picked up hours at the General Electric factory, or moved away, or become the next generation of sad jobless men. He would probably never get used to it, the way time spun everything around, making heroes out of villains and villains out of heroes. The tannery work had always been considered difficult and rugged and indispensable. But now it was said that the tannery had emptied Colton's river of salmon. There had been public meetings, and public arguments, and public attempts to make companies pay a lot of reparation money. A group of cancer patients in the area with a similar, rare, deadly form of cancer was suing the company that owned the property in an attempt to gain access to private corporate records, and every time Gene heard about the lawsuit he felt terribly sorry for the plaintiffs, not just because they were dying, but also because their last efforts seemed so futile. What could they possibly learn, at this late hour, that would make their deaths any less terrible?

When he went back into the lab, Annie was waiting in line to load her flying ship onto the conveyor belt. He followed Dary into the viewing box, a platform raised a few feet above the cement floor and enclosed on three sides by clear plastic walls. Besides protecting them from being struck, it gave them an excellent view of everyone in the room.

"Ever notice," Dary said, "how it's hip in certain places to have a child as an accessory? I mean, if you're a man," she said. "There's nothing novel about it if you're a woman. We just did as expected."

"Not you," Gene said. "You didn't do it the way anyone expected."

She smiled an indulging smile. "You never did get used to the word *donor.* What was it you called him? The Donator?"

"You wouldn't let me say *father.*"

"He doesn't get a promotion he hasn't earned."

Gene thought he saw a rare opening. "Aren't you just a little curious about him?"

There was a brief silence. Then in a cautious manner she said, "Curiosity isn't the feeling. Maybe there's something there, but it isn't curiosity. It's hard to imagine anything I could find out that wouldn't seem, well, arbitrary at this point."

"Who her father is is arbitrary?"

"Not completely. But it isn't determining, either. Annie's already who she is."

"And what if someone told you they could give you an envelope and inside was everything you could possibly want to know about this person? You're saying you wouldn't take it?"

"That's just a fantasy."

It was Annie's turn. She loaded her ship onto the conveyor belt and it climbed and climbed and then was launched by a pneumatic blast of air. It plummeted. It was remarkable how quickly it went down. There was no flying, only a swift falling and a soft upside-down landing.

"Brian would fix that in a jiffy," he said.

"Hmm. Just like he's fixing his marriage?"

"A marriage isn't anything like an aircraft," he said. "It's not under any control."

"You're always telling me things I already know."

He paused, trying to feel if this could be true. Maybe it was true some of the time, but it didn't seem like it could be true all of the time. Besides, she was the one who had brought up Brian's marriage in the first place.

"Why do you say things like that to me?" she went on. "Of course I know a marriage isn't like an airplane."

"But how would you know?"

181

16.

His daughter had violated their agreement not to get gifts for each other. It was an arrangement they had settled on after the NordicTrack episode (her idea) and the shoe rack (his), and by the time he discovered the broken agreement on Christmas morning, it was too late to do anything about it except to experience the implicit betrayal, because he had followed the agreed-upon rules in good faith and she hadn't. He was still brooding over it several hours later when Annie took the digital camera out of the box and began to show him how to use it. He half-listened to the instructions, all the while thinking that when the time came to use it, he would still have to ask somebody for help. Then she informed him that to get the photos out of the camera he would have to put them into the computer, and he lost all interest. It was a bad design, too many steps, overly complicated.

But the gift of the camera, though ostensibly dismissed, continued to occupy his mind and without any warning, it became a source of pain. Because at the end of any other Christmas he and Maida would have retreated to the bedroom and laughed about it the way they had come to laugh about the NordicTrack every time they encountered it. *That* was the gift of it, the joke in their midst. It was a special, wicked pleasure you didn't openly admit to and never stopped feeling a little guilty about—this enjoying your child's lapses in judgment, her misbegotten ideas. The guilt was a necessary part of the pleasure, and what prevented it from being mean or awful was that the person who loved your child as much as you felt the same. It was the ability to share the feeling that rendered it harmless.

The real issue with the camera, he told himself, was that Dary was sneaky, and her sneakiness consisted of being inconsiderate under the guise of being thoughtful. He was the one who had conducted himself correctly according to their agreement. Yet some part of him whispered that he was a bad father, that only a bad father would stick to a rule not to get his own child a present. He had failed to think beyond the given constraints; he was selfish and literal-minded. The fear that this might be true struck at something already weak, and he went around for the rest of the day carrying this dented organ within him.

In the evening he called Adele and told her he had to see her.

She said she was sorry, she had other plans, but she would meet him as soon as she could, which might be the next day or the day after that.

Right then he wanted to tell her he loved her. It was true, as urgent and true as the pain of missing his wife. But after he began to utter the words he thought better of it and tried to change them into something else: "I love y—"

"Sorry?"

"I love your—pie!"

She said she didn't know what he was talking about.

The one she had made him for Thanksgiving, he explained. He had never thanked her properly.

"It was good?" she said.

"The best."

"Not true."

"It was," he said. "The best strawberry-rhubarb in the state of New Hampshire."

At first the practical side of arranging to see Adele confounded him. He was uneasy about someone spotting them together in public, but he was afraid she would take offense if he suggested a motel. She didn't invite him to her apartment either, though he supposed there wouldn't have been much privacy for them anyway, with her son and her son's girlfriend hanging around.

He was still trying to think of an unobjectionable place to meet when the idea of St. Mary's came into his head.

He knew when he stumbled on it that it was irreproachable. If someone they knew happened to see them together, the church's atmosphere of decorum would inoculate them from gossip. Not that he cared what the ninety-year-old parishioners of Colton thought. All that mattered to him was preventing gossip from getting back to Dary and Ed and Gayle.

On the appointed day, there was only one other vehicle in the parking lot, a pickup truck with a water cooler bungeed to the side and a pile of scrap wood half-covered in paint. On his way into the building he passed a man in a jumpsuit on a ladder taking down boughs of evergreen strung above the double doors. Gene wondered if a considerable amount of work had been done to the building since he'd last been inside, almost

184

fifty years ago. His memory of the interior was that it was dark and crowded, the columns of the arcade intruding too much into the center of the nave, and the pendant lights with their ornate brass cages appearing too heavy for the cables on which they were suspended. He imagined Maida would have liked to have returned with him just to see what had kept them away for so long. What had they been afraid of? What did it matter if they had been married in the wrong place?

The lighting in the sanctuary had improved since the marriage ceremony, or at least since then the walls had been painted a clean institutional white, giving the impression of greater brightness. There were still pendant lights, but they lacked the ornate filigrees and they used fluorescent bulbs. The floor of the entire nave, except for the area around the main altar, was now covered in carpet, the same deep maroon that he and Dary had seen in the veterans' hall. The overall effect of the changes was to make the sanctuary appear both more welcoming and less sacred, as if in removing the gloominess, the church had also been cleansed of some of its high religious mystery.

He sat in a pew to wait for Adele. Nearby, in one of the side altars, a carved figure of Mary held a baby Jesus. There was something odd about the statue. The baby didn't look youthful. He sat perfectly upright, his full head of hair extravagantly coiffed in the style of aging men, and his eyes were dull and his expression sluggish. He looked about fifty years older than he was supposed to be, and Gene wondered if the statue had always been there. He didn't remember it from the wedding.

Only then did the strangeness of his present endeavor come to him. A voice within said, *What are you doing? Why are you here?* Of all the places he might have met Adele, why had he chosen St. Mary's? It was troubling, because it suggested a part of his mind knew something about him that the whole didn't know. He wondered if he had come back because he had once promised Maida he wouldn't, and now that she was dead and he could do whatever he wanted, it turned out he was just as vulnerable to the lure of the forbidden as everyone else. Did he want to betray his deceased wife? Of course not. But he also didn't want her to constrict him in any way.

A door opened somewhere in the building and he stood and turned around, wanting the moment of their seeing each other to coincide so he wouldn't miss the look on Adele's face. But there was no one there, just the empty rows of pews.

He sat back down and picked up one of the books in the shelf on the back of the pew. It was a hymnal, not a Bible, and he flipped through another book and then another until he found one containing the Old Testament. He opened to Deuteronomy 30:14, the verse his cousin had read without much feeling at the wedding. He still remembered the way his fifth-grade teacher, Miss Gerta, had read the same passage. *No, the word is very near to you, girls and boys, it's in your mouth,* and her own mouth had closed around the words as if it held something luscious inside. The class moved on— Miss Gerta told them to get out their notebooks and do a rumination, her word for a journal entry—but he forgot the classroom he was sitting in, and his face began to burn, and he felt that the words Miss Gerta had spoken contained a secret message about his body and its purpose. Later when he was in college he asked a chaplain if Jesus had ever been lustful. The chaplain gamely entertained his question, taking into consideration Jesus's age, his exposure to human beauty, and whether arousal in itself directly opposed any single principle of theology. "A fish swims on the first and last day of its

life, doesn't it?" the chaplain said at last. Which Gene took
to mean definitely yes.

Adele was late.

He decided he would kiss her when she arrived and that it
would be a kiss of passion. In some peculiar way he felt it was
his duty under the circumstances. He had a responsibility to
continue resisting the Church as he had resisted it for most
of his life. Years and years ago he had traded in God for a
congenial questioning of the universe's spiritual chemistry, and
the answers he generated for himself were always magnanimous
and reassuring: either there was no deity to speak of and the
world was suffused with a quality that occasionally made itself
felt as divinity, or the spirit that reigned was diffuse, pliant, and
benevolent. That there was real goodness in the world beyond
any god's doing—this seemed to him more likely than the
opposite possibility. And if in the end it turned out that what
lay beyond this world happened to follow the particular shape
the Catholics delineated, then he was counting on a loophole
that would allow him to be saved by his devotion to his wife
and child.

Now he wondered if it mattered that he was trading happiness with one beloved for happiness with another. Were some
passions worth more than others, even if you felt that something
essential about yourself remained consistent and true in the
switching around?

He felt a faint thrumming in the floor, in his feet and his
ankles, and then his head filled with the rich outcry of peal-
ing bells. There was a bright opening tone followed by a
dimmer succession, as if the later notes were plunged under a
sea of molten metal. Miss Gerta had called this effect "riding
the tail," a beautiful name for what was really a melan-

choly sound. The bells chorused resoundingly once more, then faded.

It was now impossible to deny that Adele was significantly late. His eyes returned to the aging baby Jesus, who was perhaps old enough to have lived through the agony of lust. Just then, Gene remembered something. Adele had said she would meet him only if her son's baby hadn't arrived. So the baby had to be on its way, and his life was about to change yet again. At his age he had never expected a baby to enter his life. Yet he accepted the mystery of it—how in losing his wife, he had been given another chance.

He hadn't prayed in years, but now his yearning for a new life lifted the old impediment from his soul. He prayed for Adele and he prayed for the baby. He prayed for their life together, knowing it would require everything he had to give it. A devotional feeling surged in him and it wasn't simply a devotion to her. It was a renewed devotion to his own life, because for the first time in a long time, someone needed him.

17.

ON THE SECOND-to-last night of the year, the Donnellys hosted an annual party for their friends. The Ashes attended every year and there were always familiar faces—the Harmons, the Luces, the Spectors, couples the Donnellys had befriended in Colton over the years—though the crowd also generally included some new faces drawn from among Ed's colleagues or the women with whom Gayle did charity work. One year at the party (it had to have been at least ten years ago), Ed had joked that if he was asked to tell the story of his trip to China one more time, he was going to subject everyone to a slideshow of it next year. The remark was made in jest, but some of the guests nevertheless latched onto it with enthusiasm and promised to hold Ed to it the following year, which was how the tradition of the slideshow was born. But somewhere along the way the presentations had lost the puckish spirit in which they were conceived. The mishaps and misfortunes the Donnellys endured while traveling began to be presented as inevitably strength-ening and nourishing to the family character. A wrong turn in Cuernavaca took them through a foul-smelling tunnel that led to a hidden spice market founded by the Incas, or an error in their hotel accommodations in north Cumbria resulted in their staying in the winterized barn of a local sheepherding family. Gene felt it had become almost obligatory for the assembled friends to appreciate the splendid trips the Donnellys had made to various parts of the world.

He considered bowing out this year. Annie had already decided not to go because the cousins had gone home. He'd heard nothing from Adele after she'd failed to show at St. Mary's, and his inability to reach her since then had left him restless and anxious. Anything might have happened—maybe the baby hadn't been born healthy, or some complication from labor was maybe keeping the mother in the hospital—but without knowing what it was, he worried that something else was wrong. He tried to remember the exact words of their last conversation. Had he made a misstep? Her silence gnawed at him, activating a part of him that was already insecure. But when he mentioned to Dary that he was thinking of skipping the party, she told him that he couldn't because there was going to be a surprise.

The last thing he wanted was a surprise, and he said so.

"You won't hate it" was all Dary would say.

For the occasion the Donnellys' house was lit top to bottom, with winking white lights wound around the banisters, and lamps placed in the windows, and candles arranged in twos and threes on end tables and nested into fir boughs laid across the mantel. The Christmas tree, an enormous tentacle of green life swaddled in stiff gold ribbons, still had gifts beneath it, some surplus that Gene imagined Gayle never allowed to dry up as long as guests were visiting the house. A procession of desserts with glossy chocolate tiers, concentric circles, and frosted piping stretched the length of the dining-room table on a pressed tartan runner.

Dary had insisted on his bringing a gift. It wasn't enough for her to give a gift from both of them; Gene had to hold it in his hands as he walked through the door. He added it to the stash beneath the tree and then made a circuit through the party, searching for Brian. He went upstairs and poked his head into the guest bedrooms; they appeared as they always did, immaculate and untouched. He returned to the party and asked Gayle if she expected Brian later.

"There was an argument," she said.

It was just like Gayle to say, "There was an argument"—not to assign blame or divulge what it was about. Gene trailed her around as she refreshed drinks and collected dirty dessert plates until she finally elaborated: Ed had discovered Brian smoking; Brian knew how his father felt about smoking; Ed got upset and yelled at Brian; Brian in turn got upset and called his father something that couldn't be repeated. Then Brian packed his things and left for White Pine Camp.

"Is he going to be all right?" Gene said.

"He's upset that Allison's going around telling everyone that he's mentally unstable."

"Is he?"

"He's devastated, that's all. Wouldn't you be?" She spoke with a fluttery briskness. "It's appropriate to be devastated when your life falls apart. Wow, did he really love her! And she didn't have a clue. She probably thinks *every* man will love her like that."

"You'll find a way to help him."

"Sometimes all you can do is just love your kids and hope they won't be as stupid as you were." Her face colored as if she found it distasteful, even garish, to be talking about herself. "I told Ed this was an opportunity for him. To start over in his relationship with his son."

"Someone finally had to say it to him."

"Oh, but you know Ed. Just the idea of being told in advance how he might deal with his son probably got him agitated. He doesn't like anything to be decided beforehand. Besides, he probably blames me for the argument in the first place."

"But he's never gotten along with Brian."

"Probably I ruined Brian before he was born or something like that. You know, back in those days I had a cigarette before I knew I was pregnant."

They were standing close together, closer than they'd been when the conversation began. Gene put his hand on the small of her back, allowing it to alight there a moment before pulling it away. "One cigarette didn't do anything," he said.

"Well, it turns out I don't know anything about anything." She laughed, but it was a laugh of discomfort. Her scent, some combination of flour and sweetness, made him want to touch her again. They both watched as Ed made his way toward them through the crowd. "I could have gone to college," she said, "but instead I married *that* man."

"Surely that wasn't a mistake," Gene said.

She was silent.

"You wouldn't call it a mistake," he said.

"What's a mistake?" Ed said, looking pleased with himself for having seized the end of the conversation.

"Oh—only—the chocolate ganache is a little gritty," she said.

"And I didn't notice," Gene said. "I thought it was wonderful."

"I was out of regular sugar so I substituted turbinado,"

Gayle said. "You can't use a substitute and expect the same outcome."

Ed threaded his arm around Gayle's waist and squeezed her to him. "Let me explain something to you about this woman," he said, addressing Gene. "If she wants you to compliment something, she'll tell you how awful it is."

"The ganache *was* wonderful," Gene said.

"You fell right into her trap."

Gene said, "If *I* tried to make something like it—"

"—it wouldn't be edible," Ed said. "What was it Maida used to say? That it was a miracle you could find your shoes under the bed every morning?"

"The point is," Gene said, ignoring this and speaking to Gayle, "you have no reason to doubt yourself."

A tenderness spread across Gayle's face and Gene could feel her reaching out for the next thing he would say.

Ed said, "I've always told her that when she decides to leave me, she can open a restaurant."

Gayle smiled a brave, disheartened smile. Then she excused herself, mentioning a sweet-potato pie that had to be heated up.

"Did Dary tell you she picked out some photos for this evening?" Ed said. "She found some nice old photos. Don't worry—everyone looks young. Young and happy and handsome. We had no idea how lucky we were with our problems back then."

Just then a woman Gene initially mistook for Esther Prince (she was not Esther Prince) arrived at the party, and it was evident from the restrained happiness emanating from Ed's face and the terrible effort he was making to stand still that he was eager to greet her. He promptly left Gene standing alone.

Gene heard Patty Luce say to Regina Harmon, "We *never* stay less than ten days in Burgundy—Burgundy simply can't be done in less than ten days." Soon he found himself trapped in a conversation with a man who was an emeritus professor of something. He ceased to pay close attention as soon as he discovered that whether he understood the man's work or didn't, there would be no change in the course of the conversation. A painting of a bathing nude hung on the wall slightly to the left of the professor's head, and Gene studied it as the professor went on about "the problem of speculative redundancy in a two-system model" between ample mouthfuls of chocolate ganache. The nude was holding a pitcher of water above her head and though the pitcher had not yet been tipped, though her head was still dry, her hair fell in loose waves that looked sculpted by the imminent flow of the water. Her eyes—heavy-lidded, contoured with a paste of dingy yellow and a streak of ashy violet—were half-closed, as if she'd been persuaded to get out of bed only a moment before. He'd been to enough parties to know how to sound smart about a painting like this. He had only to point out a detail such as the parakeet-green shadow on the woman's cheek where a flesh tone would have been expected and declare that the artist was a genius for knowing such a color would be exactly right in that spot.

When he was finally able to get away he went to the kitchen, where he found not Gayle but Ed and Dary. Ed had an oven mitt shaped like a lobster claw on one hand and he and Dary were drinking red wine and talking across the tiled kitchen island.

"But do you think it's common for two people to experience love the same way?" she was saying.

"You have to understand," Ed said. "The whole idea of marriage is founded on something generally recognizable to other people. It's conventional by definition."

"But marriage doesn't dictate feeling," Dary said.

"There has to be some agreement. A negotiated peace."

"That sounds so formal," Dary said, turning toward Gene for the first time. "And not especially thrilling."

"What are you talking about?" he said.

"Marriage and whether it's become obsolete," Dary said.

"And I was telling her," Ed said, "that there's some value to an official commitment. That stability's nothing to scoff at."

Gene wondered how they had arrived on the topic—whether Ed had brought it up and succeeded in engaging Dary, or Dary had sought Ed's opinion. Either way, Gene felt a pang of envy.

"But what's stability?" Dary said. "Is it staying with the person you fall in love with in your twenties when you still have a lifetime of changes ahead of you? Years and years of developing into somebody who hardly recognizes the twenty-something-year-old who made that decision?"

"You get old no matter how you do it," Ed said.

"But no agreement extends infinitely," Dary said. "Within a person, it shifts around or falls apart all the time. Why shouldn't life reflect that?"

Just then Gayle entered the kitchen and asked Ed if he was keeping an eye on the sweet-potato pie as she'd asked him to.

Ed opened the oven and rotated the pie. When this was done, he removed the lobster claw and tossed it on the island. He said, "Marriage only makes sense in cultures where divorce is acceptable."

"Why do you talk about such serious things?" Gayle scolded. "This is a party! All of you, you should be out there eating and drinking and having a good time." When none of them moved, her face grew stern. "Out!" she said, making a shooing gesture.

They filed out of the kitchen, though not before Ed grabbed a bottle of wine to bring with them. He asked Dary to help him carry up some folding chairs from the basement, and soon he and Dary and Gene were setting up the chairs in the living room.

The guests were invited to take their seats. This was the signal to some of them to hurry to the dessert table and load up their plates. The lights dimmed.

The Donnellys had driven up the California coast in the spring. Here was a stiff Gayle standing beside an erotic statue in the Hearst Castle courtyard. Here she was again fully clothed on the beach, searching for rocks to weigh down paper napkins for a picnic. Then they were loose in the streets of Istanbul—or at least Ed was for a couple of days while Gayle recuperated at the hotel (she should never have eaten that fruit salad). Men in brocaded red vests served tea on trays, and laundry flapped from TV antennas mounted on concrete balconies covered in graffiti. The summer days in Vermont came next. The Donnellys had rented a historic farmhouse with a defunct dairy, and all the grandchildren had come and played games in the pasture. Wheelbarrow contests, pail-hauling contests, wood-chopping contests, and all other manner of hearty outdoor games had been comprehensively documented, so that you might have thought the Donnellys had spent a whole season on the farm rather than just three days.

It had never failed to surprise Gene that Maida, who had

a much lower tolerance for romantic notions than he did, accepted the idea that travel represented an automatic deepening of the soul. She had always wanted to travel more than Gene did, and perhaps she also had felt, as the Donnellys appeared to, that one's trips were achievements, credentialing a life. He didn't know if he was resistant to going to new places, or just to the way some people talked about where they had been. Why did the Donnellys need an audience for their experiences?

After a brief intermission (the professor helped himself to the top tier of a ziggurat-shaped cake), the historical portion of the evening commenced. A young Gayle, pregnant with Michael, was looking charming and bashful in a navy smock dress with an appliquéd strawberry on the pocket. A baby-faced Colin threw sticks at a duck in a pond, while a gawky Brian stood slightly to the side looking on with disapproval but without intervening. A snowsuited Dary posed next to a bank of snow, the blob of the child and the blob of the snow in harmonious composition. Gene had to concede that Ed had a knack for catching people in dynamic relation to their surroundings. He himself was represented looking a bit more sunburned and soft-stomached than he remembered, his expressions surprisingly vague and abstract given the intensity of the feelings he recalled. And there was Maida: lying on her back on the dock, the water visible not as water but as a backdrop of pure light. There she was again emerging from the lake, stripping her head of its thick bathing cap, which always reminded him of a formidable prophylactic. There was a provocative twist in her smile, an expression of simultaneous indifference to and interest in the camera's attention, a feint at resistance that was both impasse and invitation. In another she was laughing girlishly with her head tossed back, her spine arching gymnastically in the way that made him crazy every time, her eyes half-closed like the nude's in the painting.

Each time a photo of her was shown, it was as if his heart was being pumped mechanically to exude its only output, love. It was urgent and automatic. Then, belatedly, his mind reminded him of Maida's death, confirming it not once but successively, as if his body might be in danger of forgetting again.

That Dary was enthralled with this period of her mother's life didn't surprise him—plenty of children possessed a curiosity about their parents' fluidity as people before they became the known characters of their world. There was something almost sweet and devotional about her fascination. That she embraced these images, that in some sense she was proud of them, suggested that her understanding of her mother was more nuanced than she let on, encompassing not only the mother of her direct experience, but also the woman she had been before Dary retroactively decided who she was.

Yet there was a moment after the projector was switched off and before the lights came up when his body whirred with an awful energy. He thought of all the times he had stood before his young wife with a camera and all the times she had dissuaded him, saying in that light, carefree tone, *No, no, I already know what I look like.* All along he was afraid that later, when they got older, there would be no images of her when she had been young and happy and beautiful. But somehow he had missed something that was happening, something that Ed had managed to capture even as it was passing Gene by. Because here she was over and over again, young and happy and beautiful.

18.

THE LAST DAY of his daughter's visit, New Year's Day, was clear and brilliant with cold sunshine. They were spending the morning at his office, sorting through and packing his old wares into boxes, the destination of which he wasn't exactly sure. Dary said he didn't have to worry about that part right away— getting things packed up was the intermediate step. She worked quickly, taping up boxes as soon as they were filled and easily filling all the boxes she had allotted herself. It was different for him—he felt he had to pause and consider every item, recalling how he had acquired it and why, knowing he wouldn't have kept it so long if it didn't have value.

At noon they paused to take stock of where they were. For the first time since they'd arrived, he sat down in his office chair, which in the process of moving things around had ended up not behind the desk but instead in the middle of the room, surrounded by his half-filled boxes. He and Dary were supposed to pick up Annie from the Donnellys' in half an hour, and he suggested it would be nice to drive out to Fisher Lake.

"Isn't Brian staying out there?" Dary said. She was sitting on his desk. The roll of packing tape she'd been using hung around her wrist like a bracelet.

"Does that affect the decision?" Gene said.

"I just find him so awkward sometimes. Is he as bad as he used to be?"

"I never found him awkward."

"The last time I saw him he was wearing adult braces. He's the only person I know who's had braces twice. I wanted to go up to him and say, 'Look, if you made it this far with your teeth, why bother with all of this now?'"

"He hasn't had braces for years."

"At least when he did, it was something to talk about."

"I bet the two of you have more in common than you think."

"Oh, please."

"You probably don't remember this, but Brian reads."

"So do eighty percent of first graders," she said, with a lightness that was acrid. "Do you remember the Christmas he went around telling everyone that perestroika was a terrible development because it would mean the end of American dominance in the world?"

"Was he right?"

"That's irrelevant! It's about a worldview. He and I probably wouldn't agree on the same map of the world."

"I see plenty of similarities between the two of you."

"Please don't say that."

"How about leaving Colton for college and never really coming back? How about the challenges of raising kids?"

"And don't forget nostalgia for the threat of nuclear catastrophe."

"How about—loneliness?"

"All right, that's enough." She slid off the desk and stood, ready for her next task.

"How about the difficulty of trying to date when you're a parent?" he said.

"I *said* that's enough." She knelt down and in a hurried, imprecise way, began closing up a box that wasn't completely full. Her hands fussed at the box's flaps and then abruptly fell still. "Where do you get this idea?" she said. "When have I ever complained of being lonely?"

"You don't have to complain about it for it to be true. I just want you to be happy."

"By foisting me off on some man you've met for thirty seconds at the airport? Or better yet, Brian Donnelly?"

"Now that's not fair. You've known Brian your whole life."

"That's like saying, 'I've smoked cigarettes my whole life, so they must be good for me.'"

"You know he comes from a good family."

"I'm not looking for another family! The one I've got is hard enough." She was consolidating herself in her gaze, hitching up in preparation for something. "Why don't you just admit you're trying to find me a husband?" she said. "That's what this is all about. *You* would be happier if I had a husband."

He paused, considering whether this was true. "I don't want you to get married for my sake," he said.

"For whose sake, then?"

"Your mother worried about you too, you know."

"And marriage solved all her problems? Is that what you're saying?"

He felt the needle inside her words.

She stood up abruptly, almost aggressively. "You know I don't need your help," she said. "You do know that, don't you?" She reached one hand above her, and touching the plaster, appeared to brace herself between the floor and the slant of the low ceiling. "Since when did you become such an expert in everyone else's happiness anyway?"

"Not *everyone's*. Just yours."

"And what makes you think you're right?"

"Because I'm your father."

"Somehow that gives you privileged insight into the matters of my psyche?"

"Most of the time, no. But in certain circumstances, yes."

"What if I don't want the life you want for me?" she said. She was looking at him with the strangest mixture of heartbreak and anger. "What if this is the way I am? What if I can't become the person you'd like me to be?"

When she said this, his whole body felt at once strangely hollow and heavy, as if something had been blown out of it years ago but the pain was coming to him only now. He wanted to shout something through that hollowness, but what he wanted to shout was not a sentence or a thought or anything he could grasp with his mind. It was a feeling he'd had his whole life, deeper than a thought, which was that there was nothing she could do to make him not love her—that no matter how many times she transformed herself, his love would transform itself to match her. This was what it was to be a parent—it was to give up control over your own love. To love where sometimes you didn't even like. It was something that could barely be expressed within yourself, and even then it made absolutely no sense.

Her face suddenly softened and seemed to arrange itself

around this new softness. Her arm came down. "What is it?" she said.

"You can be yourself," he said, "and still have other possibilities inside. A surprise or two. Maybe even a reversal."

Dary's eyes widened and fixed upon him intently. "What's yours, then?"

For a moment he thought of Adele, his unexpected feelings for her. The strain of the past two weeks without her, the anxiety of still having heard nothing from her, was only beginning to show him the strength of those feelings. Just thinking about her now he felt somehow guilty and, what was it—childish? Yes, maybe childish, because whatever it was between them, he still wanted to keep it to himself. "I stopped going to church before you were born," he offered.

"And?"

"I voted for Eisenhower the first time around. Believe me, that was a mistake."

"That's all you've got?" She attempted and failed to suppress a laugh. "I'm sorry, Dad. I'm trying to take you seriously, but it's hard. It's hard to take advice from a guy who counts Eisenhower as the major betrayal of his life."

"My feelings on plenty of other subjects have changed," he said.

She glanced at him, sidelong. "Have you ever reversed yourself about a woman?"

"I've only been devoted to one woman, you know that."

"Mom?"

"Who else!"

"I don't know—that's why I'm asking. But it goes to show you—some people don't have reversals. Maybe I'm like that."

"Oh, but plenty of people do. Have erotic—I mean, romantic—reversals."

She laughed a nervous laugh.

"What's funny?"

"That's the first time I've heard you say *erotic*," she said. "It's like we're talking about the birds and the bees thirty years too late."

19.

HE CALLED ADELE several times, hanging up just before the answering machine picked up, operating under his old teenager's belief that a person could call as many times as he wanted as long as he didn't leave behind evidence of the attempts. But when, after two more days, these phantom calls didn't bring about the desired result, he finally left a message:

Hello? Hello, Adele? This is...ah, well, I don't have to tell you. I'm at home right now—I've got the whole house to myself. Dary left behind a pair of boots she wants me to send her, so it's just me and a pair of boots here. Are you coming over? Well, I'm calling to tell you there's been a change to my, ah, calendar. Today's still fine, Wednesday's still fine, but if you're planning to come on Friday, we should talk about Friday. Right now I have a doctor's appointment. But I could change it. So, yeah, I'll be waiting to hear from you. About Friday, okay? Wow, this is a long message. I—hello? Oh. I thought you might have— but okay, I hope you're...BEEEEEEEP.

The machine cut him off.

The doctor's appointment was a purely pharmacological mission. He had run out of the sleeping pills, and his anxiety was keeping him awake at night. Though half the time he found the sleeping pills worthless, he had also come to realize that not having a supply of them caused a greater kind of suffering, because it was better to be awake in his room at night with lousy pills than it was to be awake with nothing left to try.

On the day of the appointment, Dr. Fornier performed a routine examination. He shined a bright beam into Gene's eyes, causing Gene to wonder if the doctor could detect lack of sleep in the physical tissue of his eyeballs. Gene assumed not, because when Dr. Fornier finished, he simply moved on to poking an instrument into Gene's ears, which reassured Gene that his body was normal. But when the doctor was walking the cold drum of the stethoscope across his back, something in Dr. Fornier's expression made Gene's stomach grip itself.

"Something wrong?" Gene said.

"Maybe not," said Dr. Fornier.

Dr. Fornier ordered an EKG, and an hour and a half later he declared the result presented nothing worrisome. Yet somehow the "nothing worrisome" was an indicator for further inquiry, and Dr. Fornier ordered more tests "just to cover our bases."

The hospital was connected to the medical offices by an underground tunnel that was several degrees too warm and smelled of ham-and-cheese sandwiches. Gene took an elevator to Cardiology on the third floor, where several others were waiting to see a doctor. There was an ancient-looking man, hunchbacked and stiff, attended by a younger, tired woman. A little boy with a dissident clump of hair poking up at the back of his head roamed around with a yo-yo he wildly and abruptly shot out into the room. His mother put down the magazine she was reading and asked him to be careful, and it was something she had evidently said so many times before that neither of them appeared to expect her words to change anything.

Also waiting was a rotund man with a pink face offset by a patchy gray beard. His belly, incongruously big for his frame, seemed swapped from a larger man's figure. He was seized by a coughing fit and the book in his lap fell to the floor. When the spasm ended, he looked around the room and, addressing no one in particular, said, "Pardon me, it isn't anything contagious."

Gene found a seat that wasn't directly next to him, but the man leaned over the empty seat between them anyway. "What do they have you in for?" he said. "Angina?"

Gene pretended not to be aware the man was addressing him. But the man was determined to get Gene's attention and repeated his question.

"Oh," Gene said finally. "They're just running a few tests."

"That's how it always starts." The man went back to his book, but hardly a minute passed before he leaned over again and said, "Children? Have any?"

Gene peered toward the door where nurses appeared and called patients' names. "Just one," Gene said. "A daughter."

The man nodded wordlessly and returned to his book again. Somehow he had arranged it in his lap so that every time he turned a page it made a loud, flapping noise. He appeared to dwell on something he'd just read, then leaned over a third time: "Does she know you're here?"

Gene said something about not wanting to worry her unnecessarily.

"That's good," the man said. "Keep that going for as long

as you can. They give us no choice, we have to protect ourselves."

"I really don't know what you're talking about," Gene said.

"You'll see," the man said. "One day you'll go in for some straightforward test, and before you know it your relatives will be whispering behind your back about whether you have an up-to-date will. If you don't run six miles before breakfast and later the same day eat a steak—because maybe when you were twenty-five a good day involved running six miles and eating a steak—someone will ask you if you're feeling all right. And God forbid you forget the name of the vice president's wife, or cough over the soup. You'll be dead already, as far as everyone else is concerned."

Just then a nurse emerged from the interior and called a name. The ancient-looking man shuffled across the room with his walker, and the younger woman followed behind him, carrying his papers.

"And there you have it," the man said. "We'll be lucky if we get to choose between a catheter and a bedpan."

As it turned out, Gene didn't rate highly enough to see a cardiologist. In the examination room a nurse fitted him with a small, portable heart monitor, then attached several soft foam discs to his chest. The discs—electrodes—connected to thin cords that in turn connected to a monitor, a computer about the size and weight of a small transistor radio that hung around his neck on a black nylon strap. The way the nurse explained it, it was an EKG meant to measure over time an unpredictable heart rhythm. Gene wasn't supposed to alter the course of his day because of it. If he exercised, he should continue to be active; if he was used to walking places to get around, he should maintain his routine; if he climbed onto ladders to clean the gutters of his house—here the nurse gave him a sharp look to make it clear what she thought of someone his age getting on a ladder. On the face of the monitor was a red button that he was to press at specific times—when he took medication, when he lay down to sleep—and also when he noticed, if he noticed, a sudden increase in his heart rate.

There was something disturbingly alien about the electrodes, which resembled large nipples, and the laminated wires, which were like veins extruded from his body and reattached on the outside. But it was the computer that disturbed him most of all, because it would learn things about him he couldn't be sure in advance he was willing to know.

As he buttoned his shirt over the monitor, he thought about how frightened Maida had been in the ambulance when the paramedics had put on the oxygen mask. Her look to him seemed to say that the mask was going to kill her. This wasn't true, of course, but it was also true that he never saw her alive again without the mask. In a way, that was when she had died—the moment when her face disappeared behind the mask. After that there were more interventions and other machines, and though he knew these also didn't kill her, they helped usher her into a liminal, personless state in which her body no longer seemed like it belonged to her anymore. That day in the ambulance he saw that the fear of death could kill you in more than one way: you could die from the fear of what was actually happening to your body, or you could begin to die the moment you observed other people considering your death likely. He'd seen in Maida's face that she was afraid to have him witness her in her condition. And it was as if by recognizing this look on her face—the one that said the mask would kill her—he had somehow validated her fear, so that the moment they both had the same thought it became inescapable.

There was no question in his mind as to whether he would or wouldn't tell Adele about his heart. If he acknowledged the possibility that his body had begun its terminal decline, she might find herself unconsciously less attracted to him. He intended to keep the monitor hidden beneath his shirt so she would never see him as his future decaying self.

Adele finally turned up on Monday. It had been three weeks since he'd seen her, and she had gained a little weight over the break. Her face was fuller and her hips had a buttery heaviness, a new plumpness that suited her. She was wearing over her jeans a long clingy sweater that went nearly to her knees, and he almost cried out in dismay when she took it off—he wanted to be the one to draw it over her head and cast it to the floor.

She offered no explanation for her absence. Her expression— officially attentive, yet personally uninterested—told him to surrender his banal, parochial desire to restart their relations by making her account for their time apart. In a way it was the first demand she had ever made of him and he was jarred by it. Why wouldn't she tell him where she'd been? If something significant had happened, wouldn't she want them to share it? And if it wasn't significant, why go to the trouble of keeping it from him? She didn't mention his phone message, perhaps because now that they were together, it no longer seemed relevant. But it was odd that she didn't volunteer any information about the birth of her grandchild, an event he knew had to have taken place in the interval since they'd spoken.

"How's the baby?" he finally said.

"Who?" she said.

"Your son's baby," he said. "A boy or a girl?"

She briefly hesitated, then told him it was a girl. "But they haven't decided on a name," she added, heading off his next question.

She made a big fuss over the vacuum cleaner, an old, temperamental metallic-green upright, and indicated her irritation with him for not having replaced the bag, accusing him of shortening the life of the machine. She had never scolded him before and he didn't know what to make of it. Possibly it was a sign they were further along in the relationship than he'd thought.

She began dragging around the armchairs in the living room, tugging them from their customary places where their feet had left flattened spots in the rug. When he tried to help, she said, "Don't do that, you'll just hurt yourself."

Her words sent a chill through him. He wondered if she had somehow intuited the wires under his clothes. Or if he was already unconsciously sabotaging himself, playing the role of an ailing man without being aware of it. He decided the thing to do was to turn her comment into a joke. He pretended to fall over the side of one of the chairs and landed in what he hoped was a charming, splayed heap with his arms open and his legs wide. He imagined the gesture was sufficiently forlorn and silly that she would come over to check on him and he would snap her up.

"I think I'm stuck like this," he said.

She glanced over. "You'll find a way."

"I don't know," he said, doubtfully. "I might need a tug too."

When she passed near him he trapped her between his legs, and she allowed herself to be held for a moment.

"Did you have a good visit with your daughter?" she said.

"I missed you like crazy. I was one glum bachelor."

She patted his knee—time to release her. "You seem to have recovered just fine."

She lifted his leg as though it was a log that had fallen into her path, a gesture he found confusing when he considered that the last time he had seen her, they had shared a bed. But he brushed the feeling aside because to feel anything but gladness at her presence now seemed like admitting that something irreparable had happened between them, when it hadn't. He told himself they had been apart for too long, that was it. He watched her vacuum the rug, bending over to adjust the settings on the front of the machine whenever it made a strange sound, and contented himself with admiring her generous backside.

As she was finishing, he got up and went upstairs. In the bathroom, standing in front of the mirror, he took off his shirt and began detaching the wires from their electrodes. When this was done, he stripped the electrodes from his chest. The adhesive left gray gummy circles on his skin, and he used a cotton ball doused in rubbing alcohol to get rid of them. He rolled everything—including the used cotton balls—into a towel and wedged the towel behind the pipe beneath the sink. He would cancel his appointment with the cardiologist and mail the monitor back to Dr. Fornier with a note of apology.

In the bedroom, he changed his clothes, swapping the heavy sweater he had chosen to hide the monitor for a shirt he considered more dapper. Half the closet remained filled with Maida's clothing; the rest was in her dresser. He still wasn't ready to give it to charity. It pained him to think of her special things, her fine shoes or the nightie he'd splurged on, getting picked off a rack by a stranger at the Salvation Army.

Adele was still tinkering with the vacuum when he found her downstairs and asked her to come with him.

"All right," she said, "but I'm bringing this with me."

When they were in the bedroom together he suggested she have a look at the dresser. It was just an ordinary five-drawer maple highboy with brass pulls. The stainless-steel shears that Dary had used to cut his corduroys for the beach were still sitting on top, next to a spool of navy thread.

"You've got some mending for me to do?" she said.

"Open the top drawer."

She did and peered inside. "What is it?"

"It's for you."

She pulled out the bundle of pale fabric and let its silky length fall to the floor. "A nightgown, is that it?"

He asked her to try it on.

"But I'm working," she said.

"I'm asking."

Her compliance reminded him of a sullen child's. She stripped off her shirt and tossed it to the ground, leaving on her sturdy bra with its wide straps, then marched herself out of her jeans, stomping on the crotch to get them off over her ankles. She was wearing baggy underwear. The elastic at the top rose above her navel, and around the contours of her thighs, it hung sad and puffed out. She pulled the nightgown over her head and then gripped at the sides and waist in an attempt to make it sit more evenly on her.

"Well?" she said, turning to him.

213

The lines of her underwear and bra strained against the fabric, clumping it, while the nightgown compressed her body into constricted, lumpy sections.

"It's not what you had in mind," she said.

"It's not . . . bad."

"I look like a tied-up chicken."

He tried to caress her shoulder but ended up stroking the thick bra strap.

"A fatty, tied-up chicken." She sucked in her breath.

"It was just a thought," he said. "It was just for fun."

She was putting her clothes back on. "But I'm working," she said.

Something in his gut stiffened, and a corresponding muscle on the back of his neck did the same. "Don't say that," he said. "Not when there are feelings between us."

She shook her head. "I can't anymore."

"What's wrong?"

"It was a mistake. We shouldn't have." Her face was slack, empty of possibility. "Excuse me," she said. She stepped around him and plugged the vacuum into the outlet.

The switch must have already been in the *On* position; it roared to life.

"Adele," he said.

She cupped a hand to her ear.

"You were never a mistake," he said.

She shook her head to indicate she couldn't hear him above the noise.

Very calmly then, as if this was their purpose, Gene picked up the shears from the top of the dresser and clamped them around the vacuum's cord and closed his hand. The heavy steel bit through the cord. Sparks shot out from the stubby ends of the wires. Oddly, the machine didn't go quiet instantly; it rumbled on for a moment.

Adele was aghast. "Are you a complete idiot?" she said.

"I'm falling in love."

"You're mixed up, that's all," she said. "Your wife is dead, but I can't help that."

"This has nothing to do with my wife," he said.

Adele gazed at him with gloomy indifference. But a moment later, the gloom was gone and she looked like the woman he had interviewed months ago, the one who was accommodating and plain, with no long fingernails, no hair doodads, no mounds of necklaces. She looked the same, only more tired, and she left the room without saying anything more. After a while the house was very quiet. When he went downstairs her rubber sandals were gone. She had left behind the key.

In the days that followed he found himself in a perpetual state of unrest. His calls to her went unreturned, but he still hoped to hear his own phone ring. He checked his email incessantly. Adele didn't have his email address, but that didn't stop him from hoping that if he happened to check his email on the right day at the right time, she might have figured out how to send him a message through the computer.

He clicked on all the stories on his AOL home page, and when the stories didn't refresh quickly enough, he clicked on the ads. He hadn't realized that if he kept clicking, eventually there would be links to what looked like news stories on the same pages as the ads, making it impossible to figure out what relationship, if any, either had to fact. The deeper he went into the layers of content the weirder they became, and he needed them to be weird if they were going to keep his mind off his loneliness. But whatever had been weird the day before would seem a bit ordinary the next day, so every day the stakes became a little higher, each search creating demand for accelerated weirdness. He clicked on gruesome photographs of a whale struck and killed by a Russian torpedo. He read about a service that would make a pornographic video of a pet, and he found himself purchasing a vitamin series that promised to strengthen the fibers of his penis. Among all of this he searched for Adele, half-expecting the internet to produce her for him.

He realized he didn't know the most basic things about her. He didn't know if she had grown up in Colton, or how long she had been in the area. He didn't know where she lived. He had an idea about the kind of neighborhood, probably one of the shabbier parts of town where houses with metal siding were divided into front and back units and there were old shoes hanging over telephone lines. It amazed him that you could search in this manner—you could enter the name of the searched-for person plus *shoes hanging over telephone wires*—and the internet would send you something. But the found-something was rarely the lost-something.

Once he typed into the oracle field *lost woman New Hampshire* and the search engine sent him an article about a woman who had lost so much weight so quickly her skin hung off her body in folds that could be gripped by several large plastic clips of the sort used for sealing opened potato-chip bags. The image disgusted him and saddened him and he felt as if it was causing real damage to a part of him he couldn't name, yet he couldn't look away. He went back to it every day, each time fearful it might have disappeared in the interval since he had last attended to it. In some bizarre way the image became a part of his grief for Adele.

Often he had the feeling of another sensibility behind the computer screen, an entity that knew he was there and what he liked, and on the basis of this, decided what content to send him next. He was calm as long as he was clicking through this reality. And immediately afterward, if he had been on the computer for several hours, his brain moved indolently, without any focus. But eventually the effect wore off, and his loneliness returned.

He spent many fruitless hours wondering why Adele had left him. After he had cycled through the preliminary explanations—she was not thinking clearly, she had made a mistake, already she regretted her actions but was too proud to admit it—he arrived in a darker state where certain words she had spoken early in their relationship took on new meaning. As when he recalled her affinity for depressed people. When she had first come to him he was depressed and she had been fond of him, but later, when he couldn't hide how happy she made him, she had left him. She had left him because he was too happy, that was it. Or because of the heart monitor. Everything between them had been fine before that, which suggested she had left him because she knew there was something inherently wrong with him.

Sometimes, in a bitter, desperate mood, he would drive slowly through neighborhoods looking at the women who happened to be on the sidewalk. They would often have a baby in one arm and a teetering grocery bag in another, and maybe a second or third child they were trying to persuade to get out of the car. Sometimes the children would be fighting each other over a scruffy stuffed animal or a cell phone. If the women noticed him they scoured him with wary eyes and as he drove away he felt his own mistrust of them.

He felt completely lost. For fifty years, he had belonged to someone else. First Maida, then, briefly, Adele. And now if Adele wouldn't listen to him, he wouldn't be understood. And if Adele wouldn't touch him, his body would go untouched. He was afraid he was witnessing the final defection of love from his life.

20.

HE'D DONE SOMETHING stupid. Sending the heart monitor back to Dr. Fornier—he hadn't thought it through. It hadn't occurred to him that some information about his heart was already recorded and the doctors might easily extract it. This or some version of it was what had happened, and now he was scheduled with a thoracic surgeon on Monday. Dr. Fornier called him personally Sunday night to explain why it was important to keep the appointment.

When he woke up Monday morning it was snowing heavily. A vast smothering whiteness extended between the houses. The asphalt had disappeared under a broad avenue of snow. He recalled a promise he'd made to Dary about not driving when the roads were bad. It seemed the most harmless kind of promise to break for a doctor's appointment, but he found himself indecisive about it, afflicted by the peculiar logic of superstitious fear. This fear told him that inevitably because he had remembered his promise and considered ignoring it, this would be the day he would get into a terrible accident. He hated asking anyone for a favor, but his discomfort was lessened by knowing Gayle would think nothing of giving him the ride.

Half an hour before the appointment, Ed came to the house to collect him. Gene felt a jab of annoyance at Gayle's assumption that she and Ed were interchangeable. Maybe if he were accustomed to the idea of his body as irreparably fragile, it wouldn't have mattered, but he wasn't yet prepared to acknowledge this to himself, and he certainly wasn't ready to talk about it with another man. When Ed asked him about the appointment, Gene told him it was a routine mole check with a dermatologist.

In her office, the thoracic surgeon showed him on her computer several grainy images, fields of black interrupted by upside-down fans of light. On one of these she pointed to a mottled black-and-white oval protruding into the surrounding darkness. It was a small growth on the left side of his heart. She called it a *mass* at first and then, after assuring him it was almost certainly not cancer, switched to calling it a *tumor*, which was its rightful name, though Gene preferred to continue thinking of it as a mass. It was, the surgeon explained, the potential cause of his disorganized heartbeat. Leaving it there introduced the possibility of several bad outcomes: the tumor could eventually block the flow of blood to his heart; or a piece of it could break off and block the blood flow to other parts of his body, including his brain; or the broken-off bits could insinuate themselves into other parts—his brain, his limbs, his eyes. She recommended taking it out right away.

"It's a fairly straightforward procedure," she said. "Resection of the left atrium wall, maybe with a little pericardial reconstruction and repair of the mitral valve."

It occurred to him these words would mean something to Ed,

but to him they simply sounded frightening. He asked if his heartbeat would go back to normal after the surgery.

"We won't really know until we get inside and take a look around," she said.

He attempted to clarify. Was she saying that she could cut something out of him, and after all of that, he might still be left with the same problems he had now?

"As you'd expect," she said, "we see a stratification of favorable and unfavorable outcomes based on the presence or absence of certain clinical markers. We also have to take into account baseline prognostic factors."

"What's that?"

"The factors that might affect the success of the treatment. Age, for instance. Advanced age creates a bit more of a challenge, but the majority of my patients are like you."

"Old," he said.

"Advanced."

After the appointment, Ed suggested they drive out to the coast and find a place to have lunch. They drove east and then north into Maine, blasting out of the tree line into a landscape assaulted by the storm. The shrubs, wiry and stunted, looked as if they had been screwed into the earth with brute force. Dirt mingled with the snow at the side of the road, forming a deep brown slush. The sluice got picked up by the tires and splattered the car's windows with dirty water.

Gene didn't much feel like talking. Inwardly he was still going over everything the doctor had told him. But every time he tried to recall her specific phrases, his mind leaped ahead and summed it up as "You're going to die."

They stopped for lunch at the Pomonock Resort and Club.

The Pom was an odd establishment because it aspired to be more exclusive than it was, enticing members with the prestige of perks ostensibly just for them, while remaining accessible to anyone willing to pay its steep fees. In the 1970s, when Ed was vigorously building up his practice, he had joined with the encouragement of an older colleague. Then it seemed there were two Eds, the one who openly deprecated the club and its kind, maintaining that his membership was a pragmatic but disagreeable necessity for his business, and the other Ed, a man of rarefied talents who from time to time deserved to enjoy a voluptuous meal in an elite setting. Some internal concession allowed him to remain untroubled by this division, and he appeared to participate in this genteel world without considering himself of it. By the time he no longer needed the club for his medical practice, he had integrated it into his life without causing himself any distress.

The dining room was filled with large things: large tables of burled wood, large chairs with the elongated profiles of thrones, a large, vaguely medieval stone fireplace that was missing only a whole roasted pig to complete the tableau. The room always felt empty and drafty no matter how many people were in it, or how big the fire was.

Ed ordered the prime rib and Gene ordered a hamburger. The food arrived on white square plates that resembled orthodontically perfected teeth. After the waiter made a formal presentation of the pepper mill and the pepper was deemed acceptable, the waiter said, "I'll be right back with some share plates for you, Mr. Donnelly."

Whenever Gene was at the Pom, he thought of Brian Donnelly's wedding reception, which had taken place in this exact room. Halfway through the evening the DJ had handed out blow-up musical instruments, inflatable electric guitars and trumpets and saxophones, and the guests were invited to wail on them on the small stage in front of the DJ's stand. Michael, by then amiably wasted, had decided that everyone in the wedding party should be bonked on the head with a purple saxophone. Colin made an effort to restrain him, cordially at first and then more insistently, but Michael had forty pounds on him and pushed him away forcefully enough that Colin fell backward over a chair. Then—rather heroically, Gene recalled—Brian escorted his bride off the dance floor and returned to dump a pitcher of ice water over Michael's head. It had all ended in laughter, after a second cousin was recruited to whisk Michael away from the party.

Gene said, "Remember the time Brian dumped water over Michael's head, and the DJ played 'You Shook Me All Night Long,' and everyone danced on the wet floor with bare feet?"

"I hate that song," Ed said. "I never liked it, even when it was popular."

"We had fun," Gene said. "You're forgetting that part."

"Brian said to me, 'How could you? How could you let him do this?' As if I was responsible for his brother's drinking."

"It was his wedding," Gene said. "You can't blame him."

Ed's lips curled in a slight sneer. "He seems to have no problem blaming me for things."

"I'm sorry I brought it up," Gene said.

"Now what exactly did the dermatologist say?"

"A growth. No—a *mass.*"

"But what did she say about cancer?" Ed said. He had eaten most of his prime rib and was using the table bread to sop up the juices.

"It isn't."

"You know what? Ninety-nine percent of our conversations from here on out will be about our health—health or death, it's all the same. It's completely stupid to get old."

"But *your* health is fine," Gene said. "You don't have to worry."

"Who knows what's coming? Even if *I'm* fine, I'm not looking forward to watching my friends die."

"If I died—would that really be so awful?"

Ed scowled. "Are you honestly asking me that?"

"Maybe some part of you would be a little—relieved?"

"You're crazy."

"But the Ashes never really made it up to your standards."

"Did the doctor say the mass was in your brain?"

"Remember how we used to talk in college? About having an important life and doing important things? Maida and I—we didn't succeed, did we?"

"You can't think that's what I think."

"I have no idea."

"Do you know what Gayle does when she wants to drive me crazy? She'll say, 'Do you really love me?'"

"What does that have to do with anything?"

"You tell me."

They sat there for a moment in silence. Then Ed said softly, "You know, right after Maida died I cried every time I saw my boys." He paused, giving the impression he might have more to say, but he didn't go on.

Gene asked him why.

"I don't know, it just happened. It was embarrassing. Not just for me, but for the boys. They love to tease me about getting infirm, but if I actually admit to *feeling* old—if I suggest mortality isn't just an abstract concept for me anymore—they totally freak out."

"We're not the same person, you know," Gene said.

"Who said we were?"

"I mean me and Maida. You tell a story about her death like it could just as easily be about me, but we're not the same."

"I *know* that," Ed said. "I know that better than anyone. Don't forget I'm the one who put the two of you together."

In that moment Gene hated Ed for his arrogant belief that other people were only bit players in the fascinating drama of his life. He wanted to tell Ed that he had an entire life Ed knew nothing about, a lover with whom the sex was still surprising and the intimacy unobligated. Just thinking of his secret made him feel powerful. But then, of course—the affair was already over. The power he'd imagined himself having was already gone.

Ed paid for lunch and they walked outside without talking and got into the car.

"Should I take you home now?" Ed said.

"Do what you like," Gene said.

"I'm asking."

"You do what you like."

Ed drove a little farther north. They got out of the car at the small park on the tip of the point. A lighthouse, white with an iron collar, stood across the sea channel on a barren island of rock. The wind diced the waves on all sides and the water charged over the snow-covered rocks at the base of the light-house. A plaque, bronze and substantial, described the practices of the former keepers who had lived there, men who in times of stormy weather had tied their wives to the lighthouse ladder to keep them from drowning.

Ed turned his back to the sea and leaned against the rail. "Look," he said. "I'm sorry about what I said earlier at the club."

There was a brief silence in which he seemed to weigh how to press forward. "Can I buy you a drink? Will you let me do that?"

The bar in York had dark paneling instead of windows. Every inch of space on the walls displayed something: schoolhouse clocks that had stopped ticking; World War II infantry helmets; empty matchboxes; ax-heads; and an array of decommissioned or pilfered signage, including one that said WATCH FOR CHILDREN THEY ARE EVERYWHERE. Their server was a woman in fur-lined boots with the tooth of an animal strung around her wrist. She wasn't old or young, beautiful or ugly. She seemed to occupy that indeterminate position in the middle of life where you're afraid to expect more and also afraid not to.

Ed delayed her departure from their table by dithering over what his drink would be. "If you don't mind my asking," he said, "what kind of animal does that tooth belong to?"

She laughed as if he'd proposed something tricky. "I'll tell you what," she said. "If you can guess it, this round's on me."

She left them to tend another table and when she returned she said, "Well? Any guesses?"

"May I have another look?" Ed said. The woman held out her wrist. Ed clasped it gently and nudged the tooth from side to side with his thumb. Then his eyes met hers and in his expression were the first stirrings of delight, as if he had momentarily forgotten that this wrist was attached to a face and now he had the pleasure of discovering it again. He said, "I thought they stopped importing these long before you were born."

"That's your guess?"

"You can't fool me with that baby face of yours. If this is authentic, you got it from your grandmother."

Her mouth registered defiant skepticism, but her eyes shone

with some weightless feeling. She took her hand away from him, but almost apologetically, as if it was a thing that belonged equally to them. Then she asked him what he did for a living, and when he told her she said, "You work at one of the hospitals around here? My sister's a nurse at Bridgeway General."

"I try my best to avoid hospitals," he said.

"You aren't one of those traveling doctors they send off to the latest crisis, are you? My sister used to date one of them. Every time he wanted to go to bed with her, he started speaking French."

Ed replied, *"Je ne parle pas français et encore moins au lit. Sauf si bien sûr je suis avec une belle Française."*

The woman laughed uncertainly. "So what kind of doc are you?"

"I work for myself. I have a small practice I have no intention of growing, but it seems to get bigger every year in spite of my attitude."

"Some people just can't help being successful," she said. "I wish I was one. But I'd settle for being married to one—that'll do too." She laughed with the confidence he'd find her gall charming. "You let me know if you hear of any openings, okay?"

She left them and returned a few minutes later with their drinks. Ed took out his wallet and tried to pay for them but she refused the money. "Don't be silly," he said, but at the same time he was preening, as if he believed she had behaved correctly in their situation, because he wasn't obliged to pay for making another person feel good.

The woman had other tables to tend and didn't spend time at theirs after that, but something in Ed had changed nonetheless. There was an air of bravado about him, a swooping energy loose in his gestures and his voice. He began to talk loudly about a topic he seemed to know an infinite amount about, the recorded images and sounds that had been sent into space on *Voyager 2,* including an image of the very same lighthouse they had just visited. This collection, he said, would supply extra-terrestrials with a compendium of life on Earth: the sounds of whales, tractors, wild dogs, a heartbeat, a baby crying, foot-steps, a Beethoven symphony, "Johnny B. Goode"—even the recorded brain waves of a woman thinking about falling in love. Gene said very little but Ed continued on hardly without pause anyway. He seemed to take it for granted that another person would find captivating what captivated him. In this moment Gene wanted to hate Ed, to dismiss his sermon as pure unthink-ing egotism. But it was more than that. It was honestly joyful, delivered in the thrall of vitality and optimism. A person like Ed imagined in color and listened to his dreams, and two days after a conversation it didn't suddenly occur to him what he had actually wanted to say. He felt at home in the world, like a spirit or an animal, and on the rare occasion when he sensed himself struggling, it only filled him with wonder and deepened his sympathy for everyone else. Gene could know all this and still know almost nothing about what it was like to be Ed.

When they got to the car it was beginning to snow.

"Why do you think they included the brain waves of the woman thinking about love?" Gene said.

"The greatest power on earth," Ed said, with awe in his voice.

They started toward home. Handfuls of snow flung at the windshield, small detonations of brightness caught by the sweeping lights of a passing car. A string of shuttered road-side motels, grim and abandoned for the season, appeared suddenly and then were sucked away into the darkness.

"Did you love my wife, Ed?" Gene said. He'd had no premonition of the question before it came out of him.

"We all loved her."

"But did you love her the way a man loves a woman?"

Ed's hands slid to the top of the steering wheel. "I don't know how to answer that. I'm a man and she's a woman, so I guess you could say I loved her the way a man loves a woman."

"Did you love her the way I loved her?"

Ed reached for the radio knob, pressed it, then immediately seemed to think better of it and pressed it again. He appeared to bring renewed concentration to the act of driving. "I wouldn't begin to tell anyone how they loved another person," he said. "How does it go? 'Love—that's a private catastrophe.'"

"Ours wasn't."

"Then it wasn't."

There was a pause in which they both seemed to be searching for something else to say.

"Why did she like you?" Gene said.

"I'm sorry?"

"What was it she saw in you?"

"Oh—gosh. I guess we recognized something familiar in each other. Something we had in common that maybe made us different from the kind of people we'd grown up with."

"What was that?"

"I'm not sure I can explain."

"You must have some idea."

There was a silence.

Gene tried again: "You must have thought about it."

Some expression rotated across Ed's face. It came and went so quickly—and was replaced by an expression of determined patience—that Gene didn't have time to interpret it.

"I don't know that it's so complicated," Ed said. "There's a kind of trust that can exist between two people who don't need much from each other—who aren't in each other's business according to the rules of their lives. Maida and I didn't use each other up. We *couldn't*. There was a deep fondness there. A genuine friendship."

"Like you and me," Gene said.

"Like you and me."

"Only *different*—your word."

"Yes."

They had made it back to Colton. Snowplows and salt trucks were already sledging the main road, flooding the smeared streets with a painful white light. They said goodbye in the car. Gene had a feeling he wouldn't see Ed again for a while.

That night he was kept awake by some tender spot in his chest where every time he breathed it seemed a bone might pop through the skin. But there was no bone, no heart bone, and if he tried to find the spot with his fingers it disappeared, fleeing somewhere else in his body where it couldn't be detected.

He was woken in the morning by the phone ringing. A woman from the hospital was trying to get him on the surgery schedule. He hadn't made up his mind whether to go ahead with it, but he didn't know how to explain what he was feeling. In a moment of panic he hung up on her. His mind felt gummed up, his decision-making faculties slowed by his impossible situation. As he understood it, the doctor had given him two choices and both called for his eventual death. He could leave the tumor in his heart alone and he could die trimming a nose hair, or he could have the tumor removed and *still* die trimming a nose hair. The thought filled him with despair.

Even the possibility that all of the problems with his heart might be fixed still ended the same way, with his dying of something else.

Where was Maida? Why couldn't she help him? Some wounded part of him still believed that it was her duty to help him. And where was Adele? He had never thought of her as a substitute for Maida—she was her own earthy entity, with her own distinct charms—but now that she too was gone he felt that he had lost both his wife and her replacement.

He thought of calling Dary to ask her what he should do. Then he remembered what the man in the waiting room had said. About how the ending would begin as soon as people knew. Dary would fly out from California and, meaning well, she would try to help him make plans for what remained of his life. But he wasn't ready to think of what remained of his life as a short block of time organized by other people.

The woman from the hospital called back to tell him the surgeon insisted on bringing him in. "This isn't a wait-and-see," she said.

Gene told her he couldn't schedule anything until he spoke to his daughter, but it was too early to call California.

He didn't want to be home when the woman from the hospital called back later in the day. The key to the Donnellys' cabin was still in the front closet, in the oversize coat that no one had claimed or worn for a very long time. He considered wearing it himself, but when he tried it on, the liner was disintegrating. It seeded small white flakes like dandruff into the wool of his sweater. He tried to brush them off but the attempt only burrowed them deeper into the wool. Then it looked like some insect had nested in the sweater and left behind little crisps of eggy vermin. He gave up and changed.

He packed a small bag of clothing and a good deal of food, the meals in the freezer that Adele had prepared for him plus butter, coffee, milk, and eggs. On his way out of town he stopped at a market to pick up cigarettes for Brian. He didn't know if Brian would still be there, but the possibility lifted his spirits.

That afternoon there were two successive winter skies, the first one a low surly plume of milky cloud dimming the light, and the second one twice as high as the first, a bright streakless blue that made the ice on the side of the road sparkle like running water. He drove past small snowcapped houses jagging smoke above the hillsides. The trees gradually moved closer to the road, until the woods appeared to lift off the ground and organize themselves as mountains.

After he passed the falls, he began to look for the turnoff. It was easy to miss—just a narrow cleft between the trees, the intersection at an oblique angle. The condition of the road on that final stretch was unpredictable at this time of year, and as he made the turn, hardened ridges of ice thumped against the car's undercarriage.

He reached the cabin just as the last of the sun was leaving the valley. Out of the corner of his eye he saw something spinning across a frozen expanse, a ghost chariot with wheels made of sparks. It was just the wind sweeping along the lake, coughing up the snow in the last of the day's light.

THREE

21.

THE CABIN LOOKED as he remembered it. Not just as he remembered it from the last time he had been there (a year and a half ago, for Gayle's birthday picnic) but according to some fixed and primitive original that seemed inalterable in his mind. The wood paneling in the main room was gouged in several places (one whole section was particularly badly damaged from the summer of indoor tricycle-riding), and some of the indentations had been filled in sloppily, with a putty lighter than the wood. A strip of blue painter's tape on the floor between the kitchen and the main room called attention to the differential in height between the linoleum and the ragged edge of the carpet. In the kitchen, beside the electric stove, open shelves displayed mismatched dishes and the bird-shaped sugar bowl from Gayle's first apartment. In the main area, beyond the woodstove, the tall shelves were chaotic with books, the usual motley assortment of popular novels and memoirs that collected at a summer place where people wanted to leave lighter than they arrived. Upstairs the homely BROKEN KNOWLEDGE sign was still hanging in the bathroom, next to a linen closet that never had a door.

Gene poked around for some indication of Brian—a bag or a pillow or something that didn't seem to belong to the cabin's general collection of extras for guests—but the presence of the cabin itself was far stronger than that of any human inhabitant. He didn't know how it would feel to be there and he was surprised it was a bit like a homecoming. It was strange how the most ordinary items could be comforting if only they were familiar: towels air-dried to a cardboardy roughness, a mineral taste in the water he associated with the lake, a small hexagon-shaped window at the top of a landing that the children, when they were young, had referred to as the fairy lookout. The cabin was almost shabby, or might have appeared that way to someone unaccustomed to it, but it reverberated with happy times in the Ashes' and Donnellys' lives, which maybe explained why it had been spared the Donnellys' vigorous impulse to remodel.

Looking over the titles on the spines in the bookshelves, Gene realized he hadn't read a book for a long time. He wasn't sure when he'd gotten out of the habit, but for years he hadn't had the motivation. Maybe this was because whenever he thought back to the evenings he and Ed had spent talking about poems in Ed's bohemian apartment, their behavior seemed somehow contrived, as if they had been merely playing the part of fervent intellectuals. At the time Gene's excitement had been real, but nine-tenths of it hadn't been about the literature; it had been about the aura of bravado surrounding what he imagined a po-etic lifestyle to be. Enchanted with their own concerns, he and Ed had treated the poems as if they were empty parentheses they could fill with any idea or emotion. When they were feel-ing lofty the poems were about the transcendence of the human spirit, and when they were feeling vulgar the poems were about the savagery of the human animal. It embarrassed him now to remember how they regarded themselves, believing in the importance of their dialogue about the nature of man and the meaning of his existence.

But this wasn't the only reason his appetite for reading literature had declined. Now that he was out of practice, he was also afraid of finding it difficult. Sometimes it required an outrageous effort, and when choosing between outrageous effort and instant satisfaction it was easier to sprint through a news story in the paper, or more recently on the computer, and then forget about it and replace it with another news story the very next day, where there was something quite pleasant about the rhythm of having to continually refill the holes in his mind left behind by the fading excitement of the fading article. Once he stopped reading books, he stopped thinking of himself as a reader. Then it became easy to say to himself that the reason he didn't read was because he wasn't a reader any more.

He tipped a book out of the shelves and read the back cover. It was a rural romance about a young widow named Lana Sky who had promised her dying husband, Edward, that she would never remarry or accept help from his brother, Edgar. There was nothing intimidating about a rural romance and this was exactly why it oppressed him—suppose his mind failed to follow the sentences the way a mind sometimes failed to follow sentences? If you were going to be vanquished, you wanted to be vanquished by Proust, Melville, *Middlemarch*. No one wanted to say the last book he ever read (the last book he gave up reading) was a rural romance featuring a heroine with a silly name. He selected two other books instead, something serious-looking about the treatment of Chinese rail workers, and a murder mystery that judging by the cover took place at a logging operation. He sat down prepared to read one or both of them and then had to laugh at himself, because in spite of having made his selections in the absence of others' scrutiny, he still hadn't chosen freely. He had chosen the books on the basis of their rightness—the serious book about the railways because it would make him an informed person about an important issue, and the murder mystery because that was the kind of indulgence you were supposed to crave and allow yourself when you went out of town. But what he actually wanted to read was a rural romance in which the characters enjoyed tawdry sexual romps, and in the end, after some confusion, true love inevitably prevailed.

He nestled into the overstuffed couch and started the romance. It wasn't so bad. The chapters went by quickly and easily.

Eventually his stomach began to rumble and he put the book down. He made a grilled cheese the way he used to for the kids, pressing it to a desirable flatness by nesting a smaller cast-iron pan inside the larger one, with the sandwich in between.

After dinner he put clean sheets on the bed in the guest room upstairs, which had been his and Maida's bedroom for many summers. The kinship he felt with the familiar pattern of orange elephants interlocking their trunks seemed as old as he was, as if he rather than Dary had lain on these sheets as a child. He could remember putting Dary down for a nap between him and Maida and reaching across the baby to touch Maida's milk-stiffened breasts.

Maida was everywhere in the cabin. Her favorite thing to do after making this bed had been to take a shower and then, giggling, slide between the clean sheets naked, her wet hair soaking the pillow and the mild vegetal smell of the soap exuding from her body. He didn't know why she loved doing this so much—it wasn't something she did at home—but he never questioned it, because her happiness seemed the obvious answer. She was also sitting in the room on the edge of the ladder-back chair, scrubbing her feet with a washcloth that she would later hang to dry on the headboard of the bed. He remembered the thick brown patches she got on her soles from stepping barefoot in pine sap, and how she would scrape at them with a dull table knife, laughing at any suggestion that she wear shoes in the future to prevent it from happening again.

It amazed him he could still remember so much about the particular way she had inhabited the world. Such intimacy, to think of these things, to know exactly the way she had cared for her own body or moved it through space. And at the same time, how ordinary, how unimportant. Yet all those years his mind had recorded it anyway. The many different versions of her: the one before she was the one he loved, the one he married, the one who continued to change in ways unseen by others. He half-wondered if he had come here to meet these successions of her. Or whether, in the wake of Adele's departure, he had come to the place where he and Maida had always been together to make himself less lonely.

But it wasn't quite true that they had always been here together. Many summers Maida had stayed on, spending extra days with Ed and Gayle and the children, after Gene had returned to Colton to run the shoe store. He had always imagined her time without him as more of the same, as a doubling or tripling of what had already happened together. But how could the things that happened with him there also happen without him? Did she still leap naked into the bedsheets? Hang dirty washcloths on the headboard? Scrape her feet with a dull table knife? He would never really know.

When he was finished fixing up the guest room, he returned to his book on the couch. The tawdry bits were beginning to seem either too salacious or not quite enough, and the love story, while replete with passion, lacked the complexity of actual love. But once he was halfway through he felt compelled to finish it, even though after a while what urged him on wasn't exactly pleasure anymore. It was more like wanting to find out all the ways in which something slightly irritating was going to fully irritate him. He pulled a crocheted blanket over his legs and ate cocoa mix straight from the package.

Once while he was reading the cabin brightened with an unnatural white light. When he looked up, a sweep of headlights was penetrating the trees. He opened the front door and walked to the end of the driveway with the blanket wrapped around him.

The lake had disappeared. It wasn't even a glint in the dark, and the lights belonged to a car much farther away than he had thought. The car wasn't coming toward the cabin. It wasn't even on the same road.

In the morning he put on his coat and borrowed a hat from the bin and went out to reacquaint himself with his surroundings. It had snowed during the night and the air above the lake was as clean and still as water. Rising to the west, the peak of Mount Orry was a patchwork of light and dark, broad fields of snow and misshapen granite outcroppings. The woods stretched in every direction that wasn't watery. Large hemlocks, their sweeping branches quivering with deposits of new snow, greened the flanks of the mountain. The tallest white pines spread great brushlike branches over the valley, and the younger trees were naked of needles except on their uppermost limbs. The leaves of the beech trees were dead but hadn't fallen off yet, and they hung upside down like dried-out tawny bats. Some of the pines had lost their bark and the exposed wood was as smooth as bone and the color of old bone. Still other trunks were splotched with medallions of lichen, their edges ragged and curling, their velvet the vivid yellow-green of a prehistoric thing refusing to die.

Some of the trees were dense with nests of snow that without warning would drop to the ground and splatter like eggs filled with slush. Every time he heard the soft splat behind him he pivoted around, half-expecting to see some animal leaping silently across his path. Once he startled a rabbit, white as the snow, and it dove into a bank where there didn't appear to be an opening, and he was left wondering if he had actually seen it.

The lake fell away in a band of shifting light. One minute it was a plug of colorlessness for a vast hole in the ground where the trees didn't grow. Then the clouds would part and the surface would sparkle like coarse sugar. It became flickering and alive on the edge of his vision.

His body felt surprisingly strong. To walk in these woods was to half-merge with a younger, healthier version of himself that had walked them countless times before. When he returned to the cabin he was surprised to see he had been gone more than an hour.

It occurred to him he should begin to consider what to do about his car, which was sitting beneath a layer of snow in the downward-sloping driveway in front of the garage. He found a shovel in the garage and began to dig it out. There wasn't enough snow to make this terribly difficult. But there was ice under the snow and when he got in the car and put it in reverse, it shimmied back and forth and then slid farther down the driveway. There was nothing to do but try again later.

After lunch—another grilled cheese, this time made directly on the woodstove—he pulled down Ed's worn copy of *Anna Karenina*. Gene disliked the book though he'd never read it, in part because he resented the claim it made on a reader's time. He found it difficult to believe any book could be worth that many hours of a person's life. Yet this same feature—the challenge it implied to the reader—created its own attraction.

Happy families are all alike; every unhappy family is unhappy in its own way.

Well, all right, that was fine—he'd heard it before, or something like it. It had a nice ring to it, and it sounded smart, but was it true? Not everything that sounded smart turned out to be true.

He read the first chapter. It was different than he expected. It ended too quickly, right in the middle of things, and there was no appearance of the famous Anna. He didn't find anything particularly special about the initial premise, but something about how unspecial it all was—the husband waking from a dream having forgotten his immediate circumstances, his irritation at having his comfortable domestic life disrupted—something about this roused his curiosity. He read another chapter. And when he finished that one, another.

It was dark by the time he put the book down.

That night he took out every can and bag and box of food he could find. Once it was all on the counter, he did an inventory: the tins of smoked fish, the cartons of salted crackers, the canisters of sugar and flour and coffee, the frozen bread and vegetables, the cheese. Between the items he'd brought and what was kept in the pantry, he was well-stocked. The ice in the driveway would eventually melt. If he ran out of supplies before then, he could walk to what the summer people affectionately called "the town"—three degraded commercial buildings at the intersection of two roads: a bar, a burger joint that was open only in the summer, and a former gas station that retained a tiny store, which kept short hours during the winter. It would be a bit of an ordeal to get there on foot, but teenagers determined to buy cigarettes did it all summer.

The only potential problem he foresaw was a shortage of coffee. There wasn't much in the cabin, and when he was packing up his car he'd grabbed by mistake the wrong can—the one containing Maida's ashes.

He began to possess the life of rustic simplicity he had always considered the true life—more difficult in some ways than life in a town, but also more authentic because whatever he did successfully he knew he had done without relying on anyone else. At first his fires were sickly smolderings that died down without constant attention, but gradually he learned, adjusting the opening of the stove's door until the fire sprang to life. He drank his coffee by the hearth and watched the dawn bleed into the clouds above the mountains, filling the sky with a pink light that appeared borrowed from the atmosphere of a far-off planet.

He discovered that he loved walking in the woods in a light snow. The snow fell with such changeability. Large flakes fell like lenses or saucers, their edges blown upward by the air, while small ones misted between the trees. Sometimes the falling snow plunged directly to the earth. At other times it drifted so slowly it seemed that the flakes themselves were still and the world was moving through them.

After the fresh air, the cold, the exercise, everything was more satisfying. His appetite, in its size and strength, connected him to a feeling he associated with an increase in life. Even his exhaustion at the end of the day was indistinct from the vitality that had spurred him to the exhaustion. When he fell asleep at night it was with that sudden encompassing of the entire body.

During the day, if he wasn't especially careful, he would catch himself drifting in and out of fantasies about Adele. In these imaginings she was always filled with regret for having broken up with him and determined to track him down. Somehow she was able to figure out where he was staying and when he opened the door, she was overcome with emotion. He would bring her inside and make her a cup of tea, but already she would be stripping off her snow-spattered clothing before the woodstove. By the time the kettle whistled, her bare legs would be wrapped around his waist and he would be moving inside her, losing himself to the fullness of her body even as he expertly maneuvered her on the floor to make sure she didn't crack her head on the edge of the hearth. (It was possible there was just such a scene between Lana Sky and her brother-in-law, Edgar.)

He rarely saw anyone except for a small, hardy woman of indeterminate age but undeniable fitness who crossed the frozen lake every afternoon on snowshoes, perhaps directing herself toward the column of smoke rising from White Pine Camp. When she reached this side of the lake she paused on what in another season would have been the Donnellys' little strip of beach. She would drink from a canteen produced from her satchel and, after hardly any rest, set back off in the direction she'd come from. Late in the afternoon a ribbon of smoke might turn in the wind above one of the large timbered houses on the opposite shore.

So life developed a pleasing rhythm. He fed the stove, he walked, he read the immense Russian novel. He felt silly for having avoided it so long. The characters were presented with great simplicity, so that without having to dwell on their virtues and vices you knew what Tolstoy wanted you to think of them. Gene disliked Anna for her revolting reflex of charming everyone as a clever way of not having to face the ugliness in herself. Dolly he found exasperating for her pretense of desiring independence from Stiva, even though she would have used it as a reason to hate him if he had given it to her. But he reserved his greatest disgust for Vronsky, whom he mocked for his foolish attempts to go into society without Anna, since Vronsky himself might have been the first to acknowledge he had wagered all of his pride, manliness, and courage on the relationship. He began to hate Vronsky just as he knew he was supposed to. He hated him for his arrogance and self-rapture and for looking at Anna with the pride of ownership. He laughed when Levin married Kitty and scorned his illusions about love, but he secretly worried for Levin because the simplicity of his life before Kitty could never be regained. It was all presented in the clearest possible way—and the pleasure of the novel was that he knew what the characters knew in their innermost souls. He experienced the satisfying elevated position you feel when watching grown-ups you know behave like spoiled children.

His main hardship, if it really could be called a hardship, was that he promptly ran out of coffee, and instead of remembering this fact and altering his morning routine to reflect it, each day he discovered the unpleasant reality anew. He would see the can of instant coffee and for a moment grow excited, forgetting what was inside and succumbing to his own ruse. It troubled him each time he remembered the actual contents. Finally he moved the can out of the kitchen, sticking it behind some books in the shelf.

22.

ON HIS FOURTH night, the scream of an owl woke him in the dark. The sound was part hiss and part croak, with a box of air rattling behind it. A barn owl, he supposed, looking for a mate or protecting a nest. The cry stopped soon after it had begun, and Gene turned over and went back to sleep.

He was tired in the morning when he went to fetch the wood from the garage. With the wood piled high in his arms blocking his sight, he forgot about the uneven transition from the linoleum to the carpet but remembered as soon as his foot caught on the ragged edge. Somehow he managed to lunge forward with a swooping motion that kept the wood from jumping out of his arms. He was aware of a grinding sensation in his ankle, but he reached the stove without dropping any of the wood.

He built the fire easily. As he watched the wood ignite, he told himself he would ice the ankle later. But he didn't think of icing it again until he'd returned from his walk, at which point it hardly seemed necessary because the ankle wasn't aching.

That night he woke again abruptly in the dark, this time

without any provocation. He tried to go back to sleep but was oddly alert. At first he thought he might read a bit more of *Anna,* but he'd entered that bittersweet period where his time left with the book was limited. He was torn between rushing toward the conclusion and stretching out the reading to extend the pleasure.

The second urge was stronger than the first, so he read another book he'd picked out from the shelves, an illustrated collection of folktales that was like a child's primer on death. Monsters and devils made regular appearances in the tales, but everywhere they went, they exhibited restraint and reason. The phantoms all possessed a genteel, courtly manner, and the most ghastly apparition was a dapper fellow in an elegant hat. Even Death, a visitor as solemn as Lincoln, behaved as though charged with having to carry out a regrettable duty. And Death was never sneaky. It gave a warning: a cough, a cold, a fever, an ominous vision, a too-powerful feeling. It helped the wood-cutter finish stacking his logs before taking him away, and when it came time for the baker's departure, it ensured the loaves he left behind wouldn't get burned. By the time each character was drawing his last breath, it was almost impossible not to feel that his time had fairly come.

When Gene woke the next morning, he felt the penumbra of derangement you feel after an unpleasant dream, as when you're still trying to persuade the dream to recede to the unreality from which it sprung. But the morning passed without incident. He tended the fire and reread the salacious scene where Edgar Sky first takes Lana.

In the afternoon, when he was on his way to feed the wood-stove and thinking about whether he should try to get more coffee, something rose out of the floor and tripped him. At first he was so relieved to have avoided the calamity of falling into the stove that the pain in his ankle seemed insignificant. Only when he pulled himself onto all fours and prepared to stand did he discover the degree to which he'd injured his ankle. A spongy softness prevented him from putting his full weight on it.

Still, it was just a sprain, or maybe not even that severe. He would ice it and rest it and it would feel better the next day.

But the next day the ankle buckled when he tried to put his weight on it.

The sprained ankle disrupted his life. Now before he went downstairs in the morning he had to plan carefully to bring with him whatever he needed for the day—there could be no spontaneous undertaking when there were fifteen steps to navigate between the first and second floors. He could carry only one log at a time from the garage, and with no surplus wood on hand, the fire often went out. By the time he'd gotten more wood to make a new one, he was often shivering badly enough that the new fire failed to warm him all the way through.

He might have gotten his blood flowing if he'd been able to go for a walk, but there could be no possibility of that when his ankle collapsed every third or fourth step. He hobbled around, making miserly lunches of warmed-up frozen vegetables flavored with shavings from an old parmesan rind. When he got into bed at night he experienced the peculiar tiredness of having steeped in a stagnant energy all day long. He would be tired but awake, awake but not keen, which resulted in his feeling tired and dull the next day.

The exhaustion made him more aware of his ankle, as if now a part of his brain was perpetually alert to the slightest discomfort in his body. He felt contempt for his limited capacity for pain, having always imagined he would be valiant in the face of injury. He remembered Maida's face filled with fear in the ambulance and wished he'd been gentler with her, more attuned to what he might have done to comfort her and less consumed by his own worry and fear.

He could no longer sleep on his back or his side. If he lay down, his heart began to quiver with strain. He slept propped up on pillows, never entirely comfortable. Some nights, when he wanted to avoid taking the stairs, the couch became his bed.

The snow continued to fall, filling the valley, and he lay in bed and read what remained of *Anna*. It saddened him to return to the book, aware that it would hasten the moment when the fates of the characters would be realized. But as he read, the pleasure he'd grown accustomed to from the story was now more difficult to achieve. Although he still felt he knew Anna and Vronsky and Levin as well as he knew himself, he was no longer sure how he was supposed to view them. That scene, for instance, where Vronsky takes up painting—what was he supposed to make of it? Was he to think it would have been better if Vronsky never attempted an art, because in his soul he was only a crass military man? What of Levin, who seemed to possess the rare gift of an innate wisdom that allowed him to discourse freely and naturally with all types of people—but who also gloated when learned men sought his opinion on important topics? And Anna—what was there to say about Anna? Her desperation, the increasingly antic quality of the deeds she undertook to avoid the loneliness and isolation that were inseparable from her position—it was awful, but he didn't know if it was awful because she was an abased creature or an exalted one. Suddenly he couldn't say that this character was good or bad or that one was complicated or simple. And the more he tried to recapture his previous understanding, the more lost he became.

He found himself arguing with Tolstoy because Tolstoy had said that people made an error in believing that happiness was the realization of desires. This was true but misleading, because *unhappiness* was also characterized by desires that went unrealized. So having your desires realized and not having them realized were both causes for unhappiness. If you were unhappy, then, how were you supposed to know whether it was because you had succeeded or failed in achieving your desires? He looked everywhere in the text but couldn't find an answer.

Then Anna died. Anna died and the book continued on. Then it came to an end. Coming to the end was like coming to an abrupt stop on a train at an undesirable provincial station and being informed only once you'd arrived that this was the last stop and all the passengers must disembark. In psychological terms, Gene didn't know where he was, or why he was there, or what he should do. Long after he put down the book he remained awake in the dark. Why had Ed recommended it to everyone? What had he thought they would understand or learn?

And now he heard Ed's voice in his head, telling Gene his relationship with Maida had been *a genuine friendship.* When a man told you he enjoyed "a genuine friendship" with your wife, it was not generally a good thing. A friendship in and of itself wasn't objectionable, but a *genuine* friendship—there was something emphatic about the word. *Genuine* passed itself off as square and wholesome, but it was one of those terms that could undermine its own meaning. It had cant. Because the idea of friendship—like most ideas advanced in a straightforward manner—didn't require emphasis or clarification to be understood. It was Ed's addition of *genuine* that seeded misgivings. If Ed's relationship with Maida was genuine, the implication was that someone else's was inauthentic or false.

Just then he began to feel his heart. He felt it as a distinct form, heavy and blunt, as if it was throwing itself from side to side in his chest, a lugubrious thing mistaking itself for something swift and nimble. At the same time his heart became a basket weaving its tight fibers across his chest, attempting to throttle the very thrashing that was also his heart. Fear seized him. He pressed his hands to his chest to try to quell the thrashing. A sound came out of him of its own accord, a dry, hoarse gasp.

He pulled himself upright and the episode ended as abruptly as it had begun.

First thing when he woke up his mind went over all of it again: *Anna,* his wife's affections, Ed's friendship with her. Certain irregularities from the past returned to him, and though they had never seemed particularly worthy of examination before, his anxiety now urged him to dissect them down to the slightest gesture. On the day Maida had gotten a heat rash and wouldn't feed Dary, why had Ed swooped in to soothe the baby, putting her in the car and driving off to get the popsicles Maida wanted? Or he recalled the day Maida swam across the lake—how after he had rowed back to the cabin, he encountered Ed, who had just woken and suggested they drive together to the other side of the lake to pick up Maida. How could Ed have known she had swum the lake if she and Ed hadn't made this plan together in advance? What else had they planned without his knowing? He couldn't decide if it was worse to think of them conspiring together after Gene had returned to Colton to work in his store, or when he was still there, an unwitting party to their smoldering affections.

Now he thought he remembered something else, a time he'd once seen Maida sitting on Ed's lap, the two of them reposing on the deck as the sun set over the lake. Everyone else was either showering or getting ready for dinner, but there they still were in bathing suits. And there was a baby in Maida's arms. Or maybe the baby was on Ed's lap. Though that hardly made sense, because both the baby and Maida wouldn't have been in Ed's lap at the same time.

Each thought gripped something inside him, pulling it upward, until he tasted bile at the back of his throat. His heart beat too high in his chest, at what seemed like the base of his neck, and at the same time, it throbbed in his groin, rapping against the hollow place where his leg met his pelvis. He was riling himself to a kind of conscious insanity, and he didn't know what purpose it served, because it would leave him only with ransacked happiness and not the definite thing he was trying to find. Yet his mind couldn't stop turning over each memory and sniffing it for signs of spoilage. He told himself it was the only way to uncover the unnamable condition that was the cause of his suffering.

"A kind of trust"—that was how Ed had described what was between him and Maida. A phrase intended to offer reassurance. And yet what was *trust* but another word for *intimacy*? Intimacy—the drawing in of someone that implied the exclusion of somebody else. If what had existed between Ed and Maida really was trust, then maybe it was Ed who was in and Gene who was out.

Was Ed capable of such a betrayal? Gene weighed Ed's fondness for women, in combination with his large appetite for pleasing himself. There was also his feeling of superiority over other people and maybe especially over Gene, a feeling that might have allowed Ed to be unusually forgiving with himself, since it was only natural that a stronger animal should take from a weaker one, and when this happened no one said it was a crime against morality.

But what about Maida? Was she the victim of a canny seducer, or had she actively conspired against Gene? And if Maida had given some part of herself to Ed, did that mean she hadn't given this part of herself to Gene? Or was it that she had held this part of herself in reserve and never given it to anyone? What was love without the whole person behind it?

A surge of nausea caused his forehead to break out in sweat. He tried to insinuate himself back into his former mental condition in which his wife's affections were familiar and known. What did it matter, after all, if Ed had a crush on her that he never acted upon? How could Gene suggest there was lasting harm in that, when he was guilty of the same with Gayle? And why should he care if at times, softened by a generous spirit, Maida had allowed Ed to think he had a chance with her? He *hadn't* had a chance with her. That was the important thing. Whatever vacillations she might have experienced in regard to Gene over the years, she'd stayed with him. Wasn't that enough? Why wasn't it enough?

There was a kind of solace in the deepest misery, the comfort of confronting the worst possible thing that could happen to a person. How keen he felt with all of his indignation concentrated on the injustice he had suffered! It was torture, it was intolerable to contemplate the sordid details of his betrayal—but it supplied a purpose. The entire beam of his existence was now focused on transmitting enmity toward the ones who had ruined his life. *My wife, my friend, my betrayal*—whenever the keenness threatened to dull, he revived it with this comforting mental chant. He had withstood the worst that could happen to a man.

But in fact, the worst was yet to come. The worst, when it arrived, sent a shock into his gut, a shower of liquid ice. The worst was—

What if Dary wasn't his?

One misgiving sired another that sired still more, until he was poisoned by his doubt.

For two bitter, incoherent days, he hardly ate, he hardly slept, he hardly did anything but cycle through a painful succession of thoughts that seized on his doubt and used his fear of the doubt growing larger to do exactly this, to enlarge it, until there was hardly anything in his mind that existed outside the doubt, and the strength of the doubt became its own persuasion.

The doubt provided explanations for long-standing mysteries. It clinched the unclinchable with its endlessly mutating logic, which proclaimed the most intolerable answer to be the only true one. Why hadn't he and Dary been able to get along with the easy rapport of other fathers and daughters? Why did things stick between them and cause pain? Why did she sometimes seem like a stranger to him, an alien being, oddly cold and unemotional, especially for a woman? What accounted for the closeness between her and Ed? Why had Ed brought her under his tutelage when she was young? Why, then and now, did Dary talk to Ed about matters she had never spoken to Gene about?

After the answer—*Because he wasn't her father*—passed through his head, something happened to him that had rarely happened before: his mind went blank. Not blank like snow, which was not blank at all but intricate and patterned, but blank like cold, a terrible frozen wash of white into the brain that stunned it motionless. His body decommissioned his brain to manage its intolerable pain. But something in his chest still spasmodically wrenched apart.

23.

HE BELIEVED HE had been at the cabin for twelve days, but he had stopped counting after finishing *Anna,* just as he had stopped cleaning up after himself. Having finished his lunch of boiled potatoes—reheated and served with ketchup—he added his dirty dishes to the others piling up. When he turned from the sink, he sensed something wasn't right in the room.

At first he couldn't figure out what it was. Then he knew.

It—death—was everywhere. It was in the lingering smell of the cooked vegetables, and in the bunched-up sheets snaking across the couch. It was in the flint of soap by the sink that shrank daily and the sponges that had the grayish cast of meat going rotten. It was in the oily stains on the dish towels. He caught a glimpse of himself in the window and was shocked by his appearance: his shoulders rounded involuntarily, his clothing hung slack on his body. He thought of the sedentary retirees in the coffee shop who waited for Ed to canter in steaming at the end of his run. These men and women had always seemed impossibly old to him, with their age-blanched faces so soft and pale they appeared interchangeable, male for female, female for male. Now he might have been one of them.

He went upstairs and got into bed and remained there for the rest of the day, though there was still light in the valley and he had not yet eaten the three canned sardines and five salted crackers he had allotted himself for dinner. Eventually the sun withdrew from the treetops and the darkness replaced it, filling in the branches with a blackness darker than the sky.

He tried to imagine Death as a benevolent companion, a friend who had accompanied him throughout his life and who had protected him from countless harms that might have intervened too soon. Hadn't Death slept in his bed when as a child he had been racked with fever? Hadn't Death swum beneath him in the lake every time he hadn't drowned? Some sustaining power had seen to it that he would make it through infancy, childhood, and adolescence, had given him the long years of marriage and fatherhood, then had extended his time yet again to allow him the birth of a grandchild. For a long time he had thought of this dispensation as a transmission of Life, but who was to say it wasn't Death all along?

But a voice within told him he was just fooling himself.

His hands were so cold they couldn't feel the sheet they were clasping. A fear that the fire had gone out came over him. He got up and the outer reaches of the room whirled around an inner black stillness. In the absence of light, he was nothing more than a pair of disembodied eyes in the dark. He touched his own face, trying to find his body and give it back to itself, but there was nothing to say if the face he touched was the face of a dead man or the face of a living one. He was afraid of his own body, afraid it would cease to exist without anyone knowing it.

He returned to the bed and curled up shivering. His body

began to convulse—elongating, contracting—as if he was retching, though his stomach was empty. The harsh involuntary movement strained everything: his throat, his eyes, his legs, his heart.

When he woke he didn't know what time it was but sensed he had slept into the afternoon. The light in the room was the same shade of watery gray as the sky above the trees. For a moment, it sounded like someone was calling him at the back of the cabin. Then the sound stopped—long enough to convince him that what he'd heard was something other than a human voice.

Then he heard something again, the thump of booted feet on the deck, followed by shouting: "Yoo-hoo, yoo-hoooo!"

He hobbled down the stairs, pulling a sweater over the clothes he had slept in.

"Yoo-hoo! I see you in there."

When he opened the door, a woman was standing there. He recognized her as the one he'd seen snowshoeing across the lake many afternoons. She was at least his age and perhaps considerably older. Child-sized, with withered skin and bitty child-sized features. Her smile, cocked and antic, dispelled any fear he might have had of receiving a solemn visitor.

She explained that her canteen was empty, and she hoped he might be able to give her a refill.

He was so surprised to be standing face-to-face with another person that for a moment he forgot she had made a request of him—it seemed the other way around. He felt such an upwelling of gratitude not to be alone that he was afraid the sentiment would gush out and she would be alarmed. It took a physical effort, a willful bracketing of himself in silence to appear, he hoped, a reasonable human being.

"You do have water?" she said, in an encouraging way.

He took her canteen and filled it at the kitchen sink.

When he returned, she wasn't waiting where he'd left her. He heard the thunk of a blade biting into resistant snow, followed by a scrape and another thunk. The absence of the shovel from the spot he'd left it, leaning against the cabin, confirmed what he already knew. Digging.

She was clearing him out of the snow. First the path that led up to the stairs of the deck, then the stairs themselves. She broke the compacted layers with quick, short jabs, then heaved the loosened snow to the side with a twist of her small torso. He stood at the top of the stairs and told her it wasn't necessary, but she showed no sign of slowing down. She continued to shovel until the path and the stairs were clear. Then she went around to the front of the house and did the walkway and the landing. When she had finished this and had asked for a box of salt and he had given it to her and she had salted the steps and the walkways and the driveway—when all of this was complete she stood on the landing with her face flushed and her boots dripping and he told her the only way he could feel right about her having dug him out was if she stayed for a cup of tea.

She was bundled in an eccentric hodgepodge of colors and textures and layers. The removal of her hat revealed a fuzzy purple ear band and a bun of wispy white hair. Beneath her outer jacket was an inner jacket, a liner of some sort, and beneath the liner was a vest, and beneath the vest a pullover with a hood. Her snow pants zipped away to reveal thick puce woolen leggings, and these leggings had matching muffs sewn around the ankles. He waited for her to make a self-deprecating remark acknowledging the peculiarity of her attire, but she proceeded to make herself comfortable in the cabin without any indication she cared what he was thinking.

She told him she was staying at her ex-husband's house across the lake. The ex-husband was apparently somewhere else— perhaps temporarily, perhaps permanently. Gene knew this only because when he mistakenly referred to her as staying *with* the ex-husband, she corrected him in a tone that was light but not wistful: "Oh, I've never been able to live with anyone. Poor Roger knew that, but he married me anyway."

She wandered through the cabin, inspecting bookshelves and objects. He wondered whether this roaming was her usual habit or whether something particular about the cabin had captivated her—and perhaps this question was inscribed on his face be- cause she said, "Don't mind me—I like to see how people have lived." She asked if he was the one reading *Anna Karenina.* "I give that book to people all the time," she said, and when he asked her why she answered, "Because everything terrible that can happen happens in it, but somehow it doesn't ruin any- thing."

When she returned from her investigation of the bathroom she said, "I'd almost forgotten about 'broken knowledge.'"

He stared at her in amazement. "You know Ed?"

"Ed who?"

When he explained, she replied, "I don't know Ed, but I do know Francis Bacon. That's his—he said wonder was broken knowledge. He wrote it defending God and the scientific method at the same time, which as you can imagine, wasn't easy to do." She paused for a moment as if she had come to the end of the thought, but then continued on. "His point was, I think, the more you know about some things, the more you know about those things, which doesn't exclude you from knowing absolutely nothing about other things. Look at him! He figured out how to prevent a chicken dinner from spoiling by freezing it, then promptly died after a walk in the snow." Then without hardly pausing she added, "Have you seen a bear?"

He remembered the last time he'd encountered a slightly batty woman. He'd mentioned the incident to Dary and she'd pounced on him for his description. Why was it, she wanted to know, that men in their later years became "sweet" and "funny" while aging woman were judged to be "unstable" and "crazy"? Now, as a thought about his visitor entered his mind, he asked himself if he was possibly being unfair. He decided it was unfair only if a woman's battiness made her less appealing, and that was not the situation here. He hadn't realized how delirious he was with the want of seeing and hearing another person, and it seemed his great luck that the one who had happened to find him was not the least bit dull. The only difficulty he foresaw would be inventing some pretext to persuade her to stay a little longer.

He said, "Are you missing a bear?"

"Well, it used to live in the blueberry bushes behind the house. Sometimes I would leave fish for it hanging on sticks. Ooh, that would make Roger *diabolical* mad. He used to say to me if I wanted a theater for slaughter would I please take it to the end of the road? I've reused that several times, by the way: 'theater for slaughter.' It has a nice ring."

He didn't need to say much to keep the conversation going. She was interested in how her own thoughts spun out, but he didn't take it for egoism. To the contrary, beneath her playful manner she seemed to have an inborn reverence for the things she spoke about. She mentioned something about her students and he decided she had probably been a university professor, someone with whom young adults searching for an indication of their purpose might have competed to have lunch. But when he asked her if she had taught at one of the nearby colleges, she laughed as though the idea was at once absurd and flattering. She was an elementary school teacher, she said, or rather she had been years ago.

"I always felt I understood children best," she said. "You can see the seed of the whole person in their faces. There's something remarkable about seeing it and having no idea what kind of seed it is and just blindly giving it everything—water, air, peanut butter—in case one of those turns out to be what it needs. That's why I liked the bear," she said. "It was just a kid when I knew it. Not a cub, not a baby, but a young thing with a real personality waiting to burst out. Adults are more tricky, in my opinion. They can be interesting, but often they try not to be."

If she had been hoping to find something in particular in the cabin, Gene now had the sense that she was disappointed. She hadn't drunk a sip of her tea, but already she was handing it back to him. It crushed him a little, this gesture of returning the tea untouched. He suggested they transfer it to her canteen so she would have something to warm her on the way back. But she told him not to bother. The canteen often leaked, sometimes slowly and sometimes all at once, and it wasn't unusual for her to get where she was going only to discover there wasn't a drop left in it.

Before long she set out from the back of the house, a small motor of intensity churning across a lakeland of snow. When she had traveled a little ways, she paused and bent down to fix one of her snowshoes. He expected she might turn back to look at him to acknowledge her own version of what he was feeling, which was the strange and intimate unlikelihood of their encounter, an event that by most measures shouldn't have happened, since there didn't seem to be many other humans for miles around. But she didn't look his way again, and when the snowshoe was fixed, she continued on.

The sun was getting lower in the sky, accelerating toward the top of the mountain. Light shivered across the ice, splintery and vanishing, as if it was being filtered through snow in the air that hadn't fallen yet. Sometimes her progress seemed as insignificant as if she was marching in place, and at other times she seemed to have jumped from one point on the lake to another, skipping what was between. The closer she got to the far side, the more difficult it became to distinguish her in the dusk. Soon she was a dark speck mingled with the last oscillations of the light. He lost sight of her, then found her again.

The last of the daylight scratched the top of Mount Orry and disappeared. Then the mountain loomed above the lake, a pit of darkness turned on its head.

When he tried to find her once more, she was gone.

24.

IT RAINED AND snowed, then snowed and rained. Icicles formed on the eaves of the cabin. For such slippery things, they were rough and knobby, lumpy like gnawed carrots. All day the icicles dripped, diminishing incrementally, and he would have thought that incrementally they would have met their ending. But they broke off suddenly, crashing to the ground.

He felt his own brokenness. He wasn't wonderfully broken, but rather ordinarily broken, like a man who has craved something his whole life that he doesn't understand. He didn't understand love. He had made an effort in his life to do mostly the right thing, the decent thing, believing that someone would love him for this. Somewhere he had gotten the idea that good conduct in this life would be rewarded with unfaltering human love. He had waited for this, not really seeing himself as an actor, not seeing his own loving impulses as something that could shape or distort or thwart. He couldn't claim that this impulse to love made a life significant or good. He could say it made pain. He could say it had hurt him.

One night he had a dream in which he saw himself arriving

at the gates of heaven. Outside the gates the Angel of the Lord asked each person who wished to enter what the purpose of his life had been. From observing those ahead of him Gene saw it didn't matter what you said: one man spoke of raising sheepdogs; another said pissing off his wife; another, while admitting he was tempted to lie, acknowledged that for him, drinking stood above all. Each man made his declaration, and each was allowed to pass. But when Gene's turn arrived, he had nothing to say.

The Angel of the Lord bent over and whispered, "Just make something up."

Gene woke with his heart knitting its tight garment over his chest. He lay there in terror, sifting his mind for possible purposes that might be belatedly superimposed on a life. Had his purpose been to "turn out" all right? To please his parents? To marry and not get divorced? To have a family?

There was a question in his mind as to whether his purpose was to be a husband and a father. This would not make him an anomaly—think of all those mothers and fathers who happily proclaimed that their sense of meaning in life derived from being the family nurturer or protector. But these proclamations always raised for him the question of whether the sentiment had been arrived at by default, as other dreams that would have required immense effort, privation, and luck ceded to a more accessible reality. The designation of importance might have been made afterward, once the reality of the child-rearing chaos began and the adult human required some self-reward for the turmoil and heartbreak he had indentured himself to. Was it possible to trick the self into an exalted sense of purpose, some condition where the trick fell away and the exaltation remained? Was it enough to say that his purpose had been to see his wife and daughter thrive? Was it truthful?

The pain he felt now wasn't in his heart—or wasn't just in his heart. It was an all-over pain, a ringing from the inside out. At first he didn't know what the pain could be if it wasn't his heart. Then he realized the pain was emanating from a thought. The thought was that maybe his purpose in life—his volitional drive, not necessarily conscious—was just this: *never to be alone.* He had married believing it would secure someone to him who would love him for the rest of his life, and once the marriage was accomplished, some part of him believed, or hoped, the matter to be settled. The other life he had sporadically toyed with, the one in which Gayle featured as his rightful mate, was the life in which he had chosen someone who would be more faithful in spirit than Maida. His child, he'd thought, would love him innately and forever; he hadn't conceived of her birth as the beginning of a story that wasn't about the fierce tribal love she would always feel for him. Maida, Dary, Ed—when in various periods of their lives each had shifted their focus away from him, he had internally accused them of trying to injure him. And maybe because of this he had missed an opportunity to understand how badly he didn't want to be alone and just how lonely the desire had made him.

It was impossible to say whether this was true. But it was substantial enough that he couldn't dismiss it, and part of the reason he couldn't was that after all of his suffering, he still didn't want to die without the people who had possibly ruined his life.

The shock of this softened something in him. His chest opened and his breathing grew more spacious. He lay quietly without clenching himself against a new tightening or racking.

When he tried to recover the intensity of his doubt about whether Dary was his daughter, he could still locate the doubt, he could still touch it. But it no longer possessed him. He knew he had been Dary's father. In his daily labors—feeding her, reading to her, brushing her teeth, putting her to bed—but also in all the overwhelming intangibles parents trafficked in, worry and criticism and catastrophic thinking and pride, and always the same tiring and unceasing mental effort toward discovering the next best way to improve her life.

It was an understanding of himself that included Maida, that bound her to him and the two of them to each other regardless of whatever might have existed or failed to germinate between her and Ed. On the basis of a perhaps faulty connection, he and Maida had still arranged to support another life and somehow they had managed to follow through on this fairly astonishing promise.

There was no name or word or admission or rumor or fact or law or legislation that could revoke this. Not at this late stage, not when the life he was beginning to lose was not the one he had imagined or dreamed of, but just the one he'd had. And what was most confusing in all of this was that his resistance to dying, his terrible despair, his terrible fear, showed him that the life he'd had—the defective one plagued with uncertainty and misunderstanding—this was the one he wanted after all.

25.

THE NEXT MORNING he woke up feeling slightly better. His ankle was still swollen but the pain throughout his body had lessened. He was able to think a little more clearly and see that the pain itself probably wouldn't kill him. And as soon as he proceeded with the belief that the pain itself did not put his life in jeopardy, the pain relaxed a little, and he relaxed a little, and some greater effort became possible. He got out of bed and tried to see what he could do for his body. He was afraid to shower and risk slipping, but he washed his face and neck and armpits at the sink. His clothes were rank from having been slept in and sweated in and dried out and sweated in again, and he balled them up and stashed them in a plastic bag. He had one pair of fresh underwear and one clean undershirt, and these he put on under his least-dank sweater and pants. He didn't much feel like eating but thought he should have something, so he boiled water for tea and steeped a desiccated pouch of herbs in a pot. And as he was sitting at the table dressed in his cleanest clothes, he understood that anyone catching a glimpse of him at that moment would not see anything unusual in his situation.

It did not entirely surprise him when after a little while he heard people outside the cabin.

Ed entered first, followed by Dary. They were saying something to each other but fell silent when they saw him. Then they began to speak at the same time. They had been worried about him and admonished him for having gone away without telling anyone where he was going. They wanted to know how long he had been here, and also, hadn't he anticipated they would be searching for him? Dary looked at him with an expression that seemed to contain many colliding feelings: weariness and anger, frustration and relief. "What were you *thinking?*" she said, and he could hear the accusation in her voice and also her attempt to suppress it so that he wouldn't mistake it for a rhetorical question, which was how he treated it anyway.

When he stood up from the table and crossed the room for his tea, there was no hiding his limp. Dary wanted to take him to a hospital immediately, but Ed said it would be wiser to examine him here first. Dary disagreed, and soon what had begun as a discussion escalated to an argument.

Gene watched them with new curiosity. Ed was didactic with Dary without any special vehemence or patience—he addressed her in the same tiresome way he often addressed Gene. And in Dary's voice he heard an exasperated, almost haughty tone, as if Ed had proposed to take away something that belonged to her.

The argument was settled when Ed and Dary each accepted the other's proposition. Ed would perform an initial examination of Gene at the cabin, and later they would take him to a hospital. With a note of discretion in her voice, as if she was volunteering to remove herself to facilitate the exam, Dary said she would walk up the road to see if she could get a signal to call Annie, who had stayed behind in Colton with Gayle.

Ed washed his hands at the sink. "Ready?" he said.

Not even if I was dead, thought Gene, but without another word he limped behind Ed into the main room and followed his instruction to lie on the couch.

Ed began moving his hands down Gene's limbs, squeezing them gently but firmly. He asked Gene to open his mouth and stick out his tongue. He slipped a hand beneath Gene's shirt and pressed deep into his abdomen, so deep it felt like he was moving organs around. Gene was afraid Ed would ask him to remove his clothes, but then the moment passed when it seemed this would have been most useful, and still Ed worked his way around Gene's body, palpating what could be palpated through his sweater and pants. Gene was shocked to see that the skin on Ed's forearms, which he remembered as cabled with muscle, sagged like stretched-out leather.

Ed spent quite a bit of time pressing on various parts of Gene's ankle and cautiously articulating it in small increments. Then he released it and said he didn't think it was broken. He went away and came back with a plastic bag filled with ice and wedged two pillows under Gene's foot and draped the ice over the ankle.

"It's just country medicine," Ed said, "but it's what you need. If we go to the hospital they'll charge you $1,000 to tell you that you need country medicine. That's what I was trying to explain to Dary, but you can't stop her from doing what she wants. She's like her mother that way."

Gene knew this was the moment. If ever he was going to ask Ed, this was the time. "Do you know what I did when I first got here?" he said.

"You busted your ankle."

"Before that, wiseass. I read *Anna Karenina.* Do you remember it?"

"Very fondly."

"After I finished it, I wondered why you'd recommended it to me."

Ed appeared interested in this line of inquiry but didn't say anything.

"It was for my betterment or some crap like that, wasn't it?" Gene said. "And, okay, I admit it, it's a pretty good book."

"One of the best."

"But that got me thinking—you've always been able to pick out the good ones, haven't you? Not just books but—everything. People, too."

Ed appeared to consider this. Then he said, "I've been feeling some regret lately."

"Oh? What about?"

"All the lives I might've had. Whether I should've done something else. Been a writer, for instance. Or lived in Alaska."

"It's not too late."

"People say that, but I don't buy it. You start explaining to yourself why your life has to be a certain way, and then, before you know it, other people are counting on those explanations to be true."

"I always had the impression you felt like you could do anything," Gene said.

"It's the other way around," Ed said. "I did the things I could excel at so I wouldn't have to fail." There was disappointment in his voice. "But maybe regret is the most useful form of memory," he said. "It reminds you that you belong in the life you already have, and not in that other one where the better version of you is doing everything better. That fantastical, wonderful life where no one ever gets mad at you and you never have to apologize."

Gene hardly knew how to respond. Was this its own tacit apology or just an evasion of one? And if it was an apology, what was it for? What had Maida been to Ed and he to Maida? The answer Ed had given was as shapeless as the flesh on Ed's forearms. Part of Gene had always longed to see Ed weakened by something. But now that Ed was not purely strong, Gene didn't feel invigorated by it. Instead he felt implicated. To pounce on Ed now, to pummel him into an admission of questionable value—it would be almost like pummeling himself.

Ed reached out and tapped Gene's shin. "How's that ankle now?" he said. "Any better?"

"Maybe a little."

Ed rose and went upstairs and was gone a short while and when he came back he had with him a small tube of cream and a faded hand towel. He removed the bag of ice and dried Gene's foot and ankle with the towel. When Gene realized Ed intended to apply the cream, he wanted to protest. But he didn't have the energy. Ed kneaded the cream into Gene's foot and the tendons of his ankle. Gene closed his eyes. The cream seemed to numb some of the pain.

He must have dozed off, because when he opened his eyes Dary was tending the woodstove and Ed was not in sight.

"Where is everyone?" Gene said, disoriented.

Dary pulled a chair next to him. She told him Ed was digging out Gene's car, and reminded him Annie was in Colton with Gayle. She had something in her lap, a large envelope printed with a blue crest. "This came to the house while you were away," she said. "I thought maybe it was important."

He asked to see it and she held it up for him. It had been sent by the lawyer, Dale Elverson, but Dary appeared not to recognize the name and he decided not to remind her. She asked him if he wanted her to open it.

The urgency he'd once felt to know what such an envelope might contain now seemed to belong to a previous life. It was difficult for him to recall exactly why or how he'd believed the envelope's contents would help him, or her.

"It's nothing," he said. "Just add it to the fire."

She got up and opened the stove door, then hesitated. He gestured for her to continue, and she placed it inside the stove. When she sat back down, her eyes were shining with a glimmer of mischief. He tried to mirror her gaiety, but even this small effort was tiring to him. He hadn't realized how exhausted he was.

"Are you tired?" she said.

"A little," he admitted.

"You must be looking forward to going home."

When he thought of the house in Colton, he could picture the house itself, the roof and its triangular bite into the sky, but when he tried to conjure up what was in the rooms themselves they were empty. It was strange because he knew the house was filled with belongings of such specificity that once they had seemed capable of embalming his marriage. Now he couldn't think of a single thing in the drawers, shelves, cupboards, or cabinets that he would rush to save if the house caught fire. What he wished was that he had something of value to give his daughter, but everything he wanted her to have didn't reside in a thing.

"Has there—?" He paused and stopped, recalibrating his question and gathering his courage. He began again in his softest, most provisional tone, a tone that suggested she could stop him from talking about this at any time. "Has there been anyone in your life?" he said.

"Are you asking if I'm alone?"

"I'm asking about love," he said, the word rushing to him before he could think it.

"If I said yes and no, both would be true," she said. When she continued, her voice seemed smaller. "The times of yes somehow wipe out the times of no. And the times of no seem to last forever and be permanent."

He cringed to hear this. "But mostly you're happy?"

"I think you and I mean different things when we talk about love."

"Then you'll explain it to me?"

"Sometimes I think it's like putting an unanswerable question out into the world and getting back another unanswerable question. Then trying to figure out if a question can answer a question."

"Can it?"

"What do you think?"

She smiled at him, her eyes radiant, her manner calm. And it amazed him and pained him all over again that she would never feel the astonishing fact of her existence the way he did. To her, she would always be only herself, but to him she was the fissure down the middle of his life, the creation into the void that had given him two worlds—the world before she came into being and the world after it. That he could feel this and she couldn't kept them inextricably bound together, at the same time that it ensured they were somewhat forsaken to each other, like amiable strangers.

"Dary," he said.

"Dad."

"Again," he whispered. "Say it again."

And she did.

When Ed came back inside, he and Dary conferred briefly. They said they were ready to take him to the hospital, and Gene relented. But first, he said, there was something he wanted all of them to do together.

Ed and Dary helped him down the stairs and across the snowy beach. The snowdrift had formed into one solid-looking piece, a thick cake they punctured with their feet as they made their way down to the frozen lake. The wind and rain had cast pine needles, still green, across the snow, and beneath the largest trees the snow top was dented with small cavities the size and shape of marbles where icy raindrops had fallen. The fitful wind drove the scent of the trees, the sharp tang of the needles, toward them in gusts. Then the wind shifted direction and smelled of nothing and was bitterly cold.

They reached the lake's edge. A few patches of new snow dotted the ice, but otherwise it was bare and white and cross-hatched with lines of deeper white. Dary, who was carrying the can containing her mother's ashes, stopped and pulled off her glove with her teeth. When she opened the can, Gene and Ed huddled around her.

The sky was matted with clouds, light gray and darker gray. The wind blew into their faces and they turned to angle themselves against it, but it seemed only to turn with them and shove at them with greater strength. The hemlocks swung at the air with their thick branches and the large pines shuddered and the small pines leaned. Gene searched the far shore for a line of smoke above a chimney, but the houses were dark and abandoned, planted like a wall on the edge of the water to keep the snowy mountains from sliding into the lake.

In the flat, diffuse light their faces looked pale and clenched. Gene had asked Ed to pick out a poem and Ed had worried there wouldn't be anything suitable in the cabin. But he had picked one out anyway, a poem Gene didn't know. Now Ed began to read it with a stiffness in his voice. At first Gene feared that Ed had chosen a poem full of unnecessary solemnity or bleakness, but it was not a bad poem after all. It broke off with a surprising line that struck him as rather wonderful: "We end in joy."

Then Dary began to shake the can with her mother's ashes over the ice. The wind blew most of the ashes back to the shore, where they clung to the snow like dirty flakes. She crouched down with what remained of the ashes, and this time tipped the can directly onto the hard surface of the lake. Some of the ashes blew back to shore and some blew across the ice, jittering and then disappearing, so that the three of them were left looking at the frozen lake itself, the silent white immensity of it. The trees were almost black against it and even the snow on top of Mount Orry looked gray compared with it.

"It's almost like a piece of the moon," Dary said.

He stepped out onto the ice. He didn't wait for them to object, he just did it, and limped his way a short distance from the shore. Any second they might come for him, but he hobbled on. He was unsure if he would make it—with every step his ankle hurt a little more and his breath quickened—but where he was going was not very far. When he got out to the place where the floating dock used to be, he paused. Something in his chest was tightening and his heart was trying to beat it back, but instead of relieving the tightness, his heart was twisting it around. He lowered himself to the ice, a motion he could control until the last few inches, when he fell. His heart—he could feel it beating all the way in the soles of his feet. He lay down on the ice with the polished moon of the lake floating all around him, and he proposed a life to Maida and then remembered he'd already lived it. He removed a glove and touched his face. It was wet, though he didn't remember crying. When he looked up, the sky was swarming with clouds. The light gray ones had merged with the dark ones, and all of them were tossing into each other.

ABOUT THE AUTHOR

Katharine Dion was born in Oakland, California. She is a graduate of the Iowa Writers' Workshop, where she was awarded the Iowa Arts Fellowship. She has also been a MacDowell Fellow and the recipient of a grant from the Elizabeth George Foundation. She lives in Berkeley, California. *The Dependents* is her first novel.